FALLEN HEROES

The first of the Millio Galaxy Quartet

Sonya Fomboud

The Millio Galaxy Quartet

Fallen Heroes

Another World

The Heir of Dirnhet

Home Galaxy

For Speedy, who was there at the beginning...

ONE

Lethe Miarren bought a mug of ale, turned away from the bar to find somewhere to sit in the drinking house and his well-ordered world turned on its head. There in a dark corner was a man with a face from a nightmare. Someone who had been held and tortured on Lriam. Not the kind of face you saw in a Sunaran drinking house. There were scars on his cheeks where the spikes had been rammed through the flesh and his lower jaw was slightly skew. There were blue metal rods, big as a baby's finger, punched into his ears and nose which acted as receivers for the energy beams transmitted from the planet where this man had suffered. Lethe knew he had been out of galaxy for over a year, but he really hoped he was mistaken. The man at the corner table looked up for a second, his eyes wary as he knew he was unwelcome. He caught the blue gaze of the man at the bar and there was a brief flash of recognition in his dark, hopeless eyes but no more.

Lethe knew then that the unthinkable did happen. He ordered a second mug of ale and went over to the table where he plonked the mug down but wouldn't sit.

"You look in need of a drink," he remarked and tried to sound as though he would do this for any beggar he pitied.

The man had to hold the mug in his fists as his hands had been crushed into cages that were half covered by dirty sleeves.

"Thanks. How did you recognise me?" he mumbled as though it hurt to speak.

"I flew with you for six years. What happened?"

A slight shrug. "One trip too many to Lriam. You know how it goes out there."

"Never thought you'd get caught."

"Neither did I. Now you'd best get out before you're seen talking to me." The man flinched. "Thought I'd be out of range of the beams here but they're upping the strength all the time. Won't be too much longer before they're on full power here and then where can I go? There's no planet further away in this galaxy."

Lethe knew he could take this man out of galaxy but the cost to himself would be punishment as bad as that which he was looking at now. He stalled for time. "How did you get this far?"

"On a shit-ship taking a cargo of excrement from Lriam to the reprocessing plant here. Reckon I must still stink of it."

"You do a bit. How long have you been here?"

"No idea." It was obvious there wasn't going to be an offer to take him out of galaxy and he had no money to pay. "Go on, get away. You've been with me too long for common charity any more."

Lethe watched as the other man drew in his breath as though in agony and rested his head on his arms for a few moments. "You can't go on like this. Lriam's got the power to blow your brains out when they transmit at full strength. So I've been told." If he took this escaped convict away he would have to accept that he could never return to that galaxy. It was a high price to pay, but his life here wasn't what you might call brilliant. Yup, it had to be a trip out of galaxy. It was the only thing to do. "You know what you need, don't you?"

"I need to cut my fucking head off but they've broken my hands to bits so I can't. Would you do it for me?"

Lethe looked on silently as the man awkwardly tipped up the mug of ale as though his elbows were locked at right angles and some of the beer slopped down his front. Lethe stopped himself from mopping it up. It was just about acceptable to buy such a wreck a drink but never, ever, help him to drink it. The stink of shit was still on his ragged, filthy clothes and his hair was matted below his shoulders. There were tufts of beard on the parts of his face where there was no scar tissue to stop the growth of the hair.

So this was what had happened to Ygoi Roemtek. Once the most celebrated pilot and bounty hunter of the Millio galaxy. Problem was, Ygoi Roemtek had been a bit of an egomaniac and when the money wasn't coming in as fast as he wanted, he would cross to the wrong side of the law. Looked like he'd crossed just once too often. It was only a matter of time before the beams got strong enough and the torture of the former hero would be completed with an ignoble explosion of his brain. One of the brightest, sharpest and wittiest brains in the galaxy too. Ygoi Roemtek was well read, well-educated and the most exacting task master Lethe had ever met. They had flown together in Ygoi's ship for six years then Lethe had passed his advanced pilot's test and they had gone their own ways. Now he earned a comfortable living as a pilot with his own ship. Now he owed the wretched Ygoi something even if it was only to shoot him to end his misery. But Lethe had made up his mind, no matter what happened to him as a consequence. He owed Ygoi more than a bolt of high-powered energy through the head.

"Go outside and I'll join you in a few minutes," Lethe offered and then realised he sounded like an executioner. To his sorrow, Ygoi accepted that was what he was.

"You can do it in here. We'll just stage an argument and you can shoot me. You are armed?"

"Yes. But I'm not going to shoot you."

"Then you can't help me. Go away." Another flinch and Ygoi's tortured head sank onto his broken arms. "Just get out of my life before they come for you too."

Lethe happened to catch the glance of some of the other drinkers and knew what Ygoi meant. It was time to go. "Don't you talk to me like that," he growled over-loudly. "I bought you a drink out of pity and that's the thanks I get?"

Ygoi hoped this would be it. A merciful execution at the hand of a friend. He rallied his last strength to make it look convincing. "Piss off."

"Don't you tell me to piss off, Shit-face. Outside." Lethe hauled the noisome Ygoi to his feet and pushed him towards the door. To his horror the other man just collapsed on the floor and clearly couldn't walk. "Oi, you," he called across to two rather drunken youths. "Help me shove Shit-face here outside then maybe the air will be a bit cleaner in here."

The youths looked at the tall blond man who wore the indigo clothes and silver shoulder flashes of a cross-galaxy pilot and swallowed their revulsion of the stinking tramp long enough to grab one arm each and hurl him physically into the searing light of the twin Sunaran suns. They left him whimpering with one arm over his streaming eyes and went back into the drinking house to open some windows.

Lethe thus found himself being regarded by curious passers-by who were clearly wondering what a cross-galaxy pilot was doing with a stinking reject from Lriam at his feet.

"Crawl, damn you," he hissed loudly at the bundle on the ground and prodded Ygoi with his toe.

"For fuck's sake just get out your gun and finish me off now," was the plea.

Lethe realised the other man was totally incapable of independent movement unless he either rolled or wriggled and from the state of his clothes that had been how he had got this far. It nearly broke his heart to think about it. "Just stay here. I've got a transporter nearby,."

Ygoi screwed up his eyes against the glare of the suns as the other man walked away and wondered where Lethe thought he was going to go. Passers-by had seen this tramp before. He had been around for a while now and wasn't any bother. Patiently waiting for something, even if only to die, too much in pain to talk much but perfectly polite when he made the effort. He was obviously an intelligent, well-educated man but he never told anything of his past life. Now he was watching someone or something, he wasn't just staring at the ground as he so often did. He kept looking down the road with tears streaming from his eyes but he never made a sound. There were several witnesses, but nobody offered help, when the cross-galaxy pilot tipped the tramp unceremoniously into the sealed back of a land transporter. Best thing for him, they thought. It was over for him now.

Lethe had never been more glad in his life to see his spaceship as he was that day. The land transporter shot into the docking bay and Lethe thankfully shut the outer doors and remotely activated all the anti-tracking devices he possessed to deflect the Lriam beams.

He opened the back of the transporter and thought for a moment that Ygoi's dearest wish had been granted and there was a corpse in the back of his transporter.

"Still alive?" he asked.

"Yes."

"Good. Out you get. Nobody can find you in here so you can have a bath and some decent food then I'm going to get you healed."

"You can't heal the wounds of Lriam in this galaxy."

"Don't tell me things I already know. For one thing I do have my cross-galaxy licence and for another do you think your injuries can be healed by the likes of my grandmother with her incantations and herbs?"

"You would have thought so once," came the reply as Ygoi's haggard face looked up. "Where is this?"

"My spaceship. I've got all the anti-tracking programs running and the water only takes thirty seconds to heat up. So you go and have a bath and I'll get the kettle on. Then I'm taking you back to Earth."

"What?"

Lethe suddenly smiled to see the hope and disbelief of the other man. He knew his mad idea was going to work. It had to. "I've managed to hack into their primitive Internet system and I've been keeping in touch with Jenni. I'll just send her a mail you're coming and we'll soon get you all mended."

"But it's been over ten years since we were there."

"Yes, and their medical science had advanced enormously. So stop feeling sorry for yourself and go and have that bath."

"I can't," Ygoi explained as his former co-pilot hauled him out of the transporter as though he had been a rag doll and dumped him on the floor. He held out his hands with their fingers twisted into fists. "I haven't been able to wipe my arse for over a year, never mind wash my hands afterwards."

Lethe looked hard at those cages. The blue trid metal of Lriam was famous. Only a very high blast of energy could cut it and it never rusted. The fingers inside were black but whether from dirt or lack of circulation he couldn't tell. To his horror the metal went under the skin at the back of the wrist and he could see the shape of it running to the elbow where it re-emerged and was welded to a band round the arm to lock the joint. Which explained why Ygoi hadn't been able to manage the mug of ale.

"Oh my fuck," he intoned. "Come on, let's wash the bits we can reach and then see what we can do with the rest of you. Do your legs work?"

"No." Ygoi hauled himself semi-upright using the other man as a crutch. "They hammered bolts through my knees. Sorry about the stink."

Lethe lifted Ygoi in his arms and was appalled at how light he was. He consciously closed his mind to the terrible smell. "At least you're alive and you've lost such a lot of weight I guess you'd fit into some of my clothes now anyway."

Ygoi almost smiled as he put his arms, child-like, round Lethe's neck. "I'll forgive you if you don't lend me any cross-galaxy blues."

The clothes had stuck to the skin of the man who hadn't been able to wash for over a year so Lethe helped Ygoi into the bath then turned the shower on him, clothes and all. He got a knife and hacked off the knotted hair while the clothes soaked through and then he finally saw the full extent of what Lriam security services could do to a prisoner.

"Not very pretty is it?" asked the man who sat naked in the bath while the hot water washed the stink and grime off his scarred and pierced skin. The blue metal had been punched through his knees to disable the joints and the pain transmitting rods were in his ears, his nose, his nipples and his navel. But it was when Lethe saw what had been pierced lower down that he was sick in the basin. He could barely bring himself to look as he helped the other man. The scars on Ygoi's face didn't look quite so bad once the tatty bits of beard had been shaved off and most of the black went from his hands once the shower water had been pumped through the cages.

"At least you smell a bit sweeter," Lethe remarked as he wrapped Ygoi in a towel. "I'll go and find you some clothes and get the kettle on." He still couldn't believe it as he crossed the corridor to the room where he slept. He would never, ever have expected to see Ygoi Roemtek in that state. A lesser man would have given up and died from the pain long ago. He could not imagine what it must have felt like as those rods were driven through the flesh. Rumour had it that the rods were heated first then shot through with a gun so the burned flesh stuck to the metal and it couldn't be removed. He chose some fairly loose garments and went back to the bathroom where he had to dress the other man then he carried him along to the kitchen where he managed to sit at the table and look around a bit.

Some of the old sparkle was back in those dark eyes. "Looks like you've done well for yourself."

Lethe shrugged. "I earn a living."

"You're not wearing a ring any more. What happened to your wife?"

Lethe gave his guest a mug of tea and remembered how he hadn't been able to drink the ale. He looked round his kitchen, grabbed the sharpest knife in his arsenal and chopped the head and end off a hollow-handled spoon. He dropped the handle into the mug and said proudly, "There you are. One drinking aid."

"Fuck me," Ygoi responded, impressed. "What made you think of that?"

"Don't know really. I'll make you some soup and you can drink that the same way. I daresay you're hungry."

"Don't get hungry any more. It's kind of hard to eat when you can't get food to your mouth with your hands. I don't have any money so I can't buy food. Some people used to give me a couple of pieces and if I saved up ten I could buy some soup or stew at a drinking house, then I had to drink it by sticking my face in the bowl. If people gave me scraps of food I couldn't eat them. You must have seen the beggars outside the prison eating the scraps people had thrown on the ground."

Lethe had seen them. Like nearly everyone else who passed by, he had had no pity for the crippled, blinded, stinking remnants of humanity. He didn't even want to think what had brought Ygoi to that state but he guessed he would be told when the other was ready to talk. He turned his mind to the more mundane and looked through his cupboards, fortunately he had done some shopping quite recently.

"Leek and potato or carrot and beetroot?"

"Whichever." Ygoi sucked the tea through the handle and watched the other man at work in his kitchen. "You never answered my question about your wife."

"No, I didn't, did I?" Lethe answered unwillingly, wishing the other man had forgotten he had asked the question in the first place and then realising that was extremely unlikely,

"So?"

"Lethe hurled potatoes and carrots into the cooker and set it to the soup setting. "She got a boyfriend."

"That's a bit hard on you, isn't it? How long were you married?"

"About a year and a half."

"You still paying her off?"

"She had sex with him. I shot the pair of them."

Ygoi nearly bit his drinking tube in half. This wasn't the absent-minded but phenomenally intelligent, rather gentle young co-pilot he had known. This was a flint-hearted mercenary who had taken the option provided by Millio galaxy custom and had killed the wife who had cheated on him. Lethe Miarren had changed and Ygoi Roemtek wasn't too sure of their relationship any more.

"Couldn't you just have ended the commitment? You waited long enough to marry her."

"What, and been like you, paying money to the slut for the rest of my life?" Lethe took the soup out of the cooker and finished it off by hand. He gave a bowl full to his guest. "Still paying that slag you committed to?"

"She committed to the other bloke soon after our commitment was formally ended. I wasn't rich enough for her. Can't imagine her without vast sums of money, can you? I think Epian's still living with her. I still miss him and she took him away from me when he was two."

"How old is he now?"

"Must be getting on for eighteen. No idea where they are or anything." Ygoi transferred the drinking aid from the tea to the soup and took a cautious suck. "You can still cook then. Where are you living now? Is your mother still on Nurtasia?"

Lethe broke up some bread and threaded a fork into the right hand cage so Ygoi could stab it and reach his own mouth. "I just live in this ship now. Don't really have a home planet any more."

"Working at the moment?"

"Just got back from a cross galaxy to Ronet. I have no idea why I went in that dive where I found you. Do you remember how we used to second-guess each other's thoughts? Perhaps you sent out some kind of help message."

Ygoi half smiled. "I'd been sending out help messages for a year but I guess you were out of range."

Lethe gave him a hug now he smelled a bit better. "You get on with lunch, we need to get you fattened up a bit. I'll go and set course for Earth. Want me to turn the lights down a bit? Your eyes look very sore."

Ygoi rubbed his weeping eyes on the shoulder of clean clothes and tried to steady his voice. "No, it's fine. I need to get used to light levels again. Can you remember the flight plan?"

Lethe had to smile. "Engraved in my memory."

"How is Jenni these days?"

"Married apparently. A couple of years after we met her. Sounds a bit like our commitment but not so binding. Some guy who works in something called the Home Office. Whatever that is."

"They have a funny set up on Earth."

"You'll never guess the best bit," Lethe announced proudly, finally able to share his crazy idea. "Her guy's brother is something called a surgeon. They make people better when they get sick and broken."

Ygoi looked at him and had forgotten that what he felt inside him was hope. "And you think…."

"Sure do. If those people on Earth can mend each other then I don't see why they can't mend you. I'll go plot the course then come back and get you to bed for some rest."

Left alone in the kitchen, Ygoi Roemtek went back to his tea and soup and didn't even care that they had got muddled in the tube.

TWO

Lady Jennifer Kirkwood-Barnes was dreaming again. Staring at her computer screen and not doing much to revise her website. Twelve years ago today her father had died, ashamed of his rebellious daughter. If only he could see her now. She could never decide whether he would have been sorry for all those things he had said. Somehow she doubted it. A melodious beep from her computer told her some mail had arrived.

From: Star Sailor 461
To: Jenni K_B
Hi, Jenni. Met up with Ygoi after all these years but he's not too good so I'm bringing him along for your man's brother to have a look at. I've located you through your Internet tracker and you seem to have enough room. See you on Tuesday. Lethe

Melancholia was replaced by panic and Jenni realised she didn't know what the hell to do. Outside she could see her husband and brother-in-law were having an all-rules-barred game of croquet, rather childish of the Home Office Under Secretary and the neurosurgeon but then it was a lovely day and they had both had a gruelling couple of weeks.

When the emails had started coming about five years earlier, Jenni had thought they were hoaxes being sent from the only other people on Earth who had known Lethe Miarren and Ygoi Roemtek so she had rung them up but they had protested innocence and she had believed them. The emails had started a few months after her husband had decided he wanted internet access at home and had encouraged his wife to do the shopping that way rather than go through the drag of driving to the supermarket. Then they had moved out to this country home and had set up its own website and the emails had followed her there from her Hotmail account even though she hadn't told the writer of her change of address. Every time she had clicked on reply in Hotmail the message had failed to be sent. But somehow things were getting through from the Ravenswood address. Rather like having a gentle hero up in the stars looking after her. And she loved his name of Star Sailor. She had remembered from her Latin lessons at school that it was a translation of astronaut. Which was a darned clever thing for a man who had been on Earth only thirty six hours to know. But then Lethe was clever. Made her feel a bit of a dunce anyway in spite of her expensive education.

She looked back at the screen. The problem was she had never told her husband. It wasn't the easiest thing in the world to say to the man you loved, "Oh, by the way, darling, I'm in email contact with a man from another galaxy." She had never even told him about those breathless hours she had spent in the company of two extra-terrestrials over ten years ago. It had been a mad, crazy day and a half and if it weren't for the fact she still exchanged Christmas cards with the Lacey family in Wiltshire it would have been too easy to call it a dream. Except the emails kept coming. It had never occurred to her that Lethe and Ygoi would ever come back. They had no reason to. There was nothing for them on Earth except the prospect of being treated like a freak show and probably sent to a psychiatric unit as a couple of dangerous nutters.

Now, it seemed, she had to walk out onto the croquet lawn and say, "Darling, we're going to have some house guests for a few days. I'm afraid one of them isn't well." She could do that. That would be all right. Then he would ask their names and think they were a bit foreign. Then he would ask how she knew them and she would have to start lying. Or appear to be completely mad She had never lied to James about anything. Not even about how she earned her living when they had met. The problem with James was he could spot a fib at a hundred paces. He was an honourable man and she owed him the same courtesy.

Look forward to seeing you. Please advise nature of "not too good" if you can. Love, Jenni.

She clicked the Send button and flung open the French windows onto the croquet lawn.

"Darling," she called. "We're going to have a couple of house guests. They've just sent an email. I'm afraid one of them's not very well and they're hoping he can rest here for a while." Oh my God, she thought to herself, do they have weird illnesses in the Millio galaxy that could infect the whole human population on Earth? Why hadn't she said no?

Sir James came across to join her, ducking the croquet ball his brother lobbed at him. "You don't sound very happy. Are they friends of yours?"

Sir David came to join his brother. "Aha! Old flames, is it?" He suddenly thought that was a bit tactless given the parlous state of his brother's marriage and gave Jenni his most charming grin. "Sorry. Tactless. Well, how many?"

"Two," the unhappy Jenni admitted, quite used to her brother-in-law's sense of humour. At least he hadn't called her a strumpet this time. "Two men, and they're not together as it were so I'll have to ask for two rooms for them."

"Well, we've got eighteen so that shouldn't be a problem. When are they coming?" her husband asked solicitously.

"Tuesday."

"Well, that's all right. We're closed on Tuesdays so you won't have Joe Public watching their arrival. Are they driving down from London?" For some reason she was looking over his shoulder. He engaged her eyes and knew she wouldn't lie to him. He began to get a bit worried. Maybe it really was an old flame. Or some other hideous secret from her miscreant past. "Jen? What's the matter?"

Jenni took a deep breath and looked her husband squarely in the eye. "They're flying in from the Millio galaxy. It's a bit beyond Jupiter, turn left at Pluto. Or maybe the other way round, I can't remember."

For a split second James thought his wife had gone completely mad. Then the penny dropped. The two men looked at each other and roared with laughter. "Good God! You mean it's those hippies from Basingstoke you met at that charity bash," James chuckled. "I suppose they'll be arriving in a purple Dormobile with green cannabis leaves painted on the sides at the least. Well, stick the van in the stables and thank God they're coming on Tuesday."

"Did you say one of them's not well?" the surgeon enquired. "Nothing contagious, I hope?"

"Not so far as I know. "Jenni didn't really know what else to say.

"And what are their names?" James asked. "You'll have to remind me, I know it was something peculiar."

"Lethe Miarren and Ygoi Roemtek." Jenni could see the wariness in her husband's eyes. "They really are friends of mine. I haven't seen them for ages, that's all." She didn't disillusion him about the hippies. After all, missing bits out wasn't quite the same as telling a bald-faced lie.

James was still a bit baffled but couldn't think what else Jenni could mean. "Well, be nice for you to see them again. You got on rather well as I remember. Come on, David, my turn to bully off, I think."

Jenni went back to the house and back to her computer screen. More mail had arrived.

Thanks, Jenni. Ygoi has been held prisoner on Lriam for a while and he's been rather badly injured and can't do much for himself at the moment. At least Earth is outside the torture beams of Lriam Security but we've got to find a way of getting the trid rods out of him as they transmit the beams. We're coming in my ship which is smaller than his old one and I've had your house up on the videoradionic. I reckon we can get down between that line of trees you've got. What have you told your husband?

Jenni smiled. *I told him you're flying in from the Millio galaxy which he thinks means you are hippies from Basingstoke. Not sure how he's going to get his head round the spaceship.* Send.

Jenni went off to find the housekeeper to ask her to make up the rooms. It was all a long way from her one-room bedsit in Kingston-on-Thames and the life she had been leading when she had met Lethe and Ygoi. She couldn't really remember too well what they looked like and hadn't got any photos of them. Lethe was tall, slim and blond and Ygoi shorter, more sturdy and dark and that was about it. They had both been very pleasant, intelligent men even if they were from another galaxy, they had completed their mission on Earth and gone away again leaving no traces they had ever been. Except the Lacey family in Wiltshire no longer had their vintage MG. She just hoped it was a very small spaceship that could be passed off as some kind of outbuilding.

"So, my love," her husband asked her across the dinner table that evening, "any further messages from the Basingstoke hippies? You said one of them wasn't well."

Jenni had made up her mind that she, at least, was going to tell the absolute truth no matter how ludicrous it sounded. "Apparently he's been imprisoned and tortured and got some rods stuck in him that need to be taken out or a pain beam can be remotely transmitted to hurt him."

"Good grief! Can't he just have a dose of the flu or something?" James asked lightly.

The mind of the neurosurgeon who sometimes worked free of charge for Medecins sans Frontieres sharpened. "Where did this happen?"

"On the planet Lriam."

"God knows where that is. Probably out in the Middle East somewhere. Or maybe Africa. What was he doing out there?"

"Knowing Ygoi probably some kind of trade mission as he would call it. You or I would call it piracy."

James leaned his elbows on the table and regarded his wife solemnly. "Have you invited a criminal to our house?"

Jenni was quite well aware of the implications of that for her husband's career. "No. I don't know whether the imprisonment was justified or not, he could have been on holiday for all I know. But he's been released and there are no charges pending in this country. Or any other country on Earth."

David checked the diary on his phone. "I've got nothing scheduled that can't be put off until Wednesday. I'd like to see this man's injuries in case it's something that needs to be taken up with the Foreign Office. Will I get straight answers out of him or will he be stoned out of his skull?"

"Oh, you'll get straight answers."

"Good. Then perhaps we'll get to the bottom of this hippie puzzle of yours," James decided. "Shall we open another bottle of Chablis just for the hell of it? What time should we expect these hippies on Tuesday?"

"I've no idea. Probably depends on the traffic," Jenni replied sweetly.

Her husband shot her a shrewd look. He still loved his wife dearly and he had a nagging feeling she was telling the truth. Which didn't make any sense whatsoever.

Sir James and Lady Kirkwood-Barnes were breakfasting in the company of Sir David Kirkwood-Barnes on that wet and cheerless Tuesday morning when the housekeeper interrupted them.

"An American gentleman to see you, Madam. I think he said his name is Mirren? He has rather a strange accent."

Jenni's heart started banging against her ribs. She had expected the roar of engines, a blast of white-hot heat from a magnificent coppery machine such as there had been last time. Anything but rain and the housekeeper. She got to her feet. "Where are they?"

"I found them on the doorstep, Madam. He says he won't come in by himself and his friend can't walk. There's another one of them sitting in the porch but I think he's a bit drunk."

Jenni almost ran from the room, much to the consternation of her husband, and went into the hall. There on the step and looking as every bit as gorgeous as she remembered was the young man with the blond hair curling to his shoulders and the slightly odd clothes that always looked so home made somehow. He was wearing a flattering shade of indigo with some quasi-military silver flashes on the shoulder and she remembered Ygoi had worn something similar last time she had seen him. Now, it seemed, the proud Ygoi was almost in rags.

"Hullo," Jenni said nervously.

Lethe gave her a hug and a kiss on the cheek and she remembered how unaffected the two had been. "You're looking good. Big house."

Jenni returned the hug. "I'll show you round it later. It's just so good to see you again."

David wiped his mouth on his napkin and bounded up from the table after a suitable time had elapsed for his sister-in-law to greet an old friend. "The Mater's old wheelchair, don't you think, Jimbo?"

James found the wheelchair in the gun cupboard and trundled it along to the front door where a good looking young man wearing hippyish clothes was chatting with Jenni and David.

But it was the other visitor who worried the doctor. "Bring the chariot, Jimbo!" the elder brother ordered. There was a thin, dark haired man sitting half curled up in the porch, his hands were clenched into fists in his lap and, on closer inspection, David could see these fists were shut in cages of peculiarly fine blue meshed chicken wire. He gently pushed back one sleeve of the man's shirt and saw the wires go under the skin. Repulsion washed over him and he looked at the scar tissue on the man's face. This he had seen before, spikes had clearly been rammed through the flesh as a form of torture and the lower jaw was out of kilter. The rods in the ears and nose were an unknown phenomenon and an experimental twist of the lobe did no good whatsoever. Clearly this victim of torture was nearly at the end of his tolerance. He didn't flinch or swear at the flexing of the ear although it obviously hurt.

"Sorry, old man. Looks like you've been through it a bit. Right, we're just going to get you into this chair and into the house then I'll have a proper look at you. Your knees been broken?" An affirmative nod. "Thought so. The bastards. Come on, I'll just have a preliminary look at you and then run you along to the hospital to get your hands cut free. I'd do it here but the wire's very close to your skin."

"You can't cut it," the American man supplied. "It's trid from Lriam and they punched it through him from his ears to his knees. Believe me, I've tried."

There is was again. Lriam. Vaguely David wondered if it was a peculiar hippy pronunciation of Libya or Guam or somewhere like that. And what the heck was trid when it was at home?

The two brothers gently lifted Ygoi into the wheelchair and he was a featherweight in their arms. There was no fat on his body, his bones stuck through his skin and they were frightened even their careful action could break his bones. He didn't say anything, just looked totally bewildered and rather lost. The brothers began to wonder if he even spoke English. James pushed him along to the morning room where the half eaten breakfast was still on the table.

"Shall we introduce ourselves?" he asked the man he had just parked at the table. "I am James Kirkwood-Barnes and this is my brother, David. I believe you know my wife already?" He noticed the man had extraordinarily dark eyes. Nice eyes bur haunted by pain. There was intelligence in their depths and eventually the man found the words he wanted to say.

"We met her once for a day or so about ten years ago. She has been in touch with Lethe via email, I believe." He paused to get his breath back as even that effort had exhausted him then he awkwardly offered his hand in greeting as he remembered Earth people did. "Ygoi Roemtek. An odd name but my family was Russian and Swedish a long time ago."

James began to relax. A lot had been explained in a few words and now it was all starting to make sense. Ygoi Roemtek's fluent English was accented, his voice was soft and his manner perfectly civil. It was odd to take a caged hand but the gesture seemed to comfort the injured man somehow. His elbow seemed rather oddly stuck too which was puzzling.

"May I call you Ygoi?" he asked, pronouncing it the Russian way. "Good. Well, eat up some breakfast then we'll let David get you sorted out. Do you like eggs and bacon or are you a toast and marmalade man?"

Ygoi looked at the odd food on the table and didn't like to try and guess where some of it had come from.

It was all rather bewildering and thought was getting to be too much effort. He looked round for the attendant Lethe just to reassure himself that he wasn't really dreaming. He hadn't finally passed out in the gutters of Sunara. He wasn't going to die any more. He was going to get better. "Just some bread will be fine. Thank you."

Lethe was quite dexterous at breaking up bread and providing a fork for Ygoi, and the others watched as the carer tended to the invalid. "You must drink something as well," he persuaded the sick man gently.

"What's wrong with your arms?" the doctor asked. "Try him with a bit of milk, Jenni my love, mash up some bread into milk and see if he can take that."

Lethe pulled up Ygoi's sleeves to show the frame round the elbows and thus revealed the barbarity of the metal under the skin.

"Good God!" James exploded. "How the hell did they do that?"

"Pushed the spikes through the arm," Ygoi explained as though it was the most obvious thing in the world. "They do your hands first."

"How do you mean, 'do'?" David wanted to know. He wondered where on Earth this man had been to get into such a state. And how had the other one found him and brought him here? There hadn't been so much as a car outside and there was no sign of luggage or anything and they looked too poor to have afforded a taxi from the station in Exeter.

As Ygoi was being fed tiny amounts of bread and milk by Jenni, Lethe explained what he had been told. "First they break your fingers to fit them in the cage and hammer the cage round. Then they put one or two spikes in on the back of your wrist and push them along under the skin to the elbows then they attach the spikes to these bands round your arms to fix the elbow as well. It's to stop you cutting your ears and nose off."

Three people used to a more humane life on Earth suddenly didn't want to eat any more breakfast.

"The rods transmit the pain beams," Lethe continued. "So far as we know Earth is outside the scope of Lriam's beams so Ygoi's safe enough while he's here but they've planted receivers in his brain. When the beams are at full strength then they can just blow your head apart whenever it suits them." He looked at the faces of the two resident men at the table. "Jenni did tell you we're from another galaxy, right?"

"We thought you were from Basingstoke," James offered. He looked at his brother and neither knew what to say. This was hardly the time to ask his wife what was really going on here. Somehow, unlikely though it seemed, it all made sense.

"What is that stuff?" Lethe asked Jenni, leaving the men to recover their wits.

"Bacon. It comes from a pig. Meat, smoked and sliced."

"And what is a pig?" Lethe thought he knew the term from somewhere but he was starting to feel very tired.

"An animal. Four legs, snuffly nose and a curly tail."

"You eat animals?" Lethe asked appalled. "Do you eat people too?"

Jenni wanted to laugh. "No, we don't eat people. We only eat some animals – sheep, pigs and cows mostly, and some birds and fish."

Lethe shuddered. "Ugh. I don't think I could ever eat anything that had been living and breathing."

Jenni patted his arm. "Then for as long as you are here you must tell people you are vegetarian."

"Vegetarian. Got it. Oh fuck it, Ygoi's gone to sleep again. He does that a lot. I'm seriously wondering if he's been drugged with some sort of slow release compound."

David checked the sleeping man's pulse. "Your friend is exhausted. I'd guess he can't sleep for long because of the pain. Can he take morphine?"

"What's morphine?"

"A pain killing drug, most often used in the last stages of life where pain relief is needed."

"Are you saying Ygoi won't live much longer?"

"I'm saying I'm amazed he's lived this long. Jimbo, I shall pop back to my surgery for a few essentials. I suggest you let this one have a sleep then try the bolt cutters on that wire. It's pretty thin, shouldn't take much to cut it."

Lethe sniffed the jar of marmalade. "What's this?"

"Marmalade," Jenni told him. "Jam made from oranges. You eat it on toast."

Lethe had to try it. "Tastes good," he decided.

James went with his brother to the door. "What do you reckon?"

"They are either the two best conmen in the world or they really are from another galaxy. They're certainly not from Basingstoke. And I don't like the look of the dark one. I think he'll be lucky to see tomorrow."

"Under hats?"

"Absolutely. God knows what'll happen if he dies on us." David walked to the corner of the stable yard where his car was parked. "Jimbo!" he bawled. "Come and see this!"

James dashed through the rain to stand beside his brother.

Just visible among the ancient horse chestnut trees of the old avenue facing the front of the house was a strange metallic craft. It looked to be about as long as a single decker bus but rather wider and if you just caught a glimpse of it and didn't know about the men in the house you could be forgiven for thinking it was a bizarre playhouse for the children of a wealthy man.

"Good God," James breathed. "Bring your specimen bottles and take some samples back to the lab on those two. Meantime I'd best get on with the bolt cutters." He went back to the house honestly not sure what he was thinking.

By the time David got back with his medical kit, Ygoi was awake and was being pushed around the house by Lethe while Jenni gave them a guided tour. She heard her husband calling them down so they used the lift that had been fitted for her late mother-in-law and arrived in the morning room where the brothers were just setting out an array of instruments, bags and bottles on the breakfast table which the housekeeper had cleared.

"Right, Ygoi, you first," David requested. "First of all I'm giving you some intravenous painkiller for immediate relief and a shot of some vitamins to give you a bit of a boost. Ordinarily I'd get you hospitalised immediately and put on a drip but I'm not sure you could cope with even that at the moment." He pushed up the other man's sleeve and shot a syringe in at the upper arm hoping that human life forms from another galaxy weren't that different from those on Earth. He looked at the caged hands and then at his brother. "I told you to get the bolt cutters on those."

"I did. They wouldn't cut."

"You're kidding me?"

James solemnly handed across a pair of cutters capable of severing a quarter-inch piece of steel. "Here you go, you try."

David inspected the wire. It flexed easily enough in his fingers so he really couldn't see the problem. He set to with the bolt cutters but, try as he might, that fine wire would not cut. Eventually, pink and perspiring, he gave up.

"What did you call this metal?" he asked.

"Trid," Lethe told him. "It's a pure metal mined only on Lriam. It's very fashionable for jewellery as it's so easily moulded. I used to wear a bracelet of it but I kind of went off it when I saw Ygoi's built-in variety."

"But if it's that malleable, how do you drive a stake of it through someone?"

"That's base trid with the impurities in it. It's mined in two forms, the stiffer base trid is found nearer the top of the mines and the deeper you go the purer the metal. It can be found in liquid form but that solidifies on contact with air."

"So if we cut off the air supply would it go back to liquid?"

"Not unless you can catch it within a day. It doesn't rust, you can't melt it with acid and once it's solidified, you can't heat pure trid high enough to soften it in any furnace known to humans. You can cut it with a high energy blast but then the heat would turn Ygoi's hands to soot if I did it to those cages."

"So how do we get your friend out of his cages?" Lethe shrugged. "I have no idea. Jenni told me you make people better so I brought him here."

"Don't you have doctors where you come from?" Lethe shook his head.

"So what happens to the sick, the old, the injured?"

"They die," Lethe said simply. "Or get better. We have a few herbs and flowers and things that help."

"So you have no doctors, no nurses, no hospitals, nothing like that?"

"No. We have a few women, well, mostly women, who have been taught how to heal with herbs and they pass the craft on. My grandmother is one of them."

"But surely it's human nature to help one another? You helped Ygoi here. Don't you believe in compassion? You just said at breakfast that you couldn't eat something that has lived and breathed, yet you would let your fellow man die from a curable disease?"

Lethe thought about that. "We don't have many diseases really. I guess if you left here sick you died of it on the way or got better so the diseases never got to our galaxy. We don't ask what people die of, we just burn them when they do. Then the ash from the bones is used to fertilise the soil."

There was something so simple, so matter of fact and so unquestioning about the young man's explanation that any thoughts he maybe really was a hippy from Basingstoke were gone for ever. A thought occurred to the surgeon.

"So the odds are your immune system is lower than ours. If you're not used to colds and flu and such you could really get laid low. What about STDs?"

"What's that?"

"Sexually transmitted diseases. Passed on between copulating adults when one is infected."

Lethe looked faintly startled. "Never heard of anything like that."

"But you do procreate through intercourse?"

"Um, yes," Lethe replied, wondering if there was any other way.

"Do you have marriage then?" Jenni asked.

"We have what is called commitment, which I suppose is the same thing. A man and a woman commit to each other for life and if it doesn't work out he has to pay her an income until she dies or commits to another relationship."

"Even if she is a higher wage earner?"

"Committed women don't earn wages. There isn't much women do to earn money really apart from working in the fields. Then after they've got themselves into the partnership it's their job to raise the children and teach them."

There was a silence in the room while those not used to such basic concepts mentally digested them. They were interrupted by the housekeeper.

"Grocery delivery is here, Madam. They've sent Coke instead of the organic Cola you ordered. Do you want me to send it back?"

"No, let Jim in the garden have it like he did last time. It'll save his wife carting it home from Tesco and I know his children get through gallons of it. I'll order some organic Cola next time. Thanks." She smiled almost apologetically at the two visitors. "I'm afraid I won't drink the stuff since someone told me it can dissolve tooth enamel overnight. But there's nothing else better with Bacardi."

The painkillers started to kick in and for the first time in months Ygoi Roemtek felt capable of rational thought and speech. "Perhaps it can also dissolve trid in that case." He wondered what Bacardi was but didn't like to ask too much at once.

Those who were more used to the properties of Coca Cola weren't convinced but anything had to be worth a try. "Good idea," Jenny agreed. "Mrs McDougall, I need the Coke and a large bowl."

The two women left the room and Jenni presently came back with two enormous bottles of brown liquid and a mixing bowl. The Coke fizzed and hissed in the bowl which she put on the table then she said to Ygoi, "OK, stick your hand in this then."

Lethe pushed Ygoi over to the table and the latter plunged his right fist into the mixing bowl.

"Anything happening?" Lethe asked after a few moments.

"Tickling a bit."

"Is that good or bad?" the doctor asked.

"Just a bit odd, really."

"Give it half an hour. Jimbo, some books, I think to support this man's arm while we see what Coca Cola can do to trid."

They sat round in various chairs in the morning room while the Coke fizzed in the bowl and the rain drummed down outside. James and David exchanged a few desultory remarks about the prospects for the cricket season but Lethe was too worried about what was going on in that bowl to ask what cricket was. He guessed it was some form of sport.

"Thirty minutes is up," Jenni announced rather obviously.

David helped Ygoi to lift his arm from the bowl. Both men stared at the hand. "Good God," David said, "I do believe it's worked. Stick your hand back for another half an hour and if that gets rid of it I suggest we go and buy as much Coca Cola as we can get and you take a bath in the stuff."

Lethe rushed across to have a look. There was no doubt about it. The trid wires were only half the thickness and in some parts completely dissolved. "That is incredible," he breathed. "No wonder you won't drink it. Reckon it will work on base trid as well?"

"One step at the time I think, don't you?" David asked kindly as he carefully replaced the twisted hand back in the Coke. "I have a bad feeling that removing the cage is only going to be the first stage in a long process."

After an hour there was no doubt about it. The cage was gone from the hand and the ends of the base trid in the arm were definitely beginning to dissolve.

"Right," James declared. "Brother and wife of mine, to the supermarkets. Buy the stuff by the trolley load. Lethe I suggest you stay here with Ygoi for now as I think you may find the delights of Tesco rather overwhelming at this stage."

The two men from Sunara watched from the morning room window as a trio of cars set off from the stable block. Ygoi looked at the freed hand in his lap and could feel the rather pleasant fizzing sensation under the skin on his arm as the ends of the base trid slowly dissolved.

"I wondered why you'd taken the bracelet off," he remarked idly. "Thank you for rescuing me. You know I can never go back, don't you?"

"Does that matter?"

Ygoi looked out at the English landscape, the soft colours even more muted by the rain and so gentle for eyes that had once been blinded by the dark. "No."

"Do you think you can learn to live here?"

"I'd guess that's what I've got to find out." He paused to get his breath and to put into words a farewell that was breaking his heart. "What I am trying to say is, don't feel you have to stay with me. You can take off any time you like and nobody will find your ship, nobody will come hunting for me from our galaxy or anything like that. I can remain unfound more easily on my own than both of us could. As I said, I can never go back. Even if they can get the trid out of my body they can't get it out of my brain and the rods are just their code for the location of the receivers. They've pierced me nine times, so there are nine receivers in my brain. That's how they could reach me on Sunara."

Lethe looked out at the landscape that was rather drab and miserable to his eyes more used to the glare of Sunara's twin suns. He and Ygoi had known each other a long time. They had travelled galaxies together and he wasn't quite sure what sort of reception he would get anyway as he wasn't sure his own actions didn't count as some form of crime. He looked at the man sitting in the wheelchair and thought again how gaunt his face looked but he hadn't heard Ygoi say so much for a long time. "I won't leave you. Not until I'm sure you'll be OK. You heard what they said, we're from Basingstoke. We're a couple of hippies. Ygoi, what the fuck are hippies?"

"I have absolutely no idea. And what else did they say we are?"

"Vegetarians. Whatever they are."

Ygoi had been well read once. "Don't eat meat." He looked round the morning room with its furniture so old but its atmosphere so welcoming. "Funny sort of a house," he remarked idly. "Bit big."

"We didn't really look into any houses last time," Lethe reminded him, heartened to hear the other man getting almost chatty. "How are you feeling?"

"Odd. As though my body's gone to sleep and left my mind behind."

Lethe gave him a gentle hug. "Told you. It's all going to get better now."

Ygoi heaved some more breath into his lungs and hoped Lethe was right. Both men jumped when a flock of rooks took off from the black poplars along the drive with a lot of cawing and flapping. They had both forgotten about birds. Looking at the alien landscape they suddenly realised just how far they had come and just how lost and vulnerable they were.

Ygoi reached out and nudged Lethe's hand with his own. "We'll survive. We've been to worse places than this one."

Lethe saw something flash past in the sky. Odd, looked like a small, cross-galaxy machine. He looked a bit harder but whatever it was had gone. They had something called aeroplanes on this planet he remembered. "Sure," he agreed. "We'll survive."

THREE

"How are you getting on?" the voice of the doctor asked and he inspected the right hand and arm of his latest patient who was gazing out of the window of the morning room. "Hm, looks like you might need surgery to remove those rods in your arm. Never mind, we've got the Coke so let's get you in the bath. We'll put you in the late Mater's suite, it's got all you need. Poor old girl had diabetes at the end and lost both legs."

Ygoi had been watching the birds on the grass outside and his eyes focussed reluctantly on the man leaning over him in the wheelchair. He had no idea what diabetes was or how you lost legs which were, presumably, attached to your hips. He tried to get his thoughts in order but although his body didn't hurt so much his mind had definitely gone wandering off somewhere.

David could tell the painkillers had kicked in and he was glad to think this man's suffering was being alleviated. He seemed to have overestimated the dose a bit but that had to be better than the acute pain. He looked at him sharply and wondered if he was going to need another shot of something to wake him up a bit. "You all right? No that's a ridiculous question to ask someone in your situation. Come on, let's get rid of the trid then we'll be more into the kind of medicine I can cope with."

"Why are you doing this?" Ygoi asked as he finally focussed this thoughts as he was wheeled along to the lift with Lethe in attendance. "To you I am a total stranger, To anyone else in the Millio galaxy I am a social outcast. Yet you are trying to heal me and your brother had no hesitation in taking my hand."

"It's what we do, James and I. He is with the Home Office and does his bit to make this country a better place to be and I am a neurosurgeon which means I mend injured brains as best I can. But I do work on other parts of the body as well. One day I will tell you about Medecins Sans Frontieres, but I'd guess this isn't a good time. So first I get the trid out of your body. I've checked the bit we've managed to get from your hands and it's not magnetic, so I'm taking you along to the hospital and giving you a scan to see exactly where those receivers are in your brain. Then I'm going to see if I can get them out before they do any damage. I'll x-ray your hands and knees too while I've got you in there so I know what I'm dealing with."

The three men went into a room on the first floor of the house. The door had been widened to allow the wheelchair to get in easily, there was a strange contraption beside the bed and the door to the bathroom slid across. Jenni and James were giggling like a pair of children as they tipped bottle after bottle of Coke into the bath.

"Right, Lethe," David instructed. "Come and learn how to use a hoist to get this mate of yours into the bath. And you, Ygoi, I hope you aren't claustrophobic as you're going in that bath ears, nose and all. We've got you a snorkel to breathe with so you won't drown."

Jenni discreetly withdrew while the men tended to Ygoi and got him undressed and into his Coca Cola bath. She went into the adjoining room where once her mother-in-law's nurse had slept and sat idly on the bed so she could look out of the window. The room was on the west side of the house and she had a good view of the spaceship. There was some rather earthy masculine laughter from the room next door and she half smiled to herself. This was all just too weird. There was a spaceship in her garden and an extra-terrestrial had just been hoisted into a bath full of Coca Cola. She sat with her elbows on her knees, head in hands, until the jolting of the bedsprings told her someone had sat next to her.

It was her husband who kissed her ear. "Well, that's your friend Roemtek totally submerged for the next hour or so. I must say I wish you'd told me about those two. Bit of a shock to the system."

"It was ten years ago," she began.

He gave her a hug and knew she didn't like to think about those days. He had remembered about her father, he knew she was heartbroken they had no children. But she had put up a wall round her feelings and he couldn't get through to her any more. "Come on, it's stopped raining. Let's go and look at the bus in our avenue."

Jenni looked into his eyes and remembered this was the man who had rescued her from her sleazy lifestyle. This was her hero. He may not have fallen from space but he was still the man who loved her. "Come on then," she agreed.

No sooner had they left the nurse's room than David poked his head round the door. "Coast's clear. Now, you come in here and tell me more about life in the Millio galaxy and the kind of barbarous mentality that will skewer a human being but won't eat meat."

Lethe sat at the table by the window and suddenly realised he was very, very tired. It had been a long worrying journey to Earth with Ygoi and now they had landed among friends, there was someone else to help and all he wanted to do was sleep.

"It's not that we won't eat meat," he yawned, trying to be polite. "It's just that no animal survived the journey to the galaxy. There are no animals for us to eat."

"But your planets can sustain life as we know it. What of the indigenous life forms before all these people arrived from Earth?"

"Never heard of any." Lethe took the few steps across to the bed, fell on his face and was asleep in seconds.

David Kirkwood-Barnes threw a duvet over the sleeping man and went off to check up on his patient. All he could see was a snorkel sticking out of a bath of Coke, which looked rather ridiculous. He went into the room on the other side of the bathroom and sat on the bed for a while. It had been a long time since he had had to sit and listen out for a patient in trouble. He settled in one of the armchairs in the room and tried to let his mind make sense of all that had happened since breakfast.

Jenni left her husband taking his time getting his head round the idea as he stood outside a spaceship. She went to the morning room to throw out the bowl of Coke, carefully carried the bowl out to the kitchen and tipped the Coke down the sink. There was a clatter of metal and a tangled lump of trid hit the stainless steel sink.

"Another of your husband's experiments?" Mrs McDougall asked, by now almost used to Sir James' occasional mad idea.

"One of Sir David's. We were taking bets on how long it would take the Coke to dissolve this metal."

"Yes, Madam. And what may I ask is that monstrosity parked in the chestnut avenue?"

Jenni and her husband had been talking about this. "It's a studio for me to do painting and things in away from the house and tourists. Sir James saw it at an exhibition in London and had it brought down ready made. I'll be looking after it myself so the staff don't need a key." It sounded pretty feeble but how else did you explain something the size of a small bungalow in your chestnut avenue?

Eileen McDougall thought it odd that a woman who did nothing all day should need to escape. She'd have done better to join in a bit more. Still, when you worked for a Home Office Under Secretary you learned not to ask questions. "How long will your guests be staying?"

"I really don't know."

"So it's two extra for lunch, is it?"

"Yes, please. And they're vegetarian. One of them will need to be given fortified drinks. David will give you the sachets if you wouldn't mind making them up."

Drinks were no problem, she had done them for years for the old lady. Vegetarians were another matter altogether. "Yes, Madam. But I'm afraid it's chops. Sir James always tells me in advance if I've got to cater for odd diets."

Jenni recognised the signs. Most of the time Mrs McDougall was absolutely lovely but every so often she got a migraine and became the rattiest woman on Earth and got very sniffy towards the woman whose lifestyle had once been rather unorthodox. "That's fine, they can just eat the vegetables. Can you find some cheese for them?"

"Yes, no problem. Sorry, not one of my better days."

"Look, tell you what. Take the afternoon off now you've started lunch. We can look after the dishwasher and you'll have your hands full tomorrow as we've got two coach parties booked in."

Sometimes there were advantages to having a lady of the house who had been used to looking after herself. "Thank you, Madam. I'll serve lunch in about half an hour then I'll go and lie down."

Jenni looked at the kitchen clock. Half an hour would just be completely the wrong time. "Go now," she said kindly. "I'll cook lunch this once, it won't kill me."

"Well don't go rearranging my kitchen like you did last time."

Mrs McDougall left the kitchen and Jenni looked at the piece of trid in her hands. She could bend it and mould it by hand, there was an iridescence to the blue that was quite beautiful considering what it had been used for. Jenni remembered to put the chops in the oven then sat at the table and started to experiment with the piece of metal.

Ygoi had lost all sense of time just lying submerged in a bath of brown liquid. He had got bored at one point and taken out the snorkel so he could try drinking the stuff but is was so nauseatingly sweet for a man not used to sugar in his diet that he had spat it out again. His mind was idly rambling on thoughts of the English countryside when strong hands grabbed his shoulders, hauled him upright and took out the snorkel. He coughed and snuffled inelegantly as the liquid got into his eyes, up his nose and into his mouth.

"Right, let's have a look at you then." David looked at the holes in the other man's ears and nose. "Well, your face is clean." The hands and elbows were free of their cages at last but there was still evidence of the rods under the skin in the arms. "Want to go back for another session or shall we get these out with a knife?"

"Knife's fine by me, I expect Lethe's got one somewhere."

"No, my good chap. I mean you go hospital and have them surgically removed. Right let's get this lot down the drain and wash you off with some clean water. Where's that handmaiden of yours got to? Fast asleep last time I saw him."

"We're not committed you know, Lethe and I."

"Do you have homosexual commitments then?"

"You're allowed one commitment of each gender if you want it. But you have to get the opposite sex commitment first. You're not allowed to have sexual partners of either gender outside commitment."

"I'm ashamed to say that all sounds remarkably civilised. And it's quite open and legal?"

"Perfectly. Lots of men encourage their wives to have a same sex commitment. Mine didn't want one, nor did Lethe's."

"You're both married then?" David hazarded trying to get his head round what on the surface sounded like incredibly loose living but there was a definite underpinning of morality there somewhere.

"No, my wife left me years ago The commitment would have been ended anyway when I went to prison. Lethe shot his."

"What?"

"It was adultery. It was his right as the cuckold to shoot both his wife and her lover, She could have shot him if he'd had sex with another woman."

"Such a curious blend of barbarity and common sense, licentiousness and morality. One day you and I must discuss the arts. Do you go to the ballet at all?"

"The what?"

"Ballet. Music and dancing. You do have dancing where you come from?"

"Yes, and music." Now it seemed he was expected to talk about Millio galaxy dance forms while sitting in a bath of some toxic brew and a man he had known only a few hours poked about with his ears and nose and tried to make his fingers unbend. Ygoi snatched his hand back but that made his elbow hurt and he didn't know which bit to nurse first.

"Sorry, old chap. Getting a bit carried away in my enthusiasm. We'll have to get the physio on you for those hands of yours. After I've mended the fingers for you, that is." He pulled out the plug and set the shower running. "Right, you sit in the rinsing water for a bit and I'll see if Lethe is awake."

Ygoi tilted his head back and let the clean water pound onto his face. Slowly, slowly the stink of shit was going from his mind and he blew bubbles out of the holes in his nose.

"Gross!" Jenni exclaimed.

"Oh, for fuck's sake. Can't a guy have a shower in peace?"

Jenni slapped the plug back in the bath again. "Trid goes solid again after a time. Don't want you blocking the drains or we'll have some explaining to do to the plumber. See?"

Ygoi tipped his head out of the running water and saw the bracelet she had made for herself. "Too late, I'd guess most of it's gone."

"Damn. Sorry, didn't mean to burst in on you."

"Ah, good," came David's tones. "The cavalry. Fetch me some towels, Strumpet, and help me get this one hoisted out. The other one's so far asleep I don't think a bomb would wake him up."

"Is he all right?" Jenni asked, still wishing he wouldn't call her strumpet, no matter how fondly it was said.

"Just asleep. Probably got some extreme form of jet lag."

The doctor inspected his patient on the bed where for so long he had nursed his own mother. "Right, well, your flesh wounds will heal themselves probably. Your scar tissue and your jaw I can't do much about now. But at the moment those are the least of your worries. Your knees are going to have to be replaced if you want to walk again – I'll know more when I've had you x-rayed. Your hands are worse and your left arm is decidedly wonky. I propose to rebreak your fingers and set them properly and repair the damaged muscle and tendon as best we can. Are you predominantly right or left handed?"

"Right," Ygoi croaked thinking it sounded like a repair job on his old spaceship. "Whose knees will I get then?"

"Artificial ones, my dear chap. Very good they are too. I think we'll have to rebreak your arm as well and put a plate in it or we'll never get your hand working properly again." David experimentally ran his fingers over Ygoi's head. "How many wires did they put in your head?"

"Nine."

David found what he was looking for. "Right, scissors please, strumpet-in-law of mine and let's cut this man's hair." A chunk of hair was experimentally cut from behind Ygoi's left ear. "Yup, thought so. A culture such as yours with no knowledge of surgery cannot operate on the brain to insert implants. There is something here just below the skin but on top of the bone which I'd guess was fired in by some kind of gun and it may be attached to a wire, probably some more of that trid, and the actual receiver is deeper inside. If you're lucky then what I can see here is the receiver itself which they will have just tucked under the skin and it will be minor surgery to explore your head for nine bumps and remove them. That I am not willing to risk without a scan. For now I would like to take some blood and tissue samples to ascertain as best I can that you will be able to withstand the anaesthetic necessary for the surgery to proceed in view of your rather extreme reaction to the painkiller. Are you still awake?"

"Just about," Ygoi agreed.

"In the meantime I prescribe rest, good food, fresh air, and gentle conversation and let's get some fat on your bones as you've to a long way to go yet. I'll give you some medication for the pain when it gets too bad and something to help you sleep at night for a few nights to get your strength up. Let's get you dressed and downstairs for lunch."

"Oh my God," Jenni remembered. "I've left the chops in the Aga."

FOUR

Lethe Miarren stretched, yawned noisily and farted rather loudly. He opened his eyes and looked at the floral curtains, the white wood furniture and the pink flower-patterned wallpaper. Now where was this? This wasn't anywhere in his spaceship that he remembered. Oh, yes. He was on Earth. This was Jenni's house and they were giving Ygoi a bath in some brown gunk called Coke. He rolled off the bed, went over to the curtains and opened them and the window to look out. The rolling English landscape was bathed in a weak, golden sun. He could understand how Ygoi's eyes, so long unused to light, could heal in this gentle one-sun planet. The light levels on Sunara were always brilliant white. Somehow even when it rained the light levels were high. Lethe inhaled the scents of an English summer dawn and sneezed violently. As he was already dressed, he ambled into the adjacent bathroom to have a pee and remembered that Earth people flushed water down their toilets. He assumed the waste reprocessing took place in each individual house in that case. Made a lot of sense, really. At least you knew whose shit it was being used to replenish your soil.

He heard a thud from the room next door and went in there through the adjoining door to find Ygoi on the floor and shuffling on his bottom towards the wheelchair.

"Want a hand?"

"Yes please, I need to get to the lavatory."

Immediate needs satisfied, Lethe got the other man settled in the wheelchair. "You're looking a lot better this morning," he remarked. "I last saw you being hoisted into a bath." He gently took Ygoi's face in his hands to scrutinise his ears and nose. "Absolutely fucking amazing. Not a sign of the stuff but those are big holes in your face."

Ygoi had to smile. "They'll close. Probably. I have had so much vegetarian food stuffed into me you wouldn't believe. To say nothing of some drink or another that Jenni says will help feed me up. Then David put me to bed and stuck another needle in my arm and I must have slept for twelve hours. You've been asleep for nearer fifteen."

"It was a long journey."

"I know. And I wasn't any use whatsoever."

Lethe ruffled the top of Ygoi's head which he found annoying but didn't say anything. "True. Come on, let's go and see what's going on at this hour of the morning."

"Jenni was telling me something about a burglar alarm," Ygoi explained as Lethe got them downstairs in the lift. "Apparently we'll be alright if we go through the kitchen to get out."

"Which way's that?"

"Absolutely no idea."

At the foot of the lift they worked out the possibilities and, to their relief, got it right first time. Mrs McDougall was just stoking up the Aga for the day's work and she shrieked in fright when the two house guests came in.

"Oh, my goodness. You two did startle me. Nobody ever gets up this early in the house usually. And there have been some very strange things happening this morning too."

"How strange?" Lethe asked, not sure if he wanted to know.

"Well, first of all it seems the drains are blocked. There's a whole flood of what smells like Coke out in the back courtyard. And then there's that studio thing in the avenue. It seems to be singing. At least there's the most peculiar noise coming from that direction and that's the only thing out there apart from the trees and I've never known them to sing before."

"You stick with the drains," Lethe advised, having guessed what she meant. "We'll got and look at the studio."

"Well, thank you," Mrs McDougall responded and decided that maybe she would go and borrow a book on vegetarian recipes from the public library after all.

It was hard work pushing a wheelchair across the grass of the parkland and the spaceship was silent when they got there.

"What do you reckon?" Ygoi asked.

Just for a second Lethe remembered when he had been the gangling co-pilot totally overawed by the cool nonchalance of Ygoi Roemtek. "No idea. Shall we go in?"

There were still some lingering traces of the smell of excrement in the spaceship so they left the door open when they went in.

"Control room first, I think," Lethe decided and he pushed the wheelchair along the corridor. "Why did the wheel become obsolete?" he mused. "Such a useful thing." He parked the chair at the control panel. "Right, let's get you logged in to the system now your arms bend in the middle then can you run the basic checks for me if I do the anti-tracking and stuff?"

"My pleasure," Ygoi answered truthfully. He offered his left wrist to the captain of the ship and watched as he was logged in. He could only be logged in as co-pilot as he was no longer cross-galaxy licensed but even that was something he had thought would never happen again. It was hard to operate buttons and switches with clenched fists instead of nimble fingers but it was good to be able to move his elbows to reach the top row of controls. "So far as I can tell all your systems are OK. Fuel's a bit low, can you top up from the sun here?"

"Anti-tracking has blown," Lethe announced and tried not to sound too worried. "We can now be found by anything from Earth radar to Lriam security beams if they can get this far."

A familiar pain shot through Ygoi's head and he caught his breath. "I think they just have. Can you mend it?"

"I don't know. I doubt it. I used to get it serviced by that place on Nurtasia. Can you?"

"For fuck's sake, I can't even think with this pain in my head. I've got no hands anyway. Where's the console? Let me try to have a look."

There came a peculiar noise half way between a whistle and a roar and Ygoi seriously thought his head was going to explode. The noise stopped and the pain in his head went away. He realised Lethe was mouthing something at him.

"What?" he asked. "I can't hear you." From a long way off he began to hear very faint tones.

"I said your ears are bleeding. We'd better get you back to the house."

"Did you hear that noise?"

"I heard something like the housekeeper said, bit like a singing sound. What did you hear?"

"Lriam security beams transmitting at full strength. Fortunately we're so far away they didn't blow my brains out. You got any trid in this machine?"

"Some of the wiring I'd guess and the outer panels are an alloy."

"It's the trid that's carrying it. All I've got left is the stuff in my brain and my arms and that's not so powerful without the external rods. He remembered something. "Oh, fuck it, Jenni's made herself a bracelet out of it. Better go and see if she's alright."

"Let's get you out of here and find out. She's probably OK as there's no trid in Earth houses. We can do the anti-tracking another time. Earth radar won't bother with us until we try to take off."

"True."

A scene of total chaos greeted them in the courtyard. There was a hole in the ground large enough to accommodate a small dog and the contents of the drains were spattered all over the walls.

Jenni and her husband were at the kitchen door and David was leaning out of an upstairs window.

"What's the damage?" David called.

"Looks for all the world as though the drains have exploded," his brother replied. "How very odd." He looked across the courtyard and saw the two house guests approaching. "Oh, hullo you two. We seem to have had a bit of an accident with the drains."

"Did you wash any trid down there after the bath?" Lethe asked.

"Well, yes, I suppose it must have got washed down with the Coke."

"You've been hit by Lriam security beams. Must have hit the trid in the drains. Jenni, is your arm alright? Ygoi said you'd made yourself a bracelet."

Jenni looked at her left arm. "Fine. It was really odd though. Just as this bang happened I got a bit of a twinge in my arm and my finger." She looked at the gold rings on her wedding finger and shrugged slightly. She saw something odd on Ygoi's face and walked across to the wheelchair. "Your ears are bleeding," she said and took his face in her hands to get a closer look. There was another whistle from the chestnut avenue, another gurgle from below the courtyard and a loud crack as the septic tank burst.

The people all backed away from the stench of the ruptured tank. Ygoi had instinctively put his fists to his head when he heard the whistle and he realised he had Jenni's hands under his own.

"Sorry," he said. "Did the beams get you too?"

"I'm more worried about your poor head," she sympathised.

"Didn't hurt that time." He took her left hand on his fist. "What is that yellow metal you're wearing?"

"Gold. We use it for our wedding rings. Oh my God. It stopped the beams from getting through the trid." She called up to the man at the window, "David, my love, raid my jewellery box for anything you can find."

"I'll ring for a plumber," James decided. "But first we have to get the trid out of the drains."

"I'll do it," Lethe offered. "I know what I'm looking for."

There were no more whistles or bangs as he searched the area round the hole in the courtyard. As he had guessed, the energy of the beams had blown the metal out of the drains. The trid itself hadn't fragmented and he found a lump of it over by one of the courtyard doors.

When he went into the morning room to join the others at the breakfast table, he found them nearly weeping with fits of the giggles and it cheered him no end to see that Ygoi had remembered how to laugh. The blue trid of Lriam had been replaced by the yellow gold of Earth and Ygoi Roemtek had rings in his ears and his nose and a chain of it round his neck.

"Is that punk or grunge?" David was just asking. "I can never remember the difference."

"Grunge, I think," Jenni told him. "All we need now is the woolly hat, the army surplus clothes and boots and he could pass for an Earthling any day of the week."

James noticed the second guest had arrived. "All quiet on the western front?" he asked then realised the analogy would be lost.

Lethe didn't have a clue what he was talking about but he guessed the meaning. "For the moment. I've got to mend the anti-tracking on my ship or else blow the thing up and accept I'm here for ever."

"Might they not send someone to find out whether Ygoi is alive or not?" James asked and was amazed at how calmly he could think of flying saucers landing in his deer park.

"Very unlikely as they don't know where we are in seven galaxies. That would have been a universal blast they sent out. Might not even have been for Ygoi if another prisoner has escaped or something. There aren't that many cross-galaxy pilots who would risk coming to Earth anyway."

"Do we have that bad a reputation?" David asked sadly.

"Yes," was the brutal reply. "You've been scouted several times in the past but there's nothing here for us and you don't bother the Millio galaxy so we don't bother you. It's just that the original colonisers of Millio were persecuted from here so it's gone down as a bad place in our folklore. They're not going to blow up your whole planet just to make sure they've finished off Ygoi. It's too big anyway. They'd be hard pushed to blow up your moon. They'll blow him up which won't be very nice for anyone caught in the immediate vicinity but they won't declare war."

"And is that supposed to make us feel better?" James asked.

"It's the truth," was the best consolation Lethe could offer.

David finished his breakfast. "Well, gentlemen and strumpet-in-law, much as I love coming to this house where life is so much more exciting than it is at home, I must be on my way as I have brains to mend and appointments to make for a certain gentleman in our party and then perhaps we may rid ourselves once and for all of any threat from Lriam and get on with mending some ordinary broken bones."

"And I am away to a Home Office that requires my services," James announced. "I won't be back until the weekend now, my love. Look after our hippies from Basingstoke. Gentlemen, what are your plans for today?"

"None," Ygoi offered for both of them.

"Shame on you. Couple of bright young things like you should be out and about and seeing life in general. You've got a whole new planet to explore now."

Husband and wife kissed vaguely, brother-in-law embraced sister-in-law and then the two brothers left the house bantering cheerfully about England's prospects in the first Test.

"Well," Jenni said to her visitors, "it's just you and me. You're not on any sort of a mission this time and one of you isn't in the best of health so we'll take it slowly. I'd guess you're not that keen on walking anywhere while there's a wheelchair to push but we can go for a drive. I'll have to take the Land Rover to get the wheelchair in as we had it adapted for James' mother. How about a trip into Exeter? It's only about twenty minutes away. The shops aren't bad so we can get you two some native clothes, and the cathedral's lovely."

"Exeter sounds fine by me," Lethe agreed. "Where's the marmalade?"

It had been a while since Jenni's mother-in-law had died and she had to admit it was a bit easier now to get a wheelchair round Exeter than it had been in the old lady's day. The shops were more accessible and they accumulated quite a few packages between them, mostly clothes for the two men whose own garments, while not exactly odd, looked a bit foreign. Clothes came from all sorts of shops from Marks and Spencer to Oxfam although the latter had taxed Jenni slightly as she had had to explain the purpose of Oxfam to two men who had never heard of charity. It was an odd world they inhabited. Human compassion was obviously not unknown in a society open with its affections, but it wasn't encouraged and it certainly wasn't harnessed for any sort of greater good. They hooked bags over the handles of the wheelchair and decided they had earned a coffee break. Shopping and learning about Earth habits and customs were decidedly exhausting to two from another galaxy.

"How long before we can get you walking again?" Jenni asked Ygoi as the three of them sat at a pavement table at a café near the cathedral.

He hooked one fist round the straw in his mug of latte and swirled it round but didn't have the strength to grip it. He had only had a couple of mouthfuls and now one of his greatest regrets was that only tea plants had made it to the Millio galaxy and not coffee plants. "Don't know. I think David wants to get the brain sorted out first then decide between knees and hands. He may do one of each first just to get me mobile a bit. Jenni, I am not an idiot, I know all this costs money."

"Don't worry about that now, let's just get you better. If I can't help you out as a friend then I'm not a friend worth having." Jenni was pleased to hear her voice didn't give away any doubts. OK so David wasn't going to charge to treat this patient, but it wasn't going to be cheap keeping these two for any length of time.

A busker set up an excruciating caterwauling on the other side of the square.

"I could do that," Lethe announced.

"You won't earn much money that way," Jenni laughed kindly. "Especially if you're as bad as he is. He's often here. Think he's a bit of a smackhead and needs anything to fund his habit."

"A what?"

"Drug addict," Jenni informed Lethe. "You know, imbibes prohibited substances and gets out of his mind on them. Don't you have drugs in your galaxy?"

"We have a planet called Goine where we grow bloodflowers and they are extremely narcotic so you go there to get stoned," Lethe explained. "No good being out of your mind when you've got your living to earn. Where we come from if you can't work you die of starvation."

"Like me," Ygoi put in wryly and winced as the busker's howling got even more discordant.

"Would you buy his guitar off him?" Lethe asked Jenni. "I'll pay you back from my earnings."

"Can you play?" Jenni asked amazed.

"Yes. Pity about Ygoi's hands getting smashed up, he used to be one great harp player. Most people play something. We don't have your television and radio and internet to entertain us."

"But you have the most sophisticated computers I've ever come across. You can translate instantly, fly from God knows where and land between two horse chestnut trees, but you don't have television?"

"Can't see the point of it really."

"Entertainment? Education?"

"We do our own entertainment when we can spare the time and education is passed on from mother to child. After that we teach ourselves. We have books and libraries on Nurtasia which is the least advanced of our planets but mostly we rely on our computers which hold everything from recent history to personal records like tracking information."

"Tracking what?" Jenni asked. "People or machines?"

Lethe turned over his left wrist and showed her a lump about the size of a postage stamp between the tendons and the arteries. "Every newborn is tagged and the data is updated if we get committed, pass our pilot's licence or whatever. We're all connected to computers on all the planets of the Millio galaxy. Right now our records will show us as out of galaxy, domicile unknown, and anyone with a computer can see them."

Jenni gently took hold of Ygoi's left wrist and saw he had an identical flat, square lump under his skin. "And if you take the tags out?"

"You bleed to death doing it," Ygoi told her. "Or so they say. You just don't."

There was a naivety here that puzzled Jenni. "Who's to punish you if you do? Don't you have policemen?"

"We have a system of direct punishment," Ygoi explained. "Our population isn't so big we can spare many people to be the bureaucrats." He didn't feel like explaining it all right now. "Now put us out of our misery and go and get that guy away from his guitar before he kills it."

"What do you reckon he'd take for it?" Lethe asked.

Ygoi saw the other man check something was in its proper place under his jacket against his ribs. "Forget that. You can't shoot people for a guitar on this planet."

"You have a gun?" Jenni hissed. "Don't you know that's against the law?"

"It's not your sort of a gun," Lethe muttered back. "Nobody would hear anything."

"This is ridiculous," Jenni told him. "We will go to the music shop and I will buy you a guitar. It's only over there and the wheelchair won't fit. Will you be alright here on your own for a bit, Ygoi?"

He smiled then. The saddest, gentlest smile Jenni had ever seen in her life. "Believe me, I shall be perfectly content."

Alone at the table, the man in the wheelchair idly sipped his latte coffee through a straw and remembered a dark drinking house, the stink of shit and the urine taste of Sunaran ale.

There were times when Deirdre Hunsecker wished she wasn't beautiful. Like right now, when this seriously weird guy had accosted her as she left the library in Exeter cathedral and seemed to be determined to get her to agree to have sex with him. Terrified he might try to rape her, she almost ran into the cathedral square where a busker was yelling something mildly obscene which he obviously thought was singing.

"Just fuck off," she told the creep at her side for at least the tenth time. She looked frantically round her and got some inspiration. "I'm meeting my husband at the café."

"You don't wear a ring," he persisted and tried to take her hand.

Deirdre looked round and saw a man in a wheelchair sitting alone at a table. There were bags on the chair and other cups on the table so she guessed he wouldn't be alone for long. But there were no other lone males nearby.

"Nor does he," she replied tartly and set off briskly for the man at the table, well aware she was being watched from behind. She was about to tell the truth and throw herself on the mercy of a stranger but she looked at the man as she approached him and suddenly wasn't sure if he was English.

Ygoi was looking at the cathedral and wondering how such a large building didn't fall down when a female voice interrupted his thoughts.

"Ah, excuse me, can you tell me the way to the train station?"

He looked up at an elegant, young blonde lady with legs that seemed to go on for ever, and long-lashed cool grey eyes. Before he got too interested, he forced his mind to focus on the question. "No, sorry, I've not been here long myself."

Relieved he spoke English and wasn't obviously drooling over her, Deirdre decided to risk it. "Oh, sorry. I saw the chair and I kind of thought... Say do you mind if I sit down for a minute? I've been walking round and round this place and I'd kind of like to rest a bit only there's nowhere else to sit."

That wasn't quite true, Ygoi thought looking round but when a ravishing blonde beauty asked to sit with you, you didn't say no unless you were totally paranoid. "Be my guest." He wondered if she was some kind of spy from the Millio galaxy but as she took a purse from her backpack he saw there was no tag in her wrist.

She sat down with a bit of a bump. "Hi," she said brightly. "I'm Deirdre. Sorry, this is going to sound real forward of me but could you kind of pretend we know each other? There's some creepy guy been following me."

Ygoi looked round and saw the man standing at the perimeter of the pavement tables, one hand suggestively on his crotch and an evil look in his eye. He leaned forward and gave Deirdre a kiss on the forehead as though they had been married for years. "Ygoi. It's Russian. I'd buy you a drink but I've got no money. Sorry. I'm with a couple of friends and they've gone to the music shop."

"No sweat." Deirdre raised an elegant arm which made her bangles rattle and two attendant waiters rushed forward at once. "Hi, just some iced latte please," she asked the one who got there first.

"Yes, Miss," he responded with his eyes nearly coming out on stalks. He dashed off to get the drink before he got a bit unprofessional with that one.

Deirdre looked at her new-found hero. He had the most gorgeous dark eyes she had ever seen in her life and she couldn't help brushing his long fringe of hair off his eyelashes. He had an incredible mane of thick, dark curls and she didn't remove her fingers all that quickly. "So, you're from Russia? I'd never have guessed it except you've got a bit of an accent to your English. I'd guess you've lived here quite some time."

"I first came here ten years ago."

"Oh, right. Say, do you mind me asking, but what happened to you?"

"An accident." This woman's open friendliness was rather appealing and she was incredibly hot. He could almost have thanked the pervert who had sent her his way. "Where are you from?"

She smiled then, reassured by the familiar question. "All the way from New York, New York. There isn't one US accent I can't tell from another. I'm doing some postgrad here on linguistics." The iced latte was delivered to the table and she gave the waiter such a dazzling smile as she handed over the

money Ygoi felt quite sorry for the poor man's self control.
"What about linguistics exactly?" he asked before baser thoughts crowded out his mind.
The question startled Deirdre. She wasn't used to men seeing beyond the blonde hair and the slender figure. She looked into the eyes of the man in the wheelchair but he wasn't leering at her. Perhaps he was gay. Or impotent. She didn't know much about cripples. "You really want to know?"
"I only said my name is Russian, not that I am. My family is Russian and Swedish so I have a bit of an interest in languages."
"So do you speak them both?"
"Yes. But they are rather out of date with the slang and such."
Deirdre abruptly switched to fluent Russian. "Great. I don't often get the chance to practice my Russian. Are you working here? You said you'd been here for ten years."
"No," he corrected her politely in the same language. "I said I first came here ten years ago. I had my accident abroad a couple of years ago and I've come here for some private health care which you can't get where I come from."
"Estonian," she said.
"Pardon?"
"I'd know that accent anywhere. You're from somewhere slightly east of Tallinn. Learned your Russian during the Soviet years and maybe even don't speak Estonian. Is that where you had your accident?"
Ygoi began desperately thinking of what to say. This was getting scary now, he had heard of Estonia,

didn't know what Soviet meant and he wished Jenni would come and rescue him.

"Got a friend?" asked a voice in English and the two speaking Russian almost jumped.

Ygoi felt as though he was letting his breath out. "Deirdre, I'd like you to meet Lethe. And I bet you can't place his accent. Lethe and Jenni, this is Deirdre. She's hiding out from that pervert over there."

"Hi," Deirdre gushed, a bit miffed her tete-a-tete was over and offered her hand to the other two. The blond guy was pretty good-looking but she saw the woman wore a wedding ring and guessed the two went together. That left her the hunk in the wheelchair. The guy with the sad, dark eyes and the gentlest smile she had ever seen. She saw the way the blond man was eyeing her up and knew he would not be her saviour in a crisis. "So, Lethe. Cool name. Your parents into the Classics or is it a nickname because you forget things?"

"No, it's my given name. I, do excuse me, I must sit down. It was a bit hot in the music shop." Lethe sat down between Jenni and the blonde beauty and all rational thoughts had gone from his head. Why had such a beauty come looking for help while he had been in a music shop? Here he was, perfectly able-bodied but it was the cripple in the wheelchair she had chosen. It wasn't fair.

"She's from New York," Ygoi tormented him. "Studying linguistics. I told her she'd never be able to place your accent."

Lethe couldn't think of a single thing to say.

"There's a film crew in the cathedral," Jenni told Ygoi. "We may have problems getting your chair over some of the cables. Want to risk it?"

The smackhead finished his busking in a final howl, looked in his guitar case and realised there wasn't any money in it. He stomped off in a cloud of profanities that quite shocked a couple of middle-aged ladies taking morning coffee near to the odd party of four.

"To be truthful," he said, "I am quite happy here. I could sit here all morning just watching the people going by."

"Me too," Jenni agreed. "I get so bored at home."

"Are you from Estonia too?" Deirdre asked Lethe.

"Me? No."

"Busker's gone," Ygoi told him. "You going to have a go?"

"Go on, "Jenni encouraged. "That guitar cost me enough."

His mind still full of erotic thoughts about long-legged, blonde New Yorkers, Lethe crossed the small square to where the smackhead had been busking and got the guitar out. He hung the instrument round his neck, checked the strings were in tune and forgot about everything except the music.

"He's real good," Deirdre sighed. "But you're right, I can't place his accent."

The man who had been following her walked close to the table and voiced an obscenity as he unnecessarily brushed her arm and she shrank a bit closer to Ygoi.

"That the one you've been having a problem with?" Jenni asked.

"Followed me all the way from the cathedral library. The guy's a creep. He was just kind of hanging around making remarks so I hope he's harmless. Just scary." She smiled gratefully at Ygoi. "Thanks for looking after me."

He returned the smile. "Once upon a time you would have been safer with that mucky pervert. But I've done with hurting people now."

Deirdre laid a hand on his arm and felt some odd lumps and bumps under his sleeve. This was a guy with some secrets that he wasn't going to tell her yet but she really hoped that one day he would.

"Some other time, huh?" she asked him.

Jenni ordered another coffee and left them to their chat so she could listen to the music. There was no doubt about it, Lethe Miarren could sing. As good as anything she had heard on the radio and better than a lot who made it into the charts these days. The song was a bit odd, kind of country rock but he knew how to handle that guitar all right. And the audience. They were all listening to him now, from the old ladies at the next table to a young mother whose small children had gone quiet for a moment – perhaps they were enchanted by the music too. Jenni looked from Lethe to Ygoi and saw the same charm and magnetism in them both. Something strange and alluring. Something definitely not of this world. Or maybe just not of this hard and cynical time. There was a slight scrape of chair on pavement as Deirdre moved closer to Ygoi as they talked and she still had her hand on his arm.

The film crew came out for a break into the warm sunshine where a young man was busking to an appreciative audience outside a pavement café and some passers-by had stopped to listen.

"That guy's brilliant," the cameraman remarked.

"Oi, Jake, call up Andy on his mobile and get him to hear this one. He wanted one more for that talent scout thing he's doing."

Jake rang Andy's mobile. "Hi. Can you hear the busker? Listen. I'll mail you a photo while I'm here." The camera in the phone snapped the man with the guitar and the picture went instantly to London. "He's bloody brilliant."

"Get his name and address and get his arse in my studio on Friday."

FIVE

Four slightly stunned people sat at a pavement table at a café near Exeter cathedral and didn't know quite what to say.

Lethe looked at the business card in his hand and tried to make a joke of it. "Well, at least I should earn some money if I win this contest."

"If you win that contest," Jenni reminded him, "you will have a twelve month contract with one of the biggest record companies in the world and another contract to cut your second album in Los Angeles next year. Still planning on going home?"

"I can't do it," Lethe told her.

"You'll be fine. Just pretend you're busking to all of us."

"No, I mean practically. I can't travel anywhere."

Jenni realised what he meant and wondered how he knew. "Let's wait and see if you win it first, shall we? Then we can start worrying about your passport."

"Will you come to London with me on Friday?" he asked Jenni

"Of course. We'll both come with you. Though God knows how we'll get the chair on a train but I don't really want to drive all that way in the morning."

"Drive up the day before and come stay at mine," Deirdre offered. "It's only a small place but it's not too far from where you want to go. You can get there easy on the Tube."

"I thought you lived here," Ygoi remarked, rather upset to think this blonde beauty wasn't even normally resident in Devon. He had been going to ask if he could see her again.

"I'm on a three year postgrad from Yale. Usually I work from home in London but I go to various places to do the regional accents and see if they link in to the different States back home as a result of migration between the sixteenth and eighteenth centuries. I've just done a week in Devon and found two guys with the weirdest accents I have ever come across. Lethe, you have beaten me, where are you from?"

"Nowhere really. I've always kind of moved around a bit," he improvised, hoping that would do.

He was out of luck. "But what does it say on your passport?" Deirdre persisted.

There was a short silence. Ygoi turned her face towards him with his left fist and gently, but not too quickly, kissed her on the lips. She tasted of coffee, her lips were cold from the ice in her latte but underneath that coffee and ice was a heat that rivalled his own.

"Some questions are best not asked in public," he told her softly.

Deirdre looked into his dark eyes as though mesmerised. Here was a guy who fancied her after all, but here was a guy who kissed like something out of this world. She put her hands over his multi-pierced ears and pulled his mouth back onto hers so she could take in great draughts of his strength and passion.

Jenni looked at Lethe while the snogging got a bit noisier and more passionate.

"One way to stop her asking questions, I suppose," Lethe remarked enviously. "Why did you have to get married? I fancied you ten years ago."

"Don't you fancy me now?" she asked lightly. "You wait, you'll have all the women of the world at your feet in a few months when you're the latest pop heartthrob."

"Yeah, right," he said sarkily. "And, yes, just to put the record straight, I do still fancy you, but you're married and where I come from both partners in an adulterous relationship can be shot by the other half of the commitment and it's kind of hard to unlearn all the morals you were raised on. Kissing the tonsils out of you would break all the taboos of the Millio society but it's allowed on your planet, which I don't understand, and you and James are so good together. Why haven't you got any children?"

"James has a problem with his sperm count," she said as matter-of-factly as she could, trying not to mind too much that her husband never kissed her like that any more.

"But you'd like some?"

"Yes. Come up for air, you two?" she asked just a bit too cattily for true levity, as the snogging stopped.

Deirdre looked at her watch. "Shit. My train's in about thirty minutes." She gently touched Ygoi's scarred face and kissed him quickly. "And when you get to my apartment tomorrow I am so taking you to bed you won't want to get up until Sunday morning."

He was rather shocked. "You want me to have sex with you?"

"Do you have a problem with that?" she asked, rather amused he felt he had to spell it out.

"But we're not…" he remembered where he was in time. "Married."

Deirdre addressed the other woman in the party. "Is he for real?"

"Catholic," Jenni offered, thinking quickly.

"From Estonia? I thought they were all either Protestant or atheist." Deirdre shrugged and stroked Ygoi rather familiarly on the thigh. "Up to you, lover boy. But I sure would like to take you to heaven while you're still in this life. So you just come with these two anyway and at least I can get to show you round London for a couple of days even if I can't persuade you to go back on your upbringing. Now I must find the train station." She took a diary and pen from her backpack and scribbled down an address and two phone numbers. She ripped the page out and tucked it into Ygoi's shirt pocket. "Here's my address, my home and cell phone. You going to give me yours?"

Jenni rummaged in her own bag and found one of her husband's business cards. "Ravenswood House, not the London number, that's my husband's office line. I'll give you my mobile number as that's the only one we've got at the moment."

Deirdre looked rather disappointed that she wasn't going to have a direct line to the best promise she had had in a long time. "No cell phone?" she asked him.

He held up his fists. "No hands."

Jenni got to her feet. "Come on, you lot. Deirdre, I can drop you at the station and you'll have plenty of time for your train."

Thursday was a bit of an odd day at Ravenswood House. Jenni spent a lot of time on the phone and emailing her husband and the two house guests spent a lot of time in the drawing room where there was a piano, tucked well out of the way but still an object of curiosity to the visitors passing through. The TV company had emailed through some travel instructions and a list of ten songs, one of which Lethe was to choose to perform live on Friday. Jenni had two of them in her CD collection and they had listened to both *Always a Woman* and *Let Me Entertain You* but hadn't been much inspired by either. Rather than bothering to stream the others using Jenni's internet as she had shown them, they explored the rest of her CD collection and found they quite liked The Eagles, Queen and Abba, weren't so keen on Adele but thought her songs were quite clever, and loathed Robbie Williams.

"You used to write good songs," Lethe suddenly told Ygoi. "Can't you write me one?"

"You're supposed to sing one off the list."

"I'm supposed to be a fucking hippie from Basingstoke. If there's one thing I'm not it's what I'm supposed to be."

Ygoi remembered snatches of a melody he had dreamed up in the dark, stinking prison of Lriam and began to wonder if he dare. "It's against the rules."

Lethe knew when the other man was wavering. "So write me one anyway and I'll learn one off their list as well just in case."

"Bully."

"You need it. I just wish you hadn't had your hands smashed up. I can't play the piano like you played your harp."

"Just stick with the guitar. I could never cope with that."

Lethe grumpily acknowledged to himself that his temper was ninety eight percent envy at the thought of what Ygoi and Deirdre were going to be doing that night. He fixed his mind on thoughts of adoring females with long hair and no morals. "Can't you even pluck some of the piano strings with one thumb?"

Ygoi looked at the thumbs in his lap. One had an extra bend in it just below the nail and the other was completely dislocated from the hand, neither would even twitch at his bidding. And Deirdre Hunsecker reckoned she wanted him to have sex with her. He had just about learned how to propel the wheelchair using the heels of his hands and even that hurt arms that still had rods of trid in them. What kind of protection could he offer her except, he thought with a smile to himself, of the foulest verbal kind. But then, Jenni had explained the different moral standards on Earth. He could shock half the population by kissing Lethe but nobody would care if he had sex with any woman who agreed to it. He brought his mind back to the conversation in hand.

"I can't pluck anything with anything as well you know. You've been cleaning shit off my arse for the last few weeks." He sighed. "How the fuck am I supposed to have sex with anyone the state I'm in?"

"Want to practise?" Lethe asked amusedly. "We don't need to be committed to have sex on this planet." He saw the regrets in the other man's eyes. "You'll make something up," he consoled. "She knows your hands and knees are shot to pieces and she'll make allowances. Lucky bastard." He idly strummed a few chords. "What are we going to do?" he appealed wistfully. "I know I only stand a one in ten chance of winning but what if I do? We're strangers in a foreign land and I've got no passport to go touring anywhere. You heard what Jenni said, I can't even open a bank account without some sort of paperwork."

"Yes, I know. And Jenni has a husband who works in the very Home Office which issues such paperwork. And Jenni is even as we speak doing her best to sort something out for you. I'm still the fucking bloodsucker in this place. At least you're doing something."

Lethe had to smile. "And you the hero of cross-galaxy pilots. Go on, write me a winning song."

"For the man who uses soft toilet paper on my sore bum, anything. Ready to memorise?"

Lethe closed his eyes, picked up his guitar and consciously switched on the part of his brain all Sunarans knew to access for memory purposes. "Go on."

Jenni was heartily glad to leave her Land Rover in the parking space for Flat 3 in what had once been the front garden of the place where Deirdre Hunsecker lived. It had been a long journey up from Devon. There had been roadworks on the A303, an accident on the M25 and, all in all, it was gone midnight and four hours later than they should have been. She was in a bad mood because she was tired, Lethe was in a bad mood because he was scared witless of his competition the next day and Ygoi was in a bad mood because he hurt after so long cramped up in a car. They were just thankful the lift was working as Deirdre's flat was on the third floor, up under the eaves of what had once been a fashionable town house.

Deirdre looked at the three faces on her doorstep. "Hi, guess you've had a horrible trip up here. I've made up some sandwiches if you just want to snack and fall into bed." The travellers followed her into a rather ordinary flat stuffed with an extraordinary amount of books. "This is the main room, kitchen through there. Bathroom is down this corridor. Jenni and Lethe I've put you in the guest room. Sorry you're having to share but it's twin beds, there's always the couch if one of you would rather. Ygoi, you're with me in the room at the end. I'm just in the middle of emailing my folks back home so excuse me if I leave you to sort yourselves out."

The three went into the kitchen where Lethe made some tea and they sat wearily at the table without speaking.

Lethe munched up one of the sandwiches. "These are good. Wonder what's in them."

Jenni looked. "Ham. Congratulations, you've just eaten your first pig."

Lethe gagged. "You mean, what I've just eaten, had feet and a heart and a tail and things once?"

"Once. It's dead now."

Lethe gulped some tea. "Sorry, pig," he said, "But you taste quite nice." He ate another sandwich. "Try one?" he tempted Ygoi.

Ygoi shook his head and the earrings rattled. "Too tired. Can you just get me on and off the toilet and then I'll go to bed."

"You must eat something," Lethe persisted.

"I'd be sick. I'll eat two breakfasts."

"Promise?"

"Promise."

"Come on then. But I'm measuring out the Cornflakes in the morning."

Jenni sat at the table eating the delicious sandwiches and drinking tea thinking what an incredible team those two still made until Lethe came back. "You alright with us sharing a room?"

"I am if you are. Can't vouch for your personal safety if I win tomorrow."

"Tomorrow I am going to be with James at his London club. I would have gone there tonight but there isn't a double room available. So, yes, I'll behave myself. Do you think you will win?"

"Realistically? No. I've no idea what they're looking for but I can't believe my knowledge of your music..." he stopped abruptly as Jenni nudged his foot under the table.

"Finished emailing?" she asked the woman in the doorway. "Ygoi's gone to bed already. He's in rather a foul mood as he's been stuck in a car for hours."

"Does he take medication for the pain?"

"Only when it gets really bad. He had some not long ago so he should sleep through the night."

That wasn't what Deirdre had been hoping for but she tried not to let the disappointment show. "OK, well, I'll say goodnight then. See you in the morning. Help yourselves to whatever you want if you get up before I do." Deirdre went into her room and took off her dressing gown. The man in her bed was fast asleep but he stirred a bit when she got in beside him. She felt so sorry for him lying there with his face all scarred, his hands useless and his knees locked bent. She softly kissed his cheek and noticed something odd about his pierced nose. Body piercing didn't bother her. It wasn't something she would do to herself beyond her ears and she wasn't too keen on pierced lips, but noses were OK. But the holes in Ygoi's nose were too big for a normal piercing. They looked for all the world as though he had been pierced with something the size of a matchstick. And what kind of an accident was it that had hurt his hands and knees and not his back or his legs. She sighed and snuggled up against him. She would find out in the morning.

Lethe looked at the weary woman at the table with him and wished he knew how to drive a car as the journey had tired her out and he hadn't been any help whatsoever. He guessed this wasn't the time for some lewd comments on the way Deirdre's face had fallen on learning her potential lover was zonked out for the night.

"Do you want to go and get ready for bed?" he asked her. "I'll come along later when you're all safely hidden under the sheets since we're not as inhibited as you are."

She smiled. "No, you go. I'm just waiting for James to text me."

"At this hour of night?"

"Just one thing to clear up before tomorrow. You go first."

He kissed her cheek. "See you later, then."

He was undressed and in bed when Jenni came into the room.

"All sorted," she told him. "If anyone asks you in the morning, you're a Canadian."

"What's a Canadian?" he asked sleepily.

"Something the Americans make jokes about. Tell you in the morning. Good night." Jenni smiled fondly at the man already nearly asleep in the other bed in the room. Reminding herself quite sternly that she was married now, she took her night clothes out of her bag and went to get changed in the bathroom.

Ygoi was woken in the morning by the clattering of a metal tray and he thought for one terrible moment that the Lriam guards were delivering a tray of food. He opened his eyes and looked straight down the cleavage of Deirdre Hunsecker.

"Morning," she breathed, and slid down the bed next to him. "Want some coffee?"

He caught the scent of her and the last vestiges of the stink that had haunted his mind were blown away for ever. "Not yet," he told her softly and hooked her blonde hair behind her ear as she lay next to him. "Just tell me before I make a fool of myself, are you doing this because you feel sorry for me or because you've never had a cripple before?"

She kissed him hard on the mouth then trailed one finger over his lips as she replied, "I'm doing this because I've met a guy I really hope I can get to know better. I don't invite everyone I meet to come and share my bed. Come on, I'd guess it's been a while for you. I promise I'll be gentle."

Lethe was quite surprised when Deirdre wheeled Ygoi into the kitchen herself. He had been expecting to be summoned to some dread scene of debauchery to clean up the evidence.

"Sleep well, did you?" he asked pleasantly but his voice came out all squeaky and peculiar.

Ygoi recognised the sign. "Been sick yet?"

"Twice."

"You'll get over it."

"Are you all right?" Deirdre asked as she took some cereals from the cupboard.

"It's only because he's scared," Ygoi told her heartlessly.

"I think I'd be scared too if I was about to go on national TV." She kissed her new lover on the lips. "What do you want for breakfast, sweetheart?"

"Toast and jam is fine if you've got any."

"Butter? Well, it's not really butter, it's sunflower spread."

"Yes, fine. So long as there's no meat in it."

She felt rather embarrassed. "Why didn't you say something before and I wouldn't have left you ham last night." She looked at the tub of spread in her hand. "You're OK, it's suitable for vegetarians. Now I suppose you're going to tell me you're a vegan and don't do dairy either." She smiled. "Always sounds to me like someone from another planet."

"I drink milk," he replied defensively.

"OK, OK, I'll let you off being a vegan. Jeez, no need to get huffy about it."

"Sorry, didn't mean to bite."

They exchanged another kiss. "You can bite me any time you like, lover boy." The kisses lengthened and she sat on his lap in the chair with her arms round his neck.

A bell rang somewhere in the flat. Deirdre detached herself long enough from Ygoi to say, "Can you get that please, Lethe? Probably the postman"

Get what, Lethe thought but didn't like to ask. He wandered out of the kitchen and met Jenni in the corridor.

"There's the postman in here somewhere," he informed her. "I've been sent to find him."

"Doorbell, idiot."

"Huh?"

Jenni took him by the arm. "Boy, have you got a lot to learn." She towed him to the front door where there was indeed a man outside.

"Parcel to be signed for," was his greeting and he held out a flat packet and a small device.

Lethe watched as Jenni took the tool from the man and scribbled on the device, took the packet and wished the man a polite 'Good morning' before closing the door. Now he understood. If Earth doors were kept locked for some reason, those outside had to ring a bell so anyone inside knew they were there. Made sense really. Good thing the door at Ravenswood House hadn't been locked or he'd still have been on the doorstep.

"Glad I intercepted this," Jenni muttered. "It's from James, he had it sent across by courier." She sat on the sofa and took out some papers. "Right, these are yours. This is your letter from the Home Office giving you Indefinite Leave to Remain in the United Kingdom. You are allowed to seek work here, you will get your National Insurance number and anything you earn will be taxed by our Chancellor of the Exchequer. For now you have applied to have your passport renewed but it seems to have been mislaid at the Canadian embassy. Can you go and get Ygoi out of the siren's clutches for a minute?"

There came a series of breathless gasps from the kitchen and something china smashed on the floor.

"This might not be a good time," Lethe observed dryly. "That guy's stuck in a wheelchair and he can still pull the women."

Jenni thought of the Ygoi Roemtek she had first met ten years ago. A dazzlingly good-looking twenty-something with an athletic figure, an almost aggressive sexuality and the superb self-confidence of a man who had crossed galaxies and cheated the law and got away with it. She rather preferred the man in the wheelchair who had had humility tortured into him and was proving to have a lovely sense of humour. Then again, ten years ago, Lethe Miarren hadn't been much more than a gangling adolescent, pathetically grateful that a hero like Ygoi Roemtek had signed him on as co-pilot and so uncoordinated he fell over his own feet. Now he had blossomed and the two men operated as equals. There was still something rather endearingly shy about Lethe Miarren but he had a good sense of fun when he got going. She was a bit worried about what might happen to him if he turned into an international megastar, but she couldn't really see it happening.

All was quiet in the kitchen.

"Oi, Shit-face," Lethe bellowed. "Get your over-sexed arse in here a minute. And leave her behind, you don't know where she's been."

"Why do you call him that?"

"Long story. He doesn't mind."

Ygoi bowled himself into the living room. "What?"

"Come over here and park yourself next to me," Jenni requested. "Right. Now, Lethe was the easy one and if anyone asks you he is Canadian. OK?"

"Fine."

"You, on the other hand, have had to be Estonian thanks to Deirdre. So, you have been granted refugee status and we will apply for resident status for you. You have no passport as there is no way we could do any sort of deal with the Estonians. As a refugee you are entitled to work and to healthcare but because you have no passport you cannot travel abroad unless you decide to apply for British Citizenship which will take several years. So now you're street legal. Enjoy yourselves."

The two men looked, not ungratefully, at the sheaves of paper they had been given and each thought privately that a simple tag in the wrist at birth was so much easier.

"Everything alright in here?" Deirdre enquired anxiously from the doorway.

"Yes, fine," Jenni assured her. "My husband has had Lethe's papers sent up in case he needs them today."

Deirdre came to look. "Canadian," she sighed, relieved. "I thought there was a touch of Manitoba in your vowels." She noticed Ygoi had some papers as well and thought it rather odd that he should have needed his but then guessed Jenni's husband had probably forgotten who was which and had sent both to be on the safe side. She picked up the papers and looked at them. "My own little Estonian refugee," she said fondly. "Come on, breakfast. Then I'll give Lethe his directions and I must go into the Uni to use the library for a bit today. Are you staying tonight as well?"

"Lethe and I will if that's OK by you. Jenni's meeting her husband at his club and then we're all going back to Devon tomorrow morning."

"I wish you could stay for ever, but I haven't the time to look after you properly."

"I won't be stuck in this chair for ever. And I'm sure Jenni won't mind if you come down to Devon sometimes."

"Jenni won't mind at all. Be glad of the company,'" she told them. "Right, breakfast."

Lethe rushed off to the bathroom and was sick.

"Shouldn't have eaten the pig," Ygoi bawled unsympathetically after him.

Three people soon found out that negotiating a wheelchair on the London Underground was a nightmare. It was worse than a nightmare, it was impossible. So they gave up without even getting on to the first escalator and Jenni tried to hail a taxi. It was the fifth one she hailed that agreed to take the wheelchair. So they were late at the studio. Jenni and Ygoi had quite expected to be turned away at the door but they were allowed to stay with Lethe and were eventually left with an assorted two dozen other friends and relations in a corner of the studio.

There were ten contestants altogether, all spotted at various venues in the UK by television company scouts who had gone out unannounced to hear the music on the streets. The idea, they all soon found out, was that the rehearsals and some chat were filmed in the morning and afternoon then shown that evening as part of a live broadcast to include a performance of a song and then the viewing public would be invited to phone in and say who they wanted to win.

Lethe was rather dubious about the whole thing. He was the oldest one there apart from a man with a grey beard and a very gravelly voice and the others were all very juvenile teenage or early twenties, full of their own egos and a firm belief in their own talents.

"Wonder what we're doing here?" the older man asked in a peculiar accent.

"Just a bit."

"Losing, that's what. Look at them. That's what the public wants. Children with no manners who can't sing. I've spent years on the pubs and clubs round Glasgow getting nowhere and only invited on because it would be rather unPC to have it all kids. You been in the business long?"

"Started singing when I was a child," Lethe replied politely, not really having a clue what the other was talking about.

A small, black woman bounded over to Lethe's side. "Hi, Lethe." She introduced herself, "I'm Bonnie and it's my job to look after you today. Just come over here with me for a few minutes and let me take down some details."

She sat him down on a very uncomfortable plastic chair and parked herself next to him. "OK, so you're Lethe Miarren, and you're how old?"

"Thirty two."

"And where are you from?"

He remembered what he had seen in a Home Office document only that morning. "Prince Edward Island, Canada."

"Oh." She raised her voice. "Andy! This one's a Canadian, does it matter?"

"Nah!" he shouted back. "It's part of the Commonwealth and he's the only country singer we've got."

Bonnie was all smiles. "Are you married?"

"No."

"Partner, girlfriend, boyfriend, cat, parrot, anything?"

"Still looking."

"And what do you usually do to earn a living?"

"Um, I'm a pilot I suppose."

"Really? Where do you fly to?"

"Oh, anywhere. Freight work mostly."

"OK, good. Now, part of your contract is going to be a taped interview and we'll show the best bits of that tonight. Are you happy with that?"

"Yes, fine."

"So you'll have to learn to say more than one sentence at a time, OK? Relax, Lethe, it's just a bit of fun and you can always go back to flying your aeroplanes if it doesn't work out. How long have you been in England?"

Lethe panicked and went mute.

Bonnie gave up. "Look, take five and go and loosen up a bit, OK? We'll need you for your run-through in about twenty minutes."

Lethe bolted over to his friends and perched himself on one arm of Ygoi's chair. "They're asking me all sorts of questions," he told them, "and I don't know how to answer them. Why couldn't I have been a fucking Estonian refugee? That would have given them something to talk about for ten hours. How long have I been in England?"

"Five years," Jenni told him promptly.

Lethe took some deep breaths and his heart began to slow down at last. "OK, I can remember that. I told them I'm a freight pilot which is true."

"Right. You were born on PE Island, your family moved around a lot as your father was in the export business. You qualified as a pilot after leaving university in, oh heck, I don't know, Toronto. You studied social politics and hotel management but took up flying instead and funded it by working in a bar. But you got fed up with flying and wanted to do something to help your fellow human beings so you are currently working as a carer for an Estonian refugee. You've always sung ever since you were a little boy in the choir at your local church. You believe in the sanctity of marriage, you believe in God and you like cats. Your parents are still on PE Island and you have no brothers or sisters. Got that?"

Lethe was thankful he had accessed the memory function of his brain in time. He left it open. "Have I been doing the pubs and clubs, whatever they are?"

"You've been busking as a relief from the mental strain of caring. You write your own songs but your main influences are The Beatles in their early years, Abba after they started to get bitter in their later years and Simply Red. You're strictly country, bit of bluegrass and with a token nod towards the sixties Mersey beat. You don't like rap, garage or shed and you think John Denver was the best American tenor ever. You're just a sweet little church-going country boy from PE Island."

"Got it. Thanks, Jenni. But I don't write my songs, Ygoi writes them. He wrote the one I'm going to do today. And that's another thing. I can't write."

"What do you mean, you can't write?"

"We always work from keyboards and just scan our wrist tags for signature. I can't even write my name and I've seen that I've got to sign a contract. I've never held a pen in my life."

"Just do some sort of scribble and if they ask you to print your name remember what the letters on your keyboard look like. I'll get the pair of you writing properly when we're home again."

Lethe went back to Bonnie. "Ready now," he told her cheerfully and hoped it was true.

"Great. So tell me about yourself." She made some notes from what he said and smiled. "See, not so bad. Do you have any cats at the moment?"

"No, I'm staying in Devon to do the caring so it's not my house to have a cat in."

"And do you still go to church?"

"Not any more."

"Oh, right. So you were a choirboy. Bet you looked sweet in your ruff."

He just smiled weakly and wished he could be the one sitting among the group of friends and relations while Ygoi was the one stuck out here. But then Ygoi's singing voice had never been all that good. Brilliant harp player but a rubbish singer.

"Ready for you now," Andy called and Bonnie ushered Lethe to the stage at one end of the studio.

"I'll go and sit with your friends and pick you up again afterwards," Bonnie told him. "Is the man in the wheelchair your Estonian?"

"Yes, but he speaks fluent English if you want to chat with him."

"I just might. He looks rather cute."

Lethe ground his teeth and turned his attention to the men on the stage.

"OK, Lethe. You've got your own guitar. What are you going to be singing for us?"

"It's one of my own."

Andy sighed. "You're supposed to be doing a song off the list I sent you so the backing group know what to do."

Lethe looked at the assorted musicians at the back of the stage. "I don't need anyone else. It's just me and the guitar. A harp would have been useful but I can manage without."

"A what?"

"A harp. You know, big thing like a piano on its side. You put it on your shoulder and it's got pedals round the bottom."

"I know what a harp is but I've never heard of anyone using one in pop before."

"There was that Irish woman," another man offered unhelpfully. "Sixties or seventies I think. Forget her name now. Mary somebody. Used to be a nun. I can do a synthesized harp on the keyboards if you tell me what you want."

Lethe went with him to the impressive banks of keyboards and thought the control panel of a spaceship was less complicated.

"OK, you play me your tune on your guitar and I'll run it through as a harp for you."

Lethe played his tune to the microphone, the keyboard's computer ran it through and the sounds of a harp floated across the studio in an ethereal melody that got the attention of everyone else there. The man who had written the tune thought it didn't sound too unlike his intentions but he cursed more than ever the loss of his hands as he realised how much he wanted to be able to play the harp again. He wanted to be the one out there on the platform too; not stuck in someone else's wheelchair with his mashed up hands resting on his useless knees and his mind half dulled on painkillers. It was odd how the nearer he got to a cure the less patient he became.

"Like it," the man on the keyboard said. "OK, is that it? Just set to repeat?"

"Can you play it through once, then let me and the guitar do the song and then run it through again at the end? There is another tune supposed to run at the same time as the song but I can put that on the guitar."

"No problems. OK, Andy. Ready when you are!"

Andy got Lethe into position at the central microphone. "OK, in your own time. We're not taping this one."

Lethe looked at the odd assortment of people watching him and suddenly wasn't scared any more. It was like being at home, sitting round with friends, and making music for the fun of it while the twin Sunaran suns dipped below the horizon and the still churned out something alcoholic in the corner of the room.

The audience could detect influences of John Denver in the light, lyrical baritone voice, perhaps some of the old-fashioned wit and observation of someone like Suzanne Vega in the narrative and something uniquely Lethe Miarren in the telling of the tale of a man of greatness brought to misery by a treacherous woman. It was a melancholy song performed beautifully and made some of the audience want to weep, some want to go and play out their wildest sexual fantasies and some want to do both.

Jenni put a hand on Ygoi's arm while the song was going on and felt the hard rods of trid under the softness of James' old check shirt. She couldn't help glancing across to see if he was at all affected by the song he had written. His dark eyes were watching the performer and she couldn't see his face too well from the side as his hair was in the way, but there was a twist of regret to the lines of his mouth. She rubbed his arm in what was meant to be a consoling, sisterly sort of way. He turned to look at her and gave her that sad, gentle smile that told her it still hurt inside as well as out. It was a moment of curious intimacy without a word being spoken.

The final harp solo drifted across the studio and there was a silence Andy had never experienced in all his years of pop production.

"Fuck me," he exclaimed as the hairs on the back of his neck settled down again and everyone else remembered how to breathe. "That was just totally, brilliantly, out of this world. What's it called?"

Lethe looked at the man in the wheelchair and caught his ironic smile. "*Fallen Heroes*."

SIX

Deirdre Hunsecker had watched the TV show that evening, alone on her sofa, remembering the feel and presence of the man she caught a glimpse of on the screen in one of the few audience shots, Nobody saw the writer of the song while it was being performed although Deirdre knew he was there. She had never felt so lonely in her life as she did sitting there listening and watching and missing the man she had known for less than a week. She had expected Ygoi to be exhausted when he got back to the flat in the late evening but he seemed remarkably cheerful and Jenni, before she left to go and join her husband at his club, assured Deirdre that Ygoi hadn't taken any of his sleeping pills that evening.

The erotic, demonic harp sound of *Fallen Heroes* echoed round her head as she lay beside Ygoi in her bed that night. For a guy who was all skin and bone, his stamina was incredible. She looked as him as he awkwardly rolled over next to her and smiled sleepily at her. The love she felt, the sense of completeness that washed over her as she returned the smile was something she had never felt before in her life. She reached out and gently stroked his face.

"You wrote a beautiful song," she told him.

"Thank you." Ygoi didn't know what else to say. He didn't know what she would do if he told her he had dreamed it up while held in a dark, stinking prison. That the tune had haunted him when he wasn't sure if he was asleep or awake. His culture didn't acknowledge any one god by any name but there were those who still believed in the old gods although they didn't worship, and he had sometimes wondered in the dark solitude that must have bordered madness whether it was the old gods who had sent the music to him as a solace. He couldn't tell this to Deirdre. Not yet.

He looked across at her bedside clock, glad it was digital as those round faces still defeated him. "It's nearly two o'clock and I don't reckon Lethe's home yet."

Deirdre wondered what it was he had so nearly said to her. She hoped one day he would tell her his secrets but this clearly wasn't going to be the time. "He's a grown up guy, he can look after himself even if he is from Canada. Anyway, didn't you say they were all going off to have a party?"

"True," Ygoi agreed and hoped his compatriot was surviving out there.

"I'll go make you some tea." Deirdre could sense he was uneasy about something but he wasn't going to talk about it. She didn't think it was any big issue as Lethe was perfectly capable of getting himself round London even if he was from PE Island.

She leaned on the kitchen worktop as the kettle boiled and wondered if Lethe and Ygoi were lovers. They were certainly very close and there was something about them that suggested a bond that nobody else could share. She shrugged as she dropped two tea bags into mugs. He sure didn't act gay. Neither of them did. And now Ygoi had got her drinking tea after sex which just seemed the right thing to do somehow. She smiled fondly as she thought of the man in her bed. And in the morning he was off back to Devon and God knew when she would see him again. She blinked irritably and brushed her eyes with the back of her hand. She had never fallen for a guy like this before.

There was a scuffling and a bump outside her front door and Lethe's voice called plaintively, "Deirdre? Are you in there?"

She pulled her dressing gown closed as she opened the door. "It's 2am," she told him reprovingly. "Where the hell have you been?"

He grabbed her roughly and pulled her close so he could kiss her hard on the mouth. "I have been in bed with two women, fucking them both when they weren't fucking each other. I have tried vodka, whisky, champagne, tobacco and cocaine and I feel fucking wonderful. Can I have you too?"

Deirdre tried to pull away. "No you can't! Just back off," she cautioned him, slightly louder than she had intended. "You're drunk and you're stoned. Go to bed."

He spun her round so her back slammed the front door shut. "Only if you'll come with me."

She had just raised her leg to knee him in the crotch when he suddenly squeaked and fell to the floor without another sound and just lay there. Deirdre looked towards the door to the kitchen and saw Ygoi was in the doorway. He was in his wheelchair and had an odd sort of gun on his lap which he had activated with his elbow. There was a murderous expression in his dark eyes and she was suddenly afraid of him.

"You all right?" he asked her and she knew he would never hurt her.

"Am now. What have you done to him."

"Shot him in the leg. He'll get over it in about half an hour, it wasn't set to kill. Sorry, he never could handle his drink."

"That's one hell of a silencer you've got on that gun," Deirdre mused. "You do know hand guns are against the law in this country?" She took the gun off his lap and looked at it. It was very small, had buttons instead of a trigger and felt heavy in her hand. "What kind of a gun is it? You've knocked him out cold and there's no blood on his leg, nothing."

Ygoi thought quickly. "It's a tranquilliser gun. Don't ask me where Lethe got it from. Just be grateful he left it in his room."

"And how did you get into that chair by yourself?"

He pulled her onto his lap and softly kissed her lips. "I have no idea. Something told me you were in trouble and I'd better do something about it."

She snuggled comfortingly against him and realised she was shaking. "He could have raped me if you hadn't turned up."

"I doubt it. At least I'd like to doubt it." Ygoi gave her a cuddle and guessed this wasn't the time to tell her that where he came from rape was a capital offence. Women were under the protection of a father or a husband who had the right to shoot the perpetrator, the whores of Goine were cheap if it was sex you were after, and although it happened it wasn't something you heard about often. He gently stroked the side of her face with the back of one hand. "I'm sorry he scared you. He always did get easily carried away and now he's won that competition he's just gone a bit crazy. He'll be fine in the morning. He always was a bit of a child." He lifted one breast to his mouth. "Tea?" he asked pathetically, trying to distract her from what had happened.

"Not in there," she laughed and gave him back the dart gun as she went back to the kitchen. She didn't even glance at Lethe still lying flat out on the floor of her sitting room and now snoring rather loudly.

In the morning Lethe had gone. Deirdre had found out the easiest way to give Ygoi his bath was to get in it with him and she just loved the feel of his warm skin under her hands as she rubbed in the bath gel. She could have sworn the holes in his ears and nose were getting smaller and she found it quite a turn on that his nipples and belly button were also pierced, although he didn't have rings in them and she idly wondered why. She was going to ask, but bath time never seemed the time to chat somehow.

She dressed him first and got him settled in his chair then let him go along to the kitchen on his own so he could make a start on breakfast while she finished off her make-up and hair.

"You seen Lethe since he made a fool of himself at two o'clock?" Ygoi's voice called from the living room.

"Nope. Is he in his room?"

Ygoi went to look. "No signs. Didn't sleep in the bed either."

"Darn it. Where do you reckon he's gone?"

"No idea. And I'm not wasting the day scouring London for him when I've only got you to myself for the morning. What do you want to do?"

"Well, since we're all shagged out, I'd guess we can go and look at some of the sights."

The phone rang in the flat but Deirdre was too busy snogging her lover to answer it.

"Hullo, voicemail of Deirdre Hunsecker," came a cheerful response to the answering message. "This is James Kirkwood-Barnes with a message for Ygoi.

Can you let him know he's booked for his scan on Monday morning. David should be able to start on his hands on Tuesday morning. Thanks. And see you after lunch. Look forward to meeting you. I've heard lots. Bye."

Deirdre kissed Ygoi on the nose and caught her lip on one of the rings. "I'll come see you next weekend. Promise. What made you go for the body piercing? You don't seem the type somehow."

He backed away from the absolute truth. "I was imprisoned a while ago in a country less civilised than this. I was involuntarily pierced by my torturers and they also scarred my face."

"So it wasn't an accident to your hands and knees?" she asked gently, guessing he was feeding her half-truths rather than scare her with something too barbarous to contemplate.

He shook his head.

"Jeez, that must have been horrible. You poor thing. No wonder you're here as a refugee. How did you escape?"

"In a septic tank lorry. I stank for over a year."

"So how come you've put earrings through the holes and not just let them close?"

There was a slight pause and an almost imperceptible sigh. "If you and I are still together when I am able to play *Fallen Heroes* on a harp then I will tell you."

She looked at the broken man in the wheelchair and knew he was hiding some massive secret from her. She believed then it was going to be some terrible story that would make them both cry and she didn't want him to have any more sadness in his life if she could possibly help it. The love and the pity engulfed her. "Well at least let me buy you some more masculine earrings."

"Don't buy me things, please. I can't afford to pay you back."

"I don't want paying back. You can take me on holiday when you're a millionaire from your royalties."

"My what?" he asked with images of kings and queens in his head.

"Royalties. Every time that song of yours is played or sold or anything, you as the writer get some money."

"Sounds a good way to earn a living. I must write some more."

"You need to find the guy to sing them."

"Oh, he'll turn up. He always does."

Jenni looked twice at the man in the wheelchair happily trundling around the London flat and saw the way he and Deirdre were so obviously in the intense early stages of a satisfying relationship. She and James had been as soppy as that once, she reflected bitterly. She looked at her husband but he was more interested in Deirdre's collection of books.

Jenni guessed that Deirdre had taken Ygoi shopping as there were new rings in his ears and those in his nose were smaller and thicker than the ones she had given him and he had a second chain round his neck. He was wearing black jeans, a white T-shirt and a dark green leather jacket that gave his hair a slightly reddish tinge.

She was so taken with the look of him she almost didn't hear what he was saying.

"We've lost Lethe."

"How can you lose someone six feet tall and with a giggle like he's got?" was her immediate reaction then she realised it sounded rather trivial put like that.

"He came here stoned out of his mind at two o'clock and groped Deirdre so I shot him in the leg. This morning he'd gone by the time we got up."

"You shot him?" Jenni gasped.

"It was a Tiowing. Shoots energy bolts. It only knocked him out for about half an hour, I wouldn't set it to injure him."

Energy bolts? Deirdre thought. Didn't they only happen in *Star Trek*? She stepped a bit closer to the living room door and shamelessly listened in.

"You idiot," Jenni said softly. "You've only been in this country five minutes, he's got no knowledge of the geography of the place and you've just turned him loose in London?"

"He's a fucking cross-galaxy pilot, not a total idiot. And if he can get from Sunara to Earth with a cripple on board then he can get from London to Devon on a train."

"Not without any money he can't."

The doorbell rang and James went to open the front door as there was no sign of the hostess.

Lethe Miarren breezed into the flat in an aura of cigarette smoke. "You off then?"

"Where the fuck have you been?" Ygoi challenged.

He shrugged. "Out with some people then we met up with Andy for lunch and he's given me my rehearsal schedule. Most of it's in London so the TV company have advanced me some money and I was going to start looking for a flat to rent up here. I'm sure Deirdre won't mind if I stay on for a few days."

"Deirdre will mind," she thundered from the doorway. "Do you know what you did to me at two this morning?"

"No," he said genuinely. "What did I do?"

"You stuck your hands somewhere you shouldn't, that's what. You are very welcome to stay in my apartment until you find one of your own, but I am moving out of it if you do."

"Did I? I'm sorry. They gave me about ten sorts of drink and some white powder to sniff up my nose and I really can't remember half the things I did. I won't do it again. Promise."

"Forget it. I'll find a hostel for a couple of days. Ring me on my cell when you've moved out."

"Bring your work to Devon for a while," Jenni suggested, and Ygoi was glad she had said it first.

"May I? That would be great. I'd like to be with Ygoi when he goes into hospital."

"You can't just leave Lethe on his own," Ygoi protested. "And I can't manage without him."

"Now hang on a minute, let's sort this out," James decided. "Ygoi, you have a hospital appointment in Devon on Monday. Lethe, you have commitments in London starting when?"

"Monday."

"Deirdre, you have research work that you can do anywhere or do you need the facilities here?"

"I can work wherever so long as I bring my laptop. It's just most handy living in London as I've been granted access to UCL and the British Library."

"And I have an overload of work waiting for me at the Home Office. Right, it seems to me that the best all round solution is for Lethe and me to remain in London while you ladies and Ygoi go back to Devon so he can get to his hospital appointment. We can book a nurse to tend to your wants as your current carer now has a new job to do."

"I can do it," Deirdre offered. "You don't want some strange nurse hanging round hearing his chat about energy bolts and cross-galaxy pilots."

"You heard that?" Ygoi asked. "You weren't supposed to."

"I know." She bent down and kissed the man in the wheelchair long and hard on the lips. "I love you," she told him. "Wherever you're from."

"Love you too. And I'm from Estonia, OK?"

"Whatever you say."

David Kirkwood-Barnes looked at the man sitting in the wheelchair on the other side of his desk and thought the patient's taste in carers had improved. Still obviously into long-legged blondes, at least this one was female. He sighed and put some papers on his desk.

"Bad news first?"

"Yes please."

"The lumps under your skin are just the tips of hair-fine wires going into your brain. No, finer than hairs. So fine we had to turn the scan up to maximum to see them. At the end of these wires are barbs like umbrellas which must have opened out after the wires were shot in. So we can't just pull them out, it would mean major brain surgery and, frankly, I don't want to risk it. I'm also not keen on removing the lumps as they are what are anchoring the wires. If we remove the lumps then those wires could wander off anywhere in your brain and God knows what they might do. So, I would suggest you keep your body piercings in place until we can think of a more permanent solution. Now, some good news. I've had a late cancellation so I can get cracking on your hands this afternoon. I propose to do your right one first as that is your dominant hand. I'll do it under local anaesthetic and put a screen over your arm so you don't see what's going on. Assuming there are no complications, I'll operate on your left tomorrow and you can go home on Wednesday morning. Your arms will be bandaged as I'll take those rods out for you and your fingers will be bandaged and splinted so it will look rather frightening. But not as bad as what you were used to looking at and will need to be in place for at least four weeks, after which you will come back here and we'll have another look at you. I'm guessing there will be significant muscle and tendon damage so I can't promise you will ever return to full dexterity. I gather you're a bit of a harpist? Tell that brother of mine to ring our brother George and get the old family heirloom shipped out here from his pile in Yorkshire. Nobody ever plays the damn thing and it's a shame to waste it. Soon as the bandages are off, I want you to play that harp. Best exercise you could give those hands. Promise?"

Ygoi nodded, still trying to absorb all he had been told.

"Good. Once we have your hands sorted out and you fully over that then I will do your knees. Don't want to do too much at once. That will be a general anaesthetic and you will need rather more orthodox physiotherapy after that operation. Any questions?"

"No."

"Good. I do like a compliant patient. Deirdre, you don't have to stay if you don't want to. The operation won't be a pretty sight and this one will be a bit woozy for the rest of the day as he'll be doped up on painkillers. Come and see him tomorrow morning, between hands. And bring that strumpet-in-law of mine with you, I've no doubt she's worried silly about him."

Ygoi sat in his bed in his private ward and leaned wearily back against the pillows. He couldn't remember the last time he had been so sick. His stomach hurt, his ribs hurt and there was a pounding headache behind his eyes. None of that seemed to matter quite so much when he looked at the right hand on the blue coverlet of the bed. His arm was bandaged from wrist to elbow and his hand and fingers were strapped into a most peculiar frame, but the fingers spread out long and straight from the hand. He had forgotten just how long his fingers were. His stomach heaved again and he vomited some more bile into the bowl on his lap.

"Oh dear," came the voice of the surgeon. "Did we overdo the anaesthetic?" He waited until the attendant nurse had mopped the patient's face and changed the bowl for a clean one then he dismissed her with a wave of his hand and sat on a chair at Ygoi's bedside while he thought back over the operation he had just done. It had made a change to work on a hand rather than a head but it hadn't been easy. The nails had grown blackened and twisted and the palms had had to be cut to free them. The whole hand was filthy inside once the fingers had been surgically rebroken and pulled straight and David had been bothered that someone from the pure atmosphere of the Millio galaxy would be badly affected by infection. He had given antibiotics as a precaution and that was when the adverse reactions had started.

He took two rods of blue metal from his pocket and put them on the coverlet. "You'd better keep these as I don't know what to do with them. How are you feeling?"

"Not as bad as I did a few months ago. I can cope with being a bit sick."

"Good man. All set for the second round tomorrow?"

"I am if you are. Was it bad?"

"Not very pleasant. Lot of damage caused by your nails. Odd question to ask, but your toenails aren't in such a mess."

"I had no shoes for a year. I guess they just kept breaking as I moved about."

The doctor sighed and was glad he had done his bit to rescue another soul from a life of pain. "Get some rest and I'll remind the chef it's strictly vegan for you apart from the milk."

"Don't even talk about food."

David smiled and briefly touched the other man's shoulder before he left. "You'll get over it," he said heartlessly and went to check up on a hysterectomy patient.

He would rather have done ten hysterectomies if he had known what was going to greet him when he set to work on the left hand of the Estonian refugee. The hand was by far the worse of the two and he guessed had been broken and incarcerated some weeks before the other. He had operated on victims of torture before and would never allow his mind to dwell on the suffering that must have been caused by the injuries he mended. But this was worse somehow. One hand was done and then the victim was left in what must have been agony and in the knowledge that it was going to happen all over again. After nearly an hour of tussling he advised the anaesthetist to put the patient under with a general and Ygoi Roemtek lay peacefully asleep with his eyes closed.

"Keep a strict eye on him and stand by with the resuss," he advised. "I didn't want to put this one under but I think it will be kinder." He crunched the ulna that had been originally shattered by a rod of blue metal that had now fused into it and tried again to get it out. "I think it's stuck somewhere, but I'm buggered if I can find out where. The other arm came out all right."

Pondering on the barbarity of Estonian torturers, the theatre nurse looked over the surgeon's shoulder. "I would guess it's in the elbow," she offered.

"And I'm guessing you're right," he agreed and carried on cutting along the arm.

"Hang on," the anaesthetist alerted them. "Something's not right." He fiddled with the levels and seemed to sigh with relief. "Amazing. I've got him on the dose for a ten year old child. No, still too strong. Dammit, man, what have I got to do with you? Stand by, we're losing this one."

"Stop the general," the surgeon ordered. "Just bring him round. We've still got the local in his arm."

"Oh my God," was the next response from the man dealing with the anaesthetic levels.

David had a sudden image of some dreadful extra-terrestrial happening. "What?"

"He's asleep."

"Of course he is, damn it, you've anaesthetised him."

"No I haven't. Not any more. Do you remember that Chinaman you had in for a brain tumour a few years ago? Put himself out with hypnosis? I'd swear this one's just done the same."

"Then just monitor him and leave him be. Put under or bring round at your discretion. And you," he said to the unconscious Ygoi, "should have told me that's what you were going to do. I wondered why you'd stopped chatting. Right, let's get back to this elbow. Got you at last, you little sod." The surgeon triumphantly pulled the last of the trid rods from the arms of Ygoi Roemtek and put it behind him on a metal table. "Right. Have we got the plate for the bone ready? Good, let's get on, ladies and gentlemen, then one of you can close the arm while I get on with the hand."

The nails were even longer on the left hand, the fingers were dislocated as well as broken and the dirt embedded in the palm had to be smelled to be believed. Those watching marvelled at the skill of the surgeon who sorted out, cleaned, relocated, splinted, stitched and had to use a saw on one of the nails as it was so thick and twisted.

Mentally and physically exhausted, David left his assistants to do the bandaging and he turned to pick up the rod to clean it. It wasn't on the table where he had put it. It wasn't on the floor either. He knew none of the others in the room could have taken it as they had all been busy with the operation.

"Anyone seen that rod I took out of his arm?" he asked, just in case.

They all replied in the negative.

"Very odd. Oh well, I'm sure it'll turn up." David didn't like to make a fuss in front of his theatre staff but he wasn't very happy about the idea of a chunk of trid being on the loose. "Let me know if one of you finds it, please."

He confided the loss to his sister-in-law when she came visiting the hospital that evening.

"And it still hasn't turned up?"

"No, it's all very odd. That whole theatre has been cleaned out and scrubbed down by now and still no sign of it. There is just a remote chance I misremembered the tray I put it on and it's now in one of the sterilisers but I could have sworn I put it down directly behind me. Do you think we should tell Ygoi?"

"Yes, I do. Do you want me to do it as I'm here visiting anyway?"

"No, I'll do it. I lost the thing after all. Do you suppose it's safe to go in there now?"

"No, but if we don't interrupt, they'll be eating each other until bed time." To Jenni's surprise, Ygoi and Deirdre weren't glued to each other's lips but were sitting side by side on the bed and talking quietly about something. To her annoyance, they were doing it in Russian.

"How are you feeling?" she asked rather over-brightly.

"OK, I'd guess. This one hurts more than the other one did."

"I'm not surprised," the surgeon told him. "I had a hell of a fight with that last rod in your arm. And now I can't give it to you because I've lost it."

"Odd. Still, no-one from Lriam's had a chance to get here yet so they haven't got it. Probably been thrown out with the rest of the rubbish."

Jenni looked quickly at Deirdre but she didn't look at all puzzled by the name of an alien planet. "Lethe phoned just before we left the house. He sends his love. Had a hard day in the recording studio from what I can gather. Hopes to be home next weekend and he's going to want you to write him some more songs. And I've rung James' brother George and he says he's sending the harp down as soon as he can find a removal firm to bring it. Be glad to think of someone playing it, he said."

"You really can play one of those things?" Deirdre asked.

He kissed her long and hard. "You wait until my hands are working properly. I'll show you what I can play with."

Eileen McDougall had a migraine again that afternoon. She had had a row with the man who had come to mend the septic tank the day before, she was sick and tired of looking up vegan recipes and all she wanted to do was go back to bed and take ten bottles of paracetamol.

"Good morning," a cheery voice hailed her from the back door and she just about made out the shape of a man between dancing green dots and yellow flashes before her eyes. Her headache was too bad for her to wonder how he had managed to get into the grounds, let alone up to the house. She supposed he must have come in with the tourists.

"Can I help you?"

"Is this where Lethe Miarren lives? He won that *Superstar* contest on Friday night."

Pain made her indiscreet. "When he's here, yes. He's in London at the moment. What do you want with him?"

"I just want to find out something about him, that's all. Bit of background so we get our facts right.

In pain she may have been, but Eileen McDougall knew discretion was paramount in her job and she tried very hard to focus her thoughts. "Can't help you. He's a pleasant enough gentleman even if he is a vegetarian. He just turned up here with that crippled bloke the same day a funny metal playhouse appeared in the chestnut avenue. But that's nothing to do with them. And the other day the septic tank blew up and I'd swear I've still got the stink of it in here. Now get out of my kitchen. This isn't a public access area."

There were two men in the doorway. They looked at each other and set off across the parklands to the rows of chestnut trees.

SEVEN

Jenni Kirkwood-Barnes was hard put to remember all those long days when nothing much had happened except she had got in the way of the Estate Manager, the Events Manager and all those other people who ran her house so efficiently for her. Then one wet Tuesday a spaceship had landed in her chestnut avenue and now her life just seemed to be one mad scramble every day.

There had been the tiniest whiff of scandal in one of the less reputable tabloids a couple of days after Lethe had won his competition showing how his new-found fame had gone to his head but Jenni couldn't really blame the poor chap. It must have been quite hedonistic to sweep over half of all the votes like that. Those egotistical teenagers had been rather put out that their trendy nasal whining and back-breaking choreography had been knocked out of fashion by one man, a guitar and a synthesised harp passage that had already earned its composer a tidy sum of money as it had been snapped up by an advertising agency.

The single of *Fallen Heroes* had gone in at number three and stayed there. Lethe Miarren was still up in London allegedly cutting an album and making a video to go with his single but in reality doing very little except drink away most of the advance he had been given by the television company.

Then suddenly there it was in one of the Sunday papers. Not a paper Jenni would normally have bought but someone had left it in the newspaper box at the gates of Ravenswood House.

FRAUD! the headline screamed at her. And there was a picture of her chestnut avenue with a spaceship in it and there was a rambling, sensationalist article claiming to prove that nobody of the name Miarren, Mirren, Marr or anything like it had been born on Prince Edward Island for over a hundred years. No pilot's licence had been issued to anyone of that name. He was not registered in any medical or dental practice in Britain or Canada and the University of Toronto had never heard of him. He was currently living in Ravenswood House on the edge of Dartmoor (the guessed value of the house made her almost want to laugh) the home of Home Office Under Secretary Sir James Kirkwood-Barnes, 53, who was allegedly a close personal friend of the Prime Minister and had been at school with the Home Secretary. Nobody from the house had been available for comment except an old retainer who had refused to tell the reporter where Lethe Miarren had come from. Residents in the nearby village had confirmed they had seen Lethe Miarren in the company of Lady Jenni Kirkwood-Barnes, 36, in her top-of-the-range Land Rover and they had been accompanied by a man in a wheelchair. This man, the reporter could prove (exclusively) was the one who had written the winning song *Fallen Heroes* and he was currently in this country as a refugee from the former Eastern Bloc (the reporter dared say no more for fear of an international incident) where he had been tortured for his religious beliefs. The paper was very worried on behalf of its readers that Lethe Miarren was an illegal immigrant and that thing under the chestnut trees was his mobile home.

"You all right?" James asked his wife across the breakfast table. "And why are you reading such a fascist rag?"

She showed him the headline. "Someone left it in the box."

He scanned the article. "Good God. We've really got to get our stories straight on these two. You may find our attendance at open days goes up. Can the studio be moved?"

"I'm sure it could, but where to?"

"I think we must see if we can get it into the home barn. At least then it will be out of sight and out of the rain."

Jenni turned to greet the couple who had just come into the morning room. "Hi, you two. Sleep well?"

"Yes, thank you. Have we heard from Lethe today?" Ygoi asked as he always did.

"From him, no. Of him, yes." James replied and plonked the paper in front of Ygoi on the table.

It cheered them all to see him put his long, splinted fingers on the paper to hold it down and to turn the page with his left hand. He had been home from the hospital for two weeks now and had never once said a word about the dissolute life style of his former carer. He and Deirdre were still clearly madly in love with each other and she had started to neglect her studies somewhat in order to care for her lover. She taught him how to use the recorder on the mobile phone he had finally got so he could note down his songs, singing the parts for him if it helped and picking out the tunes with one finger on the piano. They and Jenni would sometimes go out to escape from the house with its tourists coming round five days a week, and the three were often seen just sitting and talking at a pavement table at the café near the cathedral. Nobody bothered them. Nobody knew that the man in the wheelchair with his dark eyes so full of love for the blonde woman at his side had written one of the most beautiful songs to be in the charts recently. He got a few odd looks with three rings in his ears and two in his nose but the holes were closing and it would have taken a keen eye to spot that they were anything other than the work of an everyday body piercer.

"Fucking idiot," Ygoi pronounced on finishing the article. "Can I borrow the phone?"

"Help yourself," Jenni replied.

The phone was on the windowsill and Ygoi already had enough dexterity in his hands to get the receiver lodged on his shoulder and to be able to key in the number of a mobile phone which he had already memorised.

"It's me, you fucking idiot," was his abrupt salutation. "What the fuck do you think you're doing? Get your arse down here on the next train. You're in shit deeper than any excrement transporter I've ever been in." He hurled the phone back down again. "Voicemail," he told them. "Hope that was the right number."

It was scarcely an hour later and they were all still idly chatting round the breakfast table when the discordant blast of a car horn sent them all to the window which overlooked the front drive.

A superbly self-confident young man got out of a white Saab convertible and pushed his sunglasses onto the top of his head.

"Got your message!" he yelled at them so they could hear him through the closed window. "I was just going round Salisbury at the time."

Jenni opened the morning room window. "When did you learn to drive?"

"Yesterday. It's an automatic. One pedal to go and one to stop. Bloody sight easier than a spaceship. Got any breakfast left?"

When Lethe got into the house it was obvious he hadn't been to bed last night. There were shadows under his blue eyes and his gaze was distant and unfocussed.

"Well?" he asked Ygoi through a mouthful of bacon sandwich. "What's the problem? I've got four tracks on my album, they're all cover versions so I need another six from you. Have you written them yet?"

"Yes I have. Have you read today's papers?"

"Papers? Why should I read them?"

He didn't even notice the former invalid was able to pick up the paper to hand it to him.

"Because you're in it."

Lethe read the article. "So everyone thinks I'm a liar. What's wrong with that?"

"If that's what you want," Ygoi told him sharply. "I'm hoping to integrate here and I can't do that with you shooting your big mouth off. I'm not the one with the option of going home."

"Oh for fuck's sake!" Lethe suddenly yelled at him, showering them all with sandwich crumbs. He swallowed his mouthful. "Do you think that I can? I took a Lriam convict out of galaxy. If your fucking wrist tag is still active and their scouts ever get to this place it'll be me with the trid in my brain as well as you. I said goodbye to that galaxy the moment I left Sunara with your heartbeat on their monitors. So don't you fucking tell me what I should and shouldn't do."

They looked at each other then, two strangers in an alien world. Both lost, confused and rather frightened of what might happen.

"Sorry," Ygoi said sincerely. "You're right. I've been so full of my own problems I didn't really think about yours."

"How're the hands?"

"Straight."

"Good. I need you with your harp." Lethe looked at the elegant blonde woman standing behind the wheelchair. "Deirdre, I owe you an apology. Would a free concert ticket go some way towards it? I've got to go live at the Birmingham Arena next month."

Deirdre could tell the apology was sincerely meant and she guessed if she had won such a competition she too would maybe have gone a little crazy. Lethe Miarren had won one heck of a prize and the cameras were filming him living the dream. She was glad he hadn't brought a film crew with him this time.

"OK, apology accepted," she told him and the two exchanged a brief hug. "But don't do it again."

"Oh, I won't," he assured her. "Ygoi never did give me my Tiowing back and he's a much better shot than I ever was. Even with no hands," he concluded ruefully.

"Now you're here," Jenni said to him, "would you mind moving that studio of yours into the home barn? At least nobody will be able to take pictures of it then."

"True. Where's the home barn?"

"Round the back of the house. You can't miss it. It's a huge brick building next to the swimming pool."

"OK. Come on, Ygoi, I'll need a co-pilot on this one. You know what my low-level flying's like."

"True. Come on then, give me a push."

Deirdre watched the two men leave the room, bantering cheerfully about something that had mutually amused them. "He's not from Estonia, is he?" she asked, sounding rather bemused and shaken.

"What has he told you?" Jenni replied, playing for time.

"He said that when he can play me *Fallen Heroes* on the harp he will tell me the truth if we are still together."

"Think you will be?"

"I hope so. I think he's gotten me pregnant."

"Bloody hell," Jenni exclaimed. "Can you be sure?"

"No, not sure. I'm just a couple of days late this month. I'll give it a few more days."

Blissfully unaware of possible impending paternity, Ygoi was half shocked and half full of admiration for Lethe's exploits. Allowing for some elaboration it still seemed pretty impressive.

"You're learning to fit in better than I am," he remarked wistfully as Lethe stopped the wheelchair just outside the spaceship.

"I've had to," came the simple reply. "I've got an agent and he thinks I'm from PE Island anyway."

"What's an agent?" Ygoi asked, thinking how much he had to learn.

"A form of parasite," Lethe laughed as he wheeled his friend into the spaceship.

Suddenly a small, dark figure shot between the two of them, roughly pushing Lethe back against the wall with a bit of a crunch.

"What the fuck…" Lethe began. He hit a panel in the roof to open it and pulled down a gun the size of a small pistol. He threw this to Ygoi, grabbed a similar one for himself and set off in pursuit.

The figure was running for its life along the avenue of trees towards the house and Lethe chased after it, dodging behind the trees in case the one in front was armed and looked back. The figure shot into the old walled garden and Lethe stopped just outside, hidden behind the wall and panting for breath after the sprint. He held the gun to his shoulder with the barrel comfortingly against his cheek, and looked inside, cursing the low light levels of Earth as he scanned that garden but there was no sign of human life. There were several doors out, the wall was broken down in places and the fugitive could have gone anywhere.

Ygoi went round the spaceship as best he could in the wheelchair and thought of Lethe, dashing so nimbly across the grass. He felt a bit of a fool sneaking up to doors and peering round them from a wheelchair but he soon found the answer. One of the bedrooms had been slept in and nearly all the food had gone from the kitchen. There was a pile of dirty plates and bowls in the sink and the bathroom was an absolute mess. He went into the control room, logged himself in and ran the basic safety checks. All seemed to be in order. He ran some more advanced checks and found something odd.

"Got away," came Lethe's breathless voice from the doorway. "What did you find?"

"You've had a visitor. Someone has been living in here for quite a time. Which is odd considering you and I did the long journey here without seeing any signs of anyone else. And it was non-stop from Sunara so you didn't pick anyone up on the way."

Lethe remembered. "That time we came in here, after the Lriam beams hit us. It stank of shit so we left the door open. Anyone could have got in."

Ygoi raised one cynical eyebrow. "Someone who knows how to mend the anti tracking devices? I've just checked them out and they're fully operational."

"Now that is worrying. Have you left them running?"

"Yes, and switched on your refuelling. You're going to need one heck of a lot of power to clear up this mess."

The two men worked in silence for a while. Ygoi was rather limited with what he could do from his chair but they got the bedroom and bathroom sorted out and put the bedding, towels and clothes in for a wash while they got on with the kitchen.

"Your visitor made himself quite at home here," Ygoi remarked as he consigned a whole heap of rubbish to the refuse recycling system.

Lethe started the washing up, carefully putting the plates he had washed into the hot air dryer beside the sink. "Your hands up to making tea?"

"Just about."

"Would you mind? Then perhaps we can get a few things sorted out."

They sat at the table in a clean kitchen with the last of Lethe's Sunaran corn bread and a jar of Lriam tree syrup. That planet not only had the best prisons, it also had the best syrup in the whole galaxy. It was phenomenally expensive and there was a roaring trade for it on the black market in an economy where sugar was unknown.

"How much did this set you back?" Ygoi asked as he scooped a generous dollop out of the stone jar.

"Shall we just say it was payment for services rendered?"

"You been breaking the law too?"

"No, I never quite had your nerve."

"Least you got to keep you hands and your knees. OK, what do you want to sort out?"

Lethe lit a cigarette. "I know you don't approve of the way I've started living my life but it's how I cope with integrating. I have decided to go out there, grab life by the balls and get on with it. OK, so I won that crazy competition. If I hadn't, who knows? Maybe I'd be just living here like you with my head down and no chances in life. I can't just live here on Jenni's charity and do nothing. I only with I could help you because I'd guess you hate being dependent on Jenni too."

"Just keep singing my songs and I'll do OK out of the royalties." Ygoi shrugged and tried to pretend he meant it. "Maybe I'm happy living the quiet life down here with Deirdre."

"You? Fucking cross-galaxy hero and confirmed alcoholic?"

"That I never was."

"Bollocks. There wasn't anyone in the entire Millio galaxy you couldn't out drink, out swear and out shoot. You had the balls to go and do things that nobody else would even think of doing and you'd got away with it ever since you got your pilot's licence under age when you were seventeen."

"Yeah, right. And when I was thirty three they caught me doing some tree syrup smuggling and skewered the famous balls with white-hot trid."

"Didn't it hurt?"

"You ever had a chat with Lriam security?"

"No."

"The first thing they do is shoot you in the back to disable you temporarily. Then you go into prison, in the pitch dark, bit of disgusting food occasionally on a metal tray which you have to find by smell and feel or go hungry, no toilets, no wash, nothing. Then when you've lost all sense of time and your eyesight is shot they tie you in a chair and use you as a dart board with their trid guns. They started with the ears and worked downwards. By the time they'd gone below the waist I'd already been shot eight times with white-hot metal, I smelt like a funeral pyre and I was past caring. They broke my left hand soon after that. Just put it on a table in front of me and made me watch as they smashed it with a hammer. I was so far gone with the pain of it I swear I didn't feel the rods go through my arm even thought I watched them do it. Then it was back to the pitch dark again, knowing they were going to do it to the other hand as well. They told me so. So there I was with one hand and arm in pain such as I wouldn't wish on anyone and knowing it was going to happen all over again. Have you any idea what that is like?"

Lethe swore as his neglected cigarette burned down to his fingers. He dropped the butt in a saucer and lit another cigarette.

"You think that hurt?" Ygoi asked sarkily with a nod at the cigarette. "Then they took me out of the dark and shot me in the head nine times. Did a few experiments with the levels of the beams and blew up a watermelon in front of me just so I got the message. Then back to the dark again with transmissions from the beams every so often. Then they got me out again to smash up my other hand. They kept me in a bit of light after that so they could laugh at me when I couldn't eat with my hands and couldn't clean up when the food came out the other end. That was when they started shoving spikes in my face and the first time they asked me any questions. Can you believe they could do all that and not one of them ever said a single word to me until they'd nearly finished? I could have told them all I knew after half an hour in the dark and they'd have done it anyway." Ygoi took the cigarette from Lethe and took a drag on it for himself. He coughed and his eyes streamed so he gave it back. "Not that I did tell them anything. I was glad when they hammered those rods into my knees. That meant they'd done with me and I was about to be thrown out to die. I was at the prison gates and two of them were holding me waiting to throw me out with the others when the shit ship stopped to go out and it hadn't quite shut its doors properly. I don't know how I ever did it but I got out of their arms and in among that shit just as the doors closed and there was no way they were going to go looking for me among that cargo. And that's how I got to Sunara. There's no security at the reprocessing plant, who's going to go there unless he has to? So I kind of wriggled and rolled my way out and raided gutters and domestic reprocessing to stay alive. Why I ever wanted to stay alive I have no idea. Death couldn't have been any worse."

Lethe finished his cigarette. "Why have you told me all this?"

"So you understand why I'm not the gung-ho cross-galaxy pilot you once knew. And so you can understand why it won't bother me if I never go back. You could still just about get away with saying you left me somewhere. Which is why you have to decide what to do with this ship. If it was mine I'd set light to it right now."

Lethe sat back in his chair at the table. "Part of me still does want to go back. Maybe you're right, maybe I would get away with it but common sense tells me that I don't stand a chance there while you're still registered alive. Maybe I wouldn't and I'd finish up in Lriam like you. And then who would come and rescue me?"

"Then what I suggest is that you seal off the control room, make sure nobody can ever find the arsenal you've got up in the roof and we'll just tell the world that this is your studio and you and I come here to work away from the rest of the world."

Lethe felt a bit sad to think he had made his last flight cross-galaxy. That he would never fly among the stars again. "I'll think about it," he conceded and knew Ygoi knew just how he felt. "Kind of hard to say goodbye to our past."

"We have a new past now," Ygoi reminded him. "Or we will have when James has written it for us. Shall we go?"

They scanned the ship for life-forms and found none. They left the solar refuelling and the anti-tracking running, closed up the control room and the roof hold and then left the spaceship among the chestnut trees. Lethe walked beside the man who had learned to propel his own wheelchair and they went back into the house much more at peace than they had been when they left it.

"Everything all right?" Jenni asked the two men when they went into the morning room.

"Yes and no," Ygoi told her. "We'd had an intruder."

"What sort of intruder?" James wanted to know.

"We're hoping someone who slipped in when we weren't looking last time we were in there. Anyway, it's not been moved into your barn because Lethe is going to turn it into a studio. Besides which it needs to be outside for the solar refuelling to work. We need to get some food and stuff in it if we're going to be working there so I'd guess we'd better go to this Tesco you are always talking about."

"I just order off the internet," Jenni told him. "Much easier."

Ygoi looked out of the window. "No, I've done with hiding away. It's time I saw something of your world."

"Please let one of us go with you," Jenni requested. "Tesco is not an experience you should have on your own for the first time."

"How about it, Deirdre?" Lethe asked. "You're not wearing a wedding ring for one thing."

Startled by the bluntness, Deirdre glanced instinctively at the man in the wheelchair. He returned the look, but neither of them said anything. Deirdre had the most peculiar feeling that he knew just what had crossed her mind.

Jenni wouldn't look at her husband as she took off her rings. "Nor am I now. Just give me and Deirdre a few minutes to turn ourselves into a couple of sluts then Tesco won't know what's hit it. You ring your agent and tell him we're going."

Ygoi was quite shocked when Deirdre came downstairs for her shopping trip with her long blonde hair all tousled, her lips painted into a pout and so much make up on her eyes her lashes seemed to reach up to her hairline. Her skirt just about covered her buttocks, her heels were five inches high and her top was cut so low she couldn't wear anything under it so there wasn't much left to guess at. Jenni's shoes were black and high, her skirt was leather and no longer than Deirdre's and her top was short enough to show a gecko tattooed round her navel.
"Are you seriously going out like that?" Ygoi asked the woman he loved.
She put one spiked heel on his thigh and made sure he could get a glimpse of the thong she was wearing. "Oh, yes, and you're not going to undress me until we get home."
"Where did you get this stuff? Lethe asked wishing for the umpteenth time that Jenni wasn't married.
The Home Office Under Secretary and his wife exchanged a look and a secret smile but didn't say anything. Funny how they had got out of the habit recently. But it had made them both remember.
Jenni stuck her hand familiarly inside the back waistband of Lethe's jeans. "None of your business. And I intend to behave absolutely disgracefully with you but if you need to relieve your symptoms at any time, please remember I am not available."
He took her hand out again, unable to avoid noticing the look on James' face. "Then don't torment

me like that." He experimentally touched her gecko. "Is that painted on?"

"No, it's a tattoo I had done as a teenager. James rather likes it. It amuses him that an Under Secretary has a wife with a tattoo." She didn't mention his recent offer of cosmetic surgery to remove it.

"Can I have one?"

"You can have anything you like if you go to a tattoo parlour. Is that something else that never got to where you come from?"

"It is. Tattoos and Tesco. My shopping list for the day."

"It's Sunday. You won't get one today."

"OK, maybe another day. Let's get going then if we are."

Now Ygoi had some movement in his hands he was able to help transfer himself into the Saab in the front passenger seat. The two women climbed into the back and James reminded them to get the organic Cola as there was still half a bottle of Barcardi left.

Lethe's agent had done his work well. There was a man from the local paper and a small crew from the local TV station in the car park to greet the white Saab. Lethe was absolute charm with them, made sure he introduced the man who had written his winning song and let them take pictures of the two of them together. The media people really wanted pictures of the two women and finally managed to persuade Deirdre to pose with Lethe with one leg round his waist and her arms round his neck. This time she dug one sharp heel in his thigh to keep his mind focussed and the two were smiling for the lenses. When asked her name she laughed.

"If these two guys are the fallen heroes, you may call me Fallen Angel."

"And you?" they asked Jenni.

"We just call her Gecko," Deidre said quickly. "You know, she can climb up anything."

"And will you two be part of the nationwide tour when it happens?"

"We're strictly backstage," Jenni flirted outrageously. "We don't perform in public."

The media people were satisfied. Lethe Miarren had the usual morals of a pop star. The bloke in the wheelchair seemed a bit more shy and reserved and rather brighter but he wasn't saying much. Probably frightened of the Estonian police catching up with him after what had been printed that morning. When asked for Lethe's biography, the Estonian got more bolshy than shy.

"Now that's his game he's playing with you all. Not for me to spoil it."

"So you know the truth?" The TV reporter persisted.

"Yes, I do. I've known him nearly twenty years and he doesn't have any secrets from me."

"What's the price for telling us?"

"His friendship and that's something you could never afford."

"Are you gay lovers?" was the expected response.

Jenni had a sudden dread that these two would stage some homo-erotic tableau just as a wind-up as it would mean nothing to them but could probably lose Lethe a lot of record sales. She got behind Lethe and shoved her hands down the front of his jeans. "You must be joking."

Lethe knew he wasn't going to get another chance. He pulled her round to the front and kissed her hard on the mouth. And she didn't fight him one bit.

Jenni totally forgot that she was in a public car part and that this was likely to be screened in front of her husband. She had never known a kiss like it. A hard, demanding kiss, his lips teasing and tormenting her, his tongue in her mouth and his hands cupping her head so she couldn't get away. She slid her hands round inside his jeans and had a feel of the most deliciously tight, muscular buttocks she had groped for a long time.

"Oh, for fuck's sake," came Ygoi's disgusted tones and he fished her hands out again which rather ruined the kiss. "Can't you control yourselves for five minutes?"

It was a dangerous moment for the married woman. She and Lethe were so close together she could feel the hard heat of him against her and his breath was panting on her face. Right now all she wanted was to get him somewhere away from these other people and let him take her to the realms of passion she was just not getting from her husband these days.

Strong arms grabbed her waist and she sat down in a wheelchair with a bit of a bump. She looked into the dark eyes of the man whose lap she had just sat on.

"Leave him alone. You don't know where he's been."

"I know where I want him to be."

The reporters left them to it. The interviews were clearly over, not very interesting but may do to liven up an otherwise dull Sunday evening coverage. After all, even pop stars had to do their shopping sometimes. Hot women though.

"Jenni, you have left a husband at home. What do you think he'd say if you went off and had an affair with Lethe?"

She sat on his lap like a petulant child. "I don't suppose for one minute he would care. Anyway, I don't want an affair. I want one long, hard screw with a man who can give me babies. You've done it for Deirdre so why can't Lethe do it for me?"

The shock to Ygoi's brain was about the same as Lriam beams transmitting from a very long way away. He looked at the blonde woman standing rather self-consciously next to his chair and even Lethe got distracted from his own frustrations.

"What?" Ygoi asked his lover.

"I don't know for sure," she protested, thinking he was about to get mad at her. "I'm just kind of late this month, that's all. Thanks for that, Gecko," she concluded sarcastically. "Big mouth." It was an enormous consolation to her when the potential father of her child reached up to her as she bent down to him, took her face in his bandaged hands and kissed her softly on the lips.

"If you are having my child," he told her, "then I will commit to you body and mind for eternity as soon as we may. It you're not, I will commit to you anyway if you want me to."

Deirdre wasn't quite sure what he meant.

"He's asking you to marry him," Lethe translated. "We call it committing where we come from."

Deirdre Hunsecker was twenty eight years old. She was intending to finish her PhD then go off and see the world. She wanted to shag men from Toronto to

Timbuktu and then hitch herself to some Californian millionaire before she'd left her thirties. Instead of which she looked at a man in a wheelchair with someone else's wife sitting on his legs and the soft English rain started to fall on Tesco's car park.

"Will you tell me the absolute truth before I answer you?"

"Yes."

"Are you two really from another planet?"

"Does it make a difference?"

"Tell me."

Ygoi sighed once and looked into her eyes. Those cool grey eyes that could still hypnotise him. If he told her the truth she would probably think he was a nut case and would dump him. If he lied and she found out later things would be worse. Either way it looked as though he was about to get dumped.

"We're from the Millio galaxy, a bit beyond your Pluto, turn left at Jupiter. Our home planet is Sunara. I was imprisoned on the planet Lriam and wear all the ridiculous gold ornaments in my face to stop my brain being blown apart by their security beams. And that is the absolute truth. I had a wife once before but the commitment ended and she is now living with another man. We have a son who is about sixteen by now. And that is probably more of the truth than you wanted to know."

"But how did you get here? It would take us hundreds of years to get beyond Pluto."

"We can fly faster. We call it hyper luminal. Thousands of times faster than your speed of light."

"That's impossible."

"For you, at the moment, yes. If you want evidence then Lethe could take you to show you his spaceship. I can't go back to that galaxy as long as I have these implants in my brain as I guess my head would explode somewhere near Jupiter. We're not superhuman, we don't have any extraordinary powers, we have our own system of beliefs and morals and our technology has advanced in different ways from yours. We don't eat any living being and we have no God. We are responsible for our own actions, mostly carry out our own retribution and punishment and try to avoid getting caught on Lriam which is what happened to me. I broke their laws and so the greater system punished me. The greater system will hound me until I either get the implants from my brain or until I die. I have a tag in my wrist they can monitor even this far away and that will only be deactivated when my heart stops beating for more than ninety seconds."

Deirdre didn't know what to think. She was frightened, confused, excited and she knew she loved him no matter where he had come from.

"I'd love to marry you," she told him. "Right now. Baby or not."

There was a confused session of shrieking and hugging, the two women were crying and Lethe privately thought Ygoi had gone completely crazy. By committing himself to a citizen of Home galaxy he was more-or-less condemning himself never to go home to Millio.

"Come on," he told them sharply. "We've got some shopping to do."

Jenni and Deirdre mopped their eyes and went to fetch a trolley.

"How are you feeling?" Jenni asked as she wrestled to free a trolley from the line.

"I just don't know. You've known these guys for ten years, it's a bit different for you."

"James had a problem with it when I first told him. You'll get used to the idea. They really are a lovely couple of guys. As he said, got some odd ideas and a basically rather crude system of punishment but underneath it all is a kind of gentle faithfulness that you just don't get here any more."

"Lethe would have had you on a plate just now."

"Lethe is trying to live our way. And I'll tell you something else too, I'd have had him. I'm quite envious of you if you are having a baby. I think it's all that can keep me and James together now. And after all the fuss when we first got engaged too. Oh well, I suppose we've proved the critics right in the end."

Deirdre suddenly remembered something she had read in the New York papers all those years ago and she realised exactly what was going on. She pushed the squeaky trolley across to the two men. "OK, you guys, let's hit Tesco. You got a list? I know Jenni wants a baby but I don't think they sell them in here."

"What's that old fable from Nurtasia?" Ygoi asked Lethe as Deirdre kissed the top of his head.

Lethe had to think about that. "I know you need some tree syrup and those white dallyflowers. What else was it?"

"Pee, wasn't it? Among other things."

"Yes, but whose?"

"Hers, I think."

"You sure?"

"No," Ygoi had to admit. "But it wasn't my grandmother who used to mix these things. Your computer still running in the studio?"

"Yes, but we're probably out of range."

"Yup, you're probably right. Mine used to break down the other side of Ronet."

"What are you two going on about?" Jenni asked.

Lethe stopped to look at the display of fruit and vegetables and pulled her close with an arm around her waist. "It's some remedy or another that's quite famous in the galaxy if a man can't get it up for his wife."

"Oh, James can get it up alright but nothing useful happens when he does."

The two from another planet looked at each other. "Hers," they agreed.

Deirdre and Jenni found it quite exhausting going round Tesco with two men who had never been there before. They knew what a market was, could quite see why this should be a super-market but had problems coping with what humanity on Earth had done to its food. They had never heard of colourings or of artificial sweeteners, and the only forms of preserving they knew were pickling and drying. They had never come across salt or sugar didn't have a clue what a cake was and explained patiently to two idiots that they made bread by fermenting the dough to make it rise as yeast didn't grow where they came from. The gave Earth culture the upper hand in the way it could supply fruit and vegetables from all seasons at the same time and got almost indecent with a coconut as they had never seen one of those before.

"I've had one of my better ideas," Lethe announced somewhere between the bags of crisps (you do all that to a potato?) and the cartons of concentrated apple juice (can't you just press the apples?). "Why don't we cook something traditionally Sunaran for these two and James tonight to celebrate your pledge of commitment and they can come to the studio for it."

"And how am I supposed to cook with splints on my fingers?"

"Oh, run the still then. You can do that much."

"Only so long as I can ferment cranberries and apricots."

"Yo! Like the sound of that. One of your best. Jenni, where do we find cranberries? And we've still got to track down the dallyflowers."

"What are dallyflowers?" Deirdre wondered aloud.

Lethe frowned as if puzzled someone didn't know. "It's a tree. Has white flowers on it and then black berries later on. Lots of little ones in clumps."

"Elderflowers," Jenni guessed. "You're a bit early in the year. Will elderflower cordial do?"

"Absolutely no idea. How soon do you want your baby?"

"Well, fairly soon. I'm not getting any younger."

"OK we'll try the cordial. James is at home tonight, isn't he?"

"Yes," Jenni agreed doubtfully.

"Only this stuff works pretty fast so we'll get a bed made up for the pair of you."

"Does it really work?"

"Never tried it. I believe the hardest part is getting the guy to drink it as it tastes so disgusting. Mind you, couple of shots of Ygoi's brew and James'll drink anything."

They added cranberries and apricots to the trolley and put in rice and more pulses than the women knew existed but they did manage to persuade two lifelong vegans to try pasta as it was only flour and water.

"OK my round," Lethe declared at the till. "I've had so many companies offering me credit cards that I took one of them on."

Ygoi helped the women to load up the carrier bags while Lethe proudly handed across his new credit card. The bar code scanner caught the tag in his wrist, all the tills and doors locked shut and an alarm bell went off in Exeter police station.

EIGHT

"I thought it would be larger," James remarked when three people looked through the open door of the studio and saw nothing but a deserted corridor with doors leading off. He wasn't too sure an Under Secretary should be dining in a spaceship but there weren't any precedents and some of the old rebel was still alive inside.

"Ygoi's old ship was," Jenni told him and took hold of his hand as she hadn't done for years. "This one would have fitted in the cargo hold. Oh well, in we go."

The clattering of four stiletto heels in the corridor brought Lethe out from the kitchen.

"Hi," he greeted them a bit nervously. "I haven't got as many rooms as you have so I'm afraid we'll have to eat in the kitchen. Jenni, can I borrow you a minute?" He left two of the three guests in the kitchen with Ygoi who was engrossed in the still but had already brewed down the cranberries and apricots into something that would probably have been illegal on Earth, and led Jenni across the corridor into one of the bedrooms.

"OK, don't panic, I'm not going to throw myself at you. But you could have changed your clothes. James and Ygoi are going to get fucked witless tonight while I am sleeping in a lonely bed and you are flaunting your very considerable charms in front of me just to torment me. What you need to do is to take this bottle into the bathroom and pee in it. We've already put all the other stuff in it so don't spill it. Then after you've done that you'll have about half an hour to get James to drink it. I'd suggest keeping it down your shirt until we've got him half out of his mind on Ygoi's brew. It allegedly works fast so get him in here as soon as you can after he's had it."

"Does it really work?" Jenni asked as she took the small blue bottle from him. "He wasn't keen on IVF. Making babies in test tubes," she explained.

"Don't think I would be either," he replied, still wondering how you did that.

There came a raucous blast of Deirdre laughing in the kitchen.

"Sounds like Ygoi's brew is ready. Come and try it."

The three guests thought it was the most delicious meal they had ever had. It wasn't that the ingredients were strange, it wasn't even the intelligent cooker that knew how to do soups, risottos, stir fry or whatever it was asked to do that made it so wonderful. It was probably something to do with the cranberry and apricot gin that was so sweet on the tongue and then seemed to blow a hole in the back of your head when you swallowed it. After about three small glasses each, Deirdre had to rush off to the bathroom to be sick and Jenni went with her to make sure she was all right.

Jenni came back on her own. "Poor thing's a bit rough. That'll ruin her PhD prospects if she is pregnant. Any of that risotto left, chef?"

"Sure, give me your bowl."

The bowl came across with a small blue bottle hidden in it and Lethe dutifully tipped the foul-smelling brew over the succulent and fluffy chick pea risotto.

Jenni persuaded her mellow husband to have another shot of gin then she shamelessly sat astride him on his chair and lovingly fed him risotto.

"Think it's got a bit burned," he remarked drunkenly at the first taste. "Not quite so good this time."

Jenni kissed him gently. "It's the gin. Come on, they say chick peas are good for the sperm count."

He shifted a bit under her. "Speaking of which…"

"Oh no, my love. You eat every last spoonful of this and then there's a nice bedroom just over the way which you and I may share."

Deirdre staggered back into the kitchen and slumped on another chair. "Oh, God. I feel sick," she moaned. "Do you have a bed I can lie down on in here?"

"I'll show her to the other room," Lethe told Ygoi. "Even though it's your fault she's in this state."

Two men cleared up after their dinner party and tried to ignore the noises coming from the bedrooms.

"You're getting married then," Lethe remarked.

"Yup. She wants us to get married in the house here as it's licensed for weddings and have things like bridesmaids and I don't know what. I haven't got a clue what she's talking about. Jenni says I can buy old gold jewellery to make the rings but apparently women here expect something called an engagement ring which has a stone in it."

"I know the kind of thing. You'd better take Deirdre with you to choose it."

"If she stops throwing up long enough to let me."

Kitchen cleaned and tidied, the outer door was shut and the two men went off to the control room to make up their beds for the night.

"Not quite the ending I'd had in mind," Ygoi admitted ruefully as Lethe helped him from the chair onto a pile of rugs, blankets and pillows on the floor.

"Me either," Lethe agreed as he retired to his own heap and tried not to sound too smug.

The two were up first in the morning and were breakfasting on bread and tree syrup before anyone else joined them. The first person to emerge was James, clutching his head and walking rather unsteadily.

"I must ring in sick this morning. What was in that devil's brew last night?"

"Have some tea," Lethe offered and didn't answer the question.

"Thank you. Jenni is just taking a shower, I hope that's all right?" He sat at the table and thoughtfully drank a mug of tea. "Where do you get your water from?"

"Tank in the roof. It gets recycled so we only need to carry a certain amount."

"In some ways you are so advanced and in others completely barbaric," James mused but he was really too happily tired to think too much. He had found his lovely, lively Jenni again and this time he wasn't going to let her go.

Jenni almost bounced into the kitchen, her hair wet and still in her gecko-revealing top and leather skirt but minus the high heels. "Guys, I cannot thank you enough for last night," she told them and kissed them both on the cheek.

"You don't know yet," Ygoi puzzled aloud.

"No, my love," she told him and stroked his face. "But I feel it."

Eventually the fifth member of the party became rather conspicuous by her absence and they sent Ygoi along to find out what was the matter with her. He found his betrothed face down on the bed, her face a peculiar shade of greenish grey and with a much-used bucket by her head.

"Fuck off," she greeted her fiancé. "Just get the fuck out of my life. This is all your fault."

"I'm sorry," was the best he could say, unable to reach her from his chair to cuddle her which was what he so desperately wanted to do.

Deirdre struggled to sit up on the bed and managed to settle her stomach once the room had stopped whirling in circles. She looked at the plain white walls and the colourful blankets and bedcovers. It was a crazy mix of Spanish hacienda and student bedsit and there were no windows. She felt too ill to wonder where the air came from. Her eyes focussed on a very homely patchwork quilt on the bed and she suddenly felt about five years old and rather small and frightened. She started to cry and threw up again in her ever-attendant bucket. "Go away. I'll have a cup of tea if you're making one."

James and Jenni went to see the control room before the doors were closed again and they thought how simple it all looked. There was a central console with two chairs at it but all there was on this console was a tiny black panel which Lethe explained was a scanner activated by logged-in Millio galaxy wrist tags, and what looked like a fairly conventional computer keyboard. They had been expecting vast banks of computers and switches instead of which there was just a lot of blank metal. One wall was recognisable as the workings of a computer of a power that could only be guessed at. There was a window at the front that looked out across Dartmoor, odd to think it usually looked out on the stars. It was hard to believe that this machine really could blast out of the atmosphere relying on nothing more than solar power and fly further than either of them could ever dream of going. It made their last holiday in Antigua seem a bit of an anti-climax. Lethe wouldn't take the ship up for any sort of flight, saying the fuel levels were too low for take off but really rather worried that Ygoi's head might explode if they went too close to the Millio galaxy.

Lethe very kindly helped Deirdre to get back to the house. He felt sorry for her as she was so ill and couldn't help wondering if she was reacting to something she had eaten. Probably Ygoi's gin, he decided. Her body was warm and lithe against his, he held her with an arm round her waist and every so often their hips would bump together. He would definitely have to go and get himself laid that night. This clean, country living was doing his head in.

He stopped at his car and handed Deirdre over to James. "OK, this is where I love you and leave you," he told them. "I've got to put another six songs on my album now that I've memorised them. See you all sometime. Invite me to the wedding, won't you?"

"You," Jenni told him, "are going to be best man."

"Whatever that means. Ygoi, a word, please." Alone with his friend, he asked, "You're really going ahead with this wedding? Even if she's not pregnant?"

"I said I would."

Lethe sat in the driver's seat of his car to put the two of them on the same level. "Then let me pay for your engagement ring for her. You won't get any more royalty money until the album comes out and that's not for another month."

"You haven't got any money either. Not really. All you're doing is getting into debt that you're going to have to work off. No, thanks for the offer."

The two exchanged a meaningless, Millio galaxy parting kiss then Lethe drove off and Ygoi went rather sadly into the house. He envied the other man his new lifestyle while he was shackled to a wheelchair, a house that wasn't his own, and a woman who was too sick to love him.

"You OK?" Jenni asked, seeing his mournful face.

"Fed up with being stuck in this chair."

"Only a few more weeks. Do you want to be married by then?"

"I really don't care. Shouldn't you ask Deirdre?"

"Oh dear, you have got the grumps. Well, James has retired to his study to sleep off last night's exertions, Deirdre is spending her time between your bed and your toilet so how about you and I hit Exeter and you can get a nice ring to cheer up your betrothed?"

"Don't you think she ought to choose it?"

"I think she feels so damned rotten today she'd be grateful for anything. So you've got me looking after you today. Want the loo before we leave?"

"Why is it you can always cheer me up? No, I don't need the toilet. But it'll have to be something cheap as I didn't get that much in royalties."

"Come on, grumpy bunny, let's go and climb into the Land Rover. I'll be teaching you to drive it soon with any luck."

Ygoi paid careful attention to Jenni's driving and got her to explain the principles of clutch control to him. He couldn't really see the point of it when you could get a land transporter to run at the speed of an Earth aeroplane powered by solar energy and with no gears whatsoever. But at least they knew how to mend hands and knees on this planet.

They went to a rather disreputable second-hand jeweller first where Ygoi bought himself about half an ounce of gold in the form of several outdated items.

"And you're really going to make the rings yourself?" Jenni asked as they set off to find somewhere more highbrow.

"Tradition where I come from. Be interesting to work with some of this stuff. What do you reckon its melting temperature is?"

"I have absolutely no idea. Quite a long way below that of trid I would imagine. Right, you look in the window at that lot and I'll lend you the money until you're paid again. I'd guess Deirdre's about my size as she borrowed some of my stuff yesterday."

So Ygoi looked at the stones of various colours from the white of the diamonds to the blood red of the rubies. "And you really mine all these from the earth?" he asked incredulously. "We've only got about four or five stones where I come from and they're all on Dirnhet." He looked hard at an amethyst ring. "Are you sure that isn't ienta?"

"What?"

"Ienta. It's just about that colour."

"You know your stones then," Jenni remarked. "James is hopeless. I think all he knows is diamonds."

"Which ones are the diamonds?"

"The clear ones."

"Those I like. We don't have any that colour on Dirnhet. We do have the yellow yterin which you don't seem to have. And our red hyenigon has been mined to extinction thanks to my father."

"What's he got to do with it?"

Ygoi realised he has said too much. Oh well, he wasn't going back there now so it didn't matter. "He's the feudal Lord of Dirnhet. He owns half the mining rights to it and sold off all the hyenigon he could find as it's used as the catalyst in our engines to convert sunlight to fuel."

"Bloody hell. So if you'd stayed in your galaxy you'd have inherited half a planet from him?"

"No. He's not my blood father. I was adopted. The ex-wife dumped me when she found out."

There was a bit of a silence. "Pity. You'd make one heck of a Lord." Jenni smiled fondly at the man in the wheelchair and kissed his cheek, hating to see how some bad memories had been roused. "So which one do you think Deirdre would like?"

"I need one of the diamond ones. No, two. Quite small."

"No, which ring do you want for her?"

"Jenni, I have just spent the past hour or so explaining our rather odd custom of the guy making the ring for his bride. OK, so I haven't worked with stones before but I've seen how you fix them so it won't be a problem. So we just choose the ones we want."

"You're potty."

"Probably. And that's the other thing. I've only got limited hands. So you're doing the making."

"My life was so dull before you came. Come on then, let's go and find a couple of diamonds for you.

But we'll go back to the other place. No sense in spending thousands of pounds if all you want is a couple of diamonds."

Deirdre felt a lot better by tea time and began to think she had maybe just had scare and she wasn't pregnant after all. Probably the effects of the gin Ygoi had brewed. A familiar sensation in her belly sent her off to the bathroom again then she went downstairs to find James taking a rather lonely tea in the drawing room with its view over the terrace and down the chestnut avenue where the studio stood like a benevolent sentinel.

"Ah, feel any better?"

"Much. It was something I ate."

James caught the note of relief in her voice. "You're sure it's not a baby?"

"Definitely not. I was just a few days late that's all."

James thought the poor woman looked as though her head was splitting. "Let me ring for some more tea for you. I'm afraid my wife and your betrothed aren't back from shopping in Exeter yet."

"Doesn't matter. I need to get some things sorted out in my head first. Can I talk with you?"

"Of course."

"And you won't tell anyone?"

He smiled. "I hold secrets that could bring down the government. I think you may trust me with yours."

"OK. Now. Ygoi is from another planet, right?"

"So I believe. It is rather hard to prove unless they take us to the place they call home."

"Let's assume he is. Now, I am a US citizen, I am here on a three-year visa which runs out in a bit over two years. He is, legally, an Estonian refugee. I assume there's nothing to stop us getting married here?"

"Not that I know of."

"In two years, I have to go home and he can't come with me on the papers he's got."

"You could apply to remain here."

"I could call off the whole darned wedding especially as there's no baby. I just don't know what is going to happen in two years' time when my visa runs out. I want to go home. What if your British Home Office says I can't stay? I don't know I want to stay. I love my life in New York. I have a plane ticket booked already to fly home for a few weeks next month so I can see my family. I don't want to live here."

"So why did you agree to marry a man who can't go home with you?"

"Because I love him so much it hurts. I can't bear the thought of leaving him behind. He's kind, gentle and the best lover I've ever had in my life."

There was a silence in the room. James knew it was time to tell his truth.

"I married a woman seventeen years my junior who has a gecko tattooed on her belly and who used to earn her living in a way not normally associated with the potential wife of a top civil servant whose father was a minor Earl in Yorkshire. We met at a charity function where I was sitting at the top table and she was handing round plates of food. I fell in love with her. I was reprimanded by my superiors, demoted from Permanent to Under Secretary at work and the scandal nearly brought down the government of the day. Out of all my family only my brothers

David and Barnabas would acknowledge Jenni as my fiancée. We stuck it out. Now we've been married for nearly nine years, my family grudgingly admits she exists but were never happier than recently when it looked as though our marriage was failing. Thanks to the arrival of our two extra-terrestrial friends, I can now say with all honesty, Jenni and I are back on track and have seldom been happier."

Deirdre knew then that she had remembered the newspaper stories correctly. The high-powered civil servant and the call-girl. The scandal had even made news across the Atlantic. "So what are you saying?"

"Follow your heart. Marry the man you love and maybe in two years' time US emigration laws will have changed, you could be on your way to a second set of triplets and you might want to stay here after all. Carpe diem. Take the best lover you have ever had and be happy with him for as long as you may."

"You're right. Can we marry here? I want to do it before rationality takes over and I break both our hearts."

"I spoke to the Events Manager just before lunch. We can plead a strong case for a special licence in view of the groom's health and you can have this place Tuesday next week at 10.30. Will it be a quiet wedding?"

"Very. I'll tell my parents when it's all over."

"No. Bad policy. That will alienate them against Ygoi from the start and he will be the bad boy who has stolen their daughter. I suggest you phone them tonight. News of a wedding deserves better than an email."

Deirdre sighed. "Do you think Ygoi's going to back out when I tell him there's no baby?"

James had to smile. "I think you should give him the option but he's an honourable, old-fashioned sort of a chap and I'd guess that once he's offered to marry you he won't change his mind."

"That's what I'm hoping too."

The two sat companionably in the drawing room. Mrs McDougall cleared away tea and checked they were happy with salmon for dinner, with a lentil bake for Mr Roemtek. The old clock ticked languorously in one corner and Deirdre was nearly asleep.

"It's time those two were home," James suddenly announced in the silence.

Deirdre looked at her watch. "Jeez, it's half past six. What time did they go out in the morning?"

"Just after breakfast." James went to the telephone and dialled a mobile number.

"Have you any idea what the time is?... You're where?   Doing what?... Well, don't be too much longer. The recipient and I are about to go to dine.... Yes, much better. Most likely a touch of food poisoning.... No, go ahead anyway. Yes, in a few minutes then." He turned to Deirdre. "Our two missing shoppers are in the studio making your engagement ring. Apparently they are having some problems making the diamonds stay in."

Deirdre wasn't quite sure what to expect after that. Another half hour went by before they heard Jenni and Ygoi chatting as they came along to the drawing room.

"Sorry," Jenni apologised. "I've never done goldsmithing before. But it's pretty damn good, though I say so myself."

Ygoi trundled over to Deirdre. "Feeling any better?"

"Yes, thanks, much. I'm sorry but you're not going to be a father just yet. I must have eaten something bad and, yes, I am sure. Do you want to call the wedding off?"

"Do you?"

"No. I'll be quite happy to marry you now and give you lots of kids when I've finished my PhD. Which, I might add, is not doing too good at the moment, thanks to you."

He just smiled at her, thankful she still wanted them to get married. "Hand, please."

Deirdre watched as Ygoi's elegant, splinted fingers put a ring on her wedding finger. She spared a moment to think his bandages were looking a bit grubby then turned her attention to the ring. Blue trid and yellow gold had been twisted together and two tiny diamonds set asymmetrically in the band. It was a thing of rare beauty and she couldn't believe that Jenni had made it that afternoon. She sat on his lap and wept into his neck.

"That is so beautiful," she told him. "Thank you."

He lifted her hot face from his neck and showed her the two rings in his palm. Two more twists of trid and gold but so fine and delicate they looked as though they could break. "Wedding rings. We've tested them out and you can't cut them even with a Tiowing on half blast. Do you approve or do I send my goldsmith back to work?"

Deirdre picked up the rings. "Your bandages need a wash. Ygoi, these are just so beautiful. So delicate I daren't touch them."

"You can hit them with a hammer if you like, they won't break. That gold is tough stuff, I'll give it that and I used base trid for the wedding rings. Your engagement ring is pure trid as it moulds more easily."

"And we can wear them next Tuesday. Which reminds me I must phone my parents and invite them to the wedding."

"Tuesday? But I don't get the splints off until Wednesday."

"I'll ring David," James offered. "See if we can't get you moved forward a couple of days."

David Kirkwood-Barnes unwound bandages and removed splints. "So, wedding tomorrow. All set for it?"

"Nothing to do. Deirdre originally said she wanted a big wedding with all her friends and family and now suddenly she wants it now and have a party later. She has a rather naïve idea that as soon as we're married I'll be granted entry into the States which we know isn't true as I have no passport." Ygoi looked at his hands for the first time in over a year and experimentally flexed the fingers. He couldn't really believe it.

The surgeon proudly inspected his work. "Definitely one of my better efforts. You were lucky that only the bones were broken and not your ligaments or tendons. If you're careful you should make a complete recovery. That harp come yet?"

"Couple of days ago. It's a bit different from mine, got more pedals for one thing. Amazing instrument, plays all the keys you can think of."

David smiled, glad to see the pitiful wretch in the front porch was now a cheerful and optimistic man again. "Then go home and play it for as long and as often as you can. There's no more I can do for you until I get you in for your knees next month. See you at the wedding tomorrow."

Ygoi couldn't help it. He just had to touch everything he came across all the way home. Jenni got quite fed up with him mauling the dashboard of her Land Rover and was heartily glad to see a white Saab in the drive of Ravenswood House.

Lethe Miarren had had his naturally slightly curly blond hair spiked, straightened and streaked with a honey colour although he still wore it long, and he stank of cigarette smoke. He couldn't believe how good Ygoi's hands were either.

"Fucking brilliant," he exclaimed. "Right, come on, play me a tune on your harp."

"No feet."

"Well play it without changing key. Come on, it's been years since I heard you play."

The harp was an over-ornate Victorian monstrosity somewhat out of tune but Lethe helped to tune the instrument and even offered to kick the pedals. Ygoi declined the second offer and gingerly lowered the instrument onto his shoulder. It felt ridiculously heavy and he had a sudden image of the wheelchair skidding backwards under the weight of it. He just hoped the brakes were good and rested his cheek on the frame of the harp for a moment while deciding what to play. Suddenly he saw it all again, those hideous moments when the security forces of Lriam had mashed up his hands and squashed them into cages. He lifted his head and let rip with a brilliant version of *Bat out of Hell* which he had recently decided was the best song ever written and made his chart hit a bit of a dirge. He had spent a lot of time recently learning about music.

Most of his audience had been expecting something along the lines of Bach or Mozart. Lethe hadn't been quite sure what to expect. But they all had to agree it was rather a dramatic effect.

Deirdre literally clapped her hands when he finished. He hadn't played the whole song but they had got the idea. "That is so cool," she exclaimed. "I had no idea you could play such stuff on a harp."

Ygoi's hands were hurting again but this was a good hurt. This was muscles and tendons being stretched to their limits and doing as they were asked. The days of trid cages and black nails grown into his palm were gone for ever. Idly he tinkered with the haunting melody of *Desperado*. "You can play anything you like on one of these. That's the whole point of it. Need a backing harpist in Birmingham?"

"Can you just do *Fallen Heroes* for me? That would just be so perfect if you could."

"Do I get a fee?"

"I'll make sure you do."

At ten thirty the next morning, Ygoi Roemtek married Deirdre Hunsecker by special licence in a quiet ceremony at Ravenswood House. The latest pop sensation, Lethe Miarren, was best man, Lady Jenni Kirkwood-Barnes was the bride's attendant, and Sir James Kirkwood-Barnes and his brother David were the witnesses. The bride's parents were held up in a check-in staff dispute at JFK airport in New York and the groom didn't really have anyone to invite. The rings of blue and gold metal were exchanged and the whole thing was done with a quiet dignity which impressed the registrar who usually found special licence ceremonies tended to have a mad urgency to them. He wished the newlyweds well, gave Deirdre the marriage certificates then left the wedding party to their morning coffee in the drawing room.

Mrs McDougall brought in the coffee and with her came a youth who looked as though he had been caught with his hands in the silver drawer.

"This is your intruder," she told Sir James. "Darren, one of the garden apprentices. He says he saw the door of that studio thing open and went in to have a look and got shut in. He couldn't get out so he helped himself to some of your food and got out when you came in. He told Jim in the greenhouse he'd been staying with friends. Jim found out the truth when he heard Darren on his mobile bragging to his mates he'd been trying to hotwire a spaceship."

She looked at Lady Kirkwood-Barnes who she believed to be the owner, but she was looking at the blond man on the other side of the room. "Your spaceship now," she told him.

"It's not a spaceship," Lethe pointed out rather too quickly. "You bought some old caravan or another to use as a studio and now you've very kindly said I can borrow it to make music in. Well, Darren, is this true?"

Darren just sort of grunted a bit and shuffled his feet. It was a bit frightening to come face to face with that bloke who'd won that *Talent Scout Superstar* thing on the telly that all his mates had been going on about. And Sir James knew his history of hotwiring cars that weren't his to take away. He didn't want to have to tell his probation officer he'd blown another job. He quite liked it in the garden, watching things grow and with nobody bothering him.

"Shall we compromise?" Lethe asked him kindly. "You should have asked to look round when you followed us in. We'd have let you. You shouldn't have interfered with the wiring but by some fluke your efforts to start an engine mended a problem we'd been having with the air conditioning. So shall we leave it at that?"

Everyone was surprised by the magnanimity. Not least Darren.

"Yeah, all right. Thanks," he managed to articulate and then got a bit braver. "Looks like a spaceship."

"It's an old prefab house," Jenni improvised.

Lethe was just glad the control room had been shut off. "Just forget it, OK?"

Darren's formerly resentful eyes were almost shining as he realised he had got away with it. "Thanks, mate," he managed and then shot off to his work before the housekeeper could tell him off and threaten him with his probation officer.

Mrs McDougall sniffed. "Very lenient of you if I may say so, sir."

"I believe in giving everyone one chance in life."

"That boy's had more than one chance, believe me. Are you all staying for luncheon, Sir James?"

"I'm not," Lethe replied. "Sorry, but I'm due back in London this evening so I must go."

The mention of London reminded Deirdre of her neglected studies and she sighed loudly. "Guess I'll have to be going back too some time or I'll have my professor on at me. I'm going home to the States in a few weeks and I've done nothing recently. She kissed her new husband fondly. "And that's all your fault."

"You can't both go," he protested. "Who's going to look after me?"

"You can wipe your own arse now," Lethe told him heartlessly. "And you're quite capable of getting yourself in and out of the chair. Want a lift back today, Deirdre?"

"I've only been married half an hour, give me a break!" she laughed. "I'll come up next week probably, once my family have gone. You moved out yet?"

"Um, no, actually. I quite like your flat. And James has been staying there too when he's been in London."

"Great," Deirdre exclaimed sarcastically. "I choose myself an apartment, pay the rent on it, clean it, furnish it and think it's mine for three years and now you two have moved in. Gee, thanks, guys. Real nice of you."

"I've been cleaning it," Lethe protested hotly. "And I'm more than willing to help pay the rent on it. And I'm really sorry about what I did to you there. Please let me stay. Please."

"Tell you what. You can use it while I'm here but when I want it either you move out or I want James or Ygoi as a bodyguard. Better you're in it than it stands empty to get broken into."

"Done," Lethe agreed, glad he wasn't going to have to find somewhere else to live but sad to think he had broken her trust so completely.

James was rather pleased to think of himself as a bodyguard to such a beautiful woman, but hoped it wouldn't come to a brawl. Ygoi made a mental note to go and get himself something small and lethal from the hidden arsenal in Lethe's spaceship. Just in case.

Mr and Mrs Hunsecker got out from the taxi and just looked at the frontage of Ravenswood House. They had seen their daughter's London apartment and knew she was temporarily staying with a friend but they hadn't expected anything like this much grandeur. There were two or three people gently pottering round the flowerbeds and the sounds of several vacuum cleaners running in the house so obviously servants were employed here. Suddenly their daughter came belting out of the house like a bright-eyed teenager and rapturously hugged her parents.

"I'm so glad you got here!" she exclaimed as they joyfully returned the hugs. "And I'm sorry you missed the wedding but we had the slot yesterday and wouldn't have gotten another for months. Come on in and meet my husband." She giggled rather self-consciously. "Sure can't get used to calling him that."

The parents were satisfied that their daughter was happy, but they were still a bit bothered she had married in such haste.

"Is everything OK, honey?" her mother asked her.

Deirdre knew exactly what she meant. "Fine. Ygoi and I haven't been up to anything we shouldn't have. You're not going to be grandparents until after I've finished my PhD." She hooked her hands through their arms. "Come on in, this place opens to the public in about half an hour and I'm sure you don't want to be a couple of exhibits."

Her mother was on her left side and noticed the strange rings her daughter was wearing. "Honey, where did you get those rings? They are gorgeous. What are they made of?"

The lie had been agreed. "Gold and steel. The steel's been treated not to rust which is why it's blue. Ygoi designed them and Jenni made them. Come on and meet them both." It was only as she escorted her parents into the morning room that she suddenly remembered she had forgotten to tell them that their son-in-law was in a wheelchair. Probably because she didn't really notice it any more.

Mr and Mrs Hunsecker looked approvingly at the elegance of the room where two men and a woman were sitting at a table sharing a pot of coffee. For a moment they were a bit confused as one of the men was a lot older than the other two but he was the one who got to his feet and came to greet them. For one heart-stopping moment they thought their daughter had married some geriatric guy for his money,

"Mr and Mrs Hunsecker, so pleased to meet you at last. I'm James Kirkwood-Barnes and this is my wife Jenni. I think it's probably best if we leave you to get to know your son-in-law in private. I'll ask Mrs McDougall to have some more coffee brought in, if you like."

"Yes, thanks," the father of the bride replied. "Coffee would be good."

James and Jenni went out and there was a bit of a pause in the morning room. The visitors suddenly realised their son-in-law didn't lack old-fashioned manners, what he lacked was the ability to stand.

Deirdre saw the look her parents exchanged and she over-dramatized a bit in her embarrassment. "Oh my God, I didn't tell you, did I? Ygoi had an accident and broke his knees. He's having an operation on them soon. I kind of forget he's in a wheelchair."

Ygoi felt rather embarrassed too by the obvious discomfort of his parents-in-law and wasn't quite sure what to say. He offered his hand with a polite, "Pleased to meet you," and was relieved the hand was accepted.

"Deirdre tells us you're Estonian," Mr Hunsecker said to make polite conversation.

"On my father's side. My mother's family is Swedish."

"So are you a linguist too?"

"Not really. I can speak a bit of Russian and Swedish."

"Do you know the States at all?" Mrs Hunsecker tried valiantly.

"No, never been."

"Still, you're coming with Deirdre next week, aren't you?"

"I can't. I'm in this country as a refugee and don't have the papers to travel."

Parents looked at daughter and there was another silence. They really couldn't understand why their daughter, who could have had her pick of men, should have chosen a rather shy young man in a wheelchair, whose English was accented and who wasn't able to leave the country where he had sought a sanctuary.

A sturdy, middle-aged woman brought in a tray of coffee. "Would you like me to show you to your rooms now?" she asked the guests.

"Yes, thanks, that would be good," Mr Hunsecker replied. "You two coming with us?"

"Sure," Deirdre agreed. "Come on, honey, let's get you in the elevator."

It was as the parents saw the way their daughter manoeuvred the wheelchair that they realised she had married for love. The way those two looked at each other took them back more years than they cared to count and they knew then that Deirdre didn't care if her husband was a refugee. She would stay in the UK and be an illegal immigrant herself rather than lose the love of her life.

"You are still coming next week, aren't you, honey?" her mother checked.

"Sure. I've got lots of appointments scheduled with friends and two sessions with my professor at Yale. James, who you just met, works at the Home Office here. We're trying to get Ygoi's travel rights worked out and James is in contact with the US embassy to see if we can't get Ygoi US citizenship now he and I are married, or at least some kind of right of entry to the States. He won't get anything by next week but I'd lay my last dime we're with you for Thanksgiving."

The atmosphere lightened by several degrees and Mr Hunsecker smiled brightly at his son-in-law. "So, Ygoi, what did you do to earn a living in Estonia before you had your accident?"

Thankful he had a decent story to tell, Ygoi told him, "I'm a musician. I'm in the backing band for a pop concert in the Birmingham Arena in a few weeks."

"Really? What do you play?" Mrs Hunsecker, who was a bit of a clarinettist, asked.

"Harp."

"Jeez, you don't get many of them to the pound. Do you have a harp here? I'd sure like to hear you play."

"It's in the drawing room," Deirdre explained. "That's open to the public until five tonight but I'm sure Ygoi would play for you this evening."

"Of course," he agreed.

The visitors were just as impressed with the room where they would be sleeping. The view looked east across the Devon countryside and they could see several dozen cars in the car park.

"Sure is a beautiful place," Mrs Hunsecker sighed. "Are you going to live here until you come home?"

"Probably," Deirdre agreed. "We just love it here and there's plenty of room so we're not always falling over Jenni and James. I know it's stupid but we're just not thinking too hard of what's going to happen when my visa runs out."

"I'm sure Ygoi will be allowed into the States now you're married," Mrs Hunsecker tried to console and wondered just how tall her son-in-law was. He looked rather thin and slight and she couldn't imagine he was even as tall as Deirdre who stood six foot in her heels. She hoped he'd be up on his feet by Thanksgiving.

"Sure he will," Deirdre agreed, and hoped.

Mr and Mrs Hunsecker stayed at Ravenswood House for a week. They were delighted to see their daughter so happy but were rather worried that she didn't seem to be doing much studying. They finally managed to catch her alone one afternoon while her husband was on the phone to someone called Lethe. Parents and daughter went for a walk among the tourists in the grounds.

"You seem real happy," was the opening maternal salvo.

"I am."

"And how is the PhD coming on?" her father wanted to know and didn't sound quite so enchanted.

"Oh, OK I guess."

"Deirdre, we have watched you for the past few days and you haven't even touched your notes. You've only got two more years on your visa and it's a vast topic."

"Mom, I've only just gotten married. If Ygoi hadn't been scheduled for an operation on his knees we'd have been on honeymoon right now."

"Are you having a honeymoon?"

"No. Ygoi's got his operation the day I fly back to the States. His friend Lethe has sent me a ticket for his concert in Birmingham so I'll have to fly back for a couple of days for that. Wouldn't miss that for the world."

"Is that the one where Ygoi is playing his harp?"

"That's the one."

The parents admitted defeat. Their daughter had stars in her eyes and wasn't going to come down to earth and get on with her PhD just yet. They hoped her few weeks in the States would help retune her mind. Her father was a bit bothered that his daughter had married a musician rather than an intellectual but at least the guy could speak a couple of other languages.

Ygoi was a bit thrown when his parents-in-law got back from their walk round the garden and Mr Hunsecker challenged him in good Russian.

"So, Ygoi, are you looking forward to playing your harp in Birmingham? We still haven't heard you play."

"My fingers get tired, my hands were injured in the same accident that broke my knees. I'll play for you tonight if you like," he replied, thinking it polite to speak the same language.

"You're not from the Baltics."

"What?" Deirdre and Ygoi challenged together.

Mr Hunsecker continued in Russian. "Speak to me some more. Any old words will do. I just want to hear your accent."

Hoping this man didn't know what the polyglot community of the Millio galaxy could do to a bloke's vowels, he did as he was told. "Deirdre reckoned I'm from somewhere slightly east of Tallinn. It was the old Soviet Union in those days and my father was Russian so I never leaned Estonian and I haven't spoken much Russian for a long time so perhaps my accent has slipped a bit."

"Keep going."

"What do you want me to say? I can't think of anything."

"If I recite you a poem, will you say it back to me in your own accent?"

"Sure."

So Frank Hunsecker recited a poem in Russian and his son-in-law repeated it perfectly after only one listen. The two women could hear the difference in the sounds but so far as Deirdre was concerned that was because her father had learned his Russian during his time in the armed forces in the aftermath of the Cold War and her husband had learned his from Estonian ancestors. The poem rhymed better the way Ygoi said it and the words seemed to flow more easily making the original recital sound rather stilted and formal somehow.

"That is incredible," was Frank's diagnosis. "If I hadn't heard that I would never have believed it."

"What's up?" Deirdre asked.

"I'll admit I've never met a Soviet Estonian but that poem was written in Russia in the fourteenth century, so far as we know. It is about the oldest known piece of Russian literature and your husband's Russian suits it perfectly. It's like meeting a guy from Minnesota and finding he speaks fluent Chaucer."

"They probably do in Minnesota," Mrs Hunsecker laughed. "So now you know how they spoke Russian in Estonia. Don't forget the old Soviets were the oppressors so I guess they weren't too keen on speaking the language in those days. I think Deirdre's research is maybe more up to date than yours, honey, you've just spent too long reading old books."

"True," he agreed. "Tell you what, Ygoi, when you're over in the States I'll get one of my colleagues to speak Swedish to you, he holds the Chair in Scandinavian Languages at Harvard. See if you speak fourteenth century Swedish as well. Whereabouts does your mom come from?"

Ygoi was ahead of them on that one. "Some tiny village way up above the arctic circle, so, yes, I'd guess she wasn't up on the Stockholm slang. She died when I was quite small so I don't have as much Swedish as Russian."

"Oh, I'm sorry. Is you father still alive?" Frank asked.

"No, he died in the labour camps of the old USSR."

Mrs Hunsecker got down on her knees beside the wheelchair and hugged her astonished son-in-law. "Then Frank and I will be your parents now. You're too young to be on your own."

"I'm thirty five."

"You're a child. I was forty two when Deirdre was born and that was after twenty years of a childless marriage. So, you can call us Mom and Dad and you can let Frank treat you like the son he always wanted."

Frank's grin was huge. "Ever been to a ball game, son?"

If Ygoi had had a god he would have prayed. Here he was trying to integrate nicely by being all domesticated, getting married, hoping for a family and yet having to try harder to bury secrets than Lethe who was out there in the middle of life and enjoying every minute of it.

"No," he conceded. "I've never been to a ball game."

"Boy, are you in for a treat."

Mr and Mrs Hunsecker returned to the States with their daughter. They had managed to change their tickets so the family all flew back together with lots of hugs and kisses for the man going into hospital to have his knees operated on. Ygoi was just relieved to book in at the hospital and know that for the next few days nobody cared about his mind, his languages or anything remotely intellectual. He rather liked Deirdre's parents with their American enthusiasm and openness but thought she could have warned him her father was a professor of literature specialising in early Russian and Norse. He could quite see where Deirdre got her brains from. Her mother was six foot two and still beautiful and, like her daughter, very intelligent. Her field of expertise was astrophysics and he got the impression she was a bit disappointed

Deirdre had turned out a linguist rather than a scientist but loved her daughter anyway.

They had been quite complimentary about his harp playing too which had done his ego some good and he hadn't practised so much for a long time. His fingers had got soft after not playing for so long but the pads were hardening nicely by the time he got to the hospital.

Jenni had driven him there and stayed with him while he was booked in and shown his room. She even helped fold up his clothes for him when they asked him to get undressed and into his gown ready for surgery. Then she had to let him go and she watched as he was wheeled cheerfully away for the operation that was going to give him back his life. She sat in the small room on the chair by the window and watched a tractor go backwards and forwards across a field with a trailer behind it showering muck everywhere. The room was very quiet and for some reason Jenni felt rather nervous. But then she had been feeling a bit odd for the past few days.

Unaware of the apprehension of his sister-in-law, David was looking forward to restoring this young man to full mobility and came to see him in the pre-op room.

"Right, are you planning on another dose of your self-hypnosis?" he asked.

"Probably. I didn't do it consciously last time."

"Well, you made life hell for the anaesthetist and it's a different chap this time. I've warned him to monitor you closely but you're going under for a general anyway. You must realise you're about half the age of someone usually getting new knees so you'll almost certainly need to have these replaced at some time in the future. But at least we can have you walking on stage at Birmingham."

"So soon?"

"Oh, yes. No lying in bed with new joints. We'll get your operation done this morning and we'll have you on your feet this evening. No, don't start sniffling. I can't stand to see a grown man cry."

"You don't understand. Only a few months ago there was no hope for me. Then I went into a pub. Lethe walked back into my life and suddenly everything started to get better. Have you ever lived without hope?"

David was thoughtful. "No. And my only hope is that I never do. Well, I'll see you in a few minutes but you won't see me. Chat to you again when it's over."

The operation was perfectly straightforward. First the left knee was changed and then the right and David was beginning to think there weren't going to be any dramatics this time. Suddenly the heartbeat monitor gave out one long persistent beep and the blood pressure monitor started plummeting.

"What's going on?" David asked, although he already knew. "I told you to monitor in case he went into hypnosis."

"Anaesthetic levels are fine. His heart just stopped."

The medical team went into their standard emergency procedure but the patient didn't respond to manual attempts to revive him.

"Ready to shock," one of them reported.

"Stand by," the surgeon ordered and those not needed got out of the way.

"Stand clear," came the command and the electric charge made the body on the table jump. The monitor carried on whistling.

David looked at the clock. "Try again."

"Charging. Stand clear." Another jerk of the body and no response.

"Damn it, man, try again. I don't want to lose this one over a couple of knees."

The third attempt failed too. "It's no good. He's not responding."

"Eighty nine seconds," David realised with another check of the clock. "Just one more go. Please. This one's a friend of mine."

Millions of miles away a wrist tag was deactivated on a tracking system as the shock went through the body for the last time.

NINE

Ygoi was dreaming of something quite pleasant but he couldn't remember what when somebody started saying his name over and over again. He looked blearily into the eyes of the nurse in the recovery room.

"Welcome back," she said to him and smiled. "We lost you for a bit then."

"When?"

"Just now. Sir David will tell you all about it."

David was all hearty bravado when he walked into Ygoi's private room. He had asked his sister-in-law to say nothing and knew she hadn't by the way his latest patient was just sitting on the bed chatting with the woman in the chair beside him. "Well, do you like giving me frights, or what?"

"What have I done now?"

"OK, good news first. I have done an excellent job on your knees. So, off the bed and walk. Take my arm and the strumpet-in-law will take your other side and a lovelier crutch you couldn't hope to have. Except the one you are married to, of course."

"Walk? Just like that?"

"Just so. Come on. You may be a bit wobbly but we don't want you keeling over with thrombosis."

Ygoi's balance wasn't what it had been but he managed to walk the length of the room and stopped at the window to look out across the streets of Honiton. What he really wanted to do was go running down the corridors and shout his happiness to the world but accepted it could be a while yet before he could run. He hung on rather tightly to Jenni and she hugged him back.

"Well done, you," she complimented and saw the look in his eyes. The look of someone who had woken up and found it really had all been a horrible dream. And she knew there was some even better news to come. She was smiling inside and she helped the patient to turn away from the window.

"Is there some bad news?" Ygoi asked as the three walked back again.

David steered him into a chair. "Your heart stopped while you were on the operating table. We had to have four goes to get you started again. We don't know for sure but it was probably a reaction to the anaesthetic although I can't fault how it was administered. Just one of those things."

Ygoi couldn't believe what he was hearing. First he had rediscovered the simple joy of walking and now this. "How long did it stop for?"

"Does it matter?"

"To me? Yes."

David wasn't used to this reaction. This patient wasn't at all frightened by the news, in fact he seemed rather pleased. "Ninety five seconds."

"You're sure it was ninety five?"

"If you must be pedantic, ninety five point six. Why?"

Ygoi showed the surgeon the tag under the skin of his wrist. "If my heart stops beating for more than ninety seconds then my birth tag is deactivated and according to the computers of my home galaxy I am dead. That means the Lriam security beams targeted at me would have been automatically turned off on the ninety first second without heartbeat. So you are absolutely sure it was ninety five?"

Now David could understand why this man was so pleased. "Trust me, it was ninety five going on ninety six. I'd say you are safely dead in your own galaxy."

Ygoi took out all the gold from his ears and nose that had been replaced as soon as he was off the operating table. "Only one way to find out. And it also means that those implants can just stay in my brain if they're not doing any harm."

"Does it mean you can go back?" Jenni asked and wondered where that would leave Deirdre.

He thought about that. "In a way, yes. People might recognise me visually but it'll be on all the databases that I died while out of galaxy so they won't believe it's me. I still have a tag in my wrist so the only problem would be if anyone ever scanned the tag. I could probably live some sort of life back there if I wanted to."

"Do you want to?"

Ygoi got up and shuffled slowly to the window, holding on to furniture as he went. His tortured eyes looked beyond the town to that lovely, rolling landscape with its red earth and green forests. He thought of promises of Birmingham Arena and Thanksgiving. There was a future for him here now. "No. I have nothing there and I have a wife and family and friends here. I am dead in the Millio galaxy. Let those who knew me drink to my memory then let me go."

Lethe Miarren wasn't sure who would be coming in on the 12.15 train. He had a vague idea that Deirdre was away in America but guessed Jenni would travel with Ygoi even if James couldn't get time off work. He stood quite contentedly watching the passengers leaving the platform, keeping an eye open for a wheelchair and let his mind wander over the morning's work. He had finally found something he really liked doing. The musicians were all good, the songs were exhilarating and the stage crew had all been very complimentary. The TV crew looked a bit sour but he really didn't care too much about them. He had enjoyed working with the musicians even if they had been a bit sceptical when he told them he was shipping in a harpist. But there was the harp that had been ordered. Bit different from the ornate instrument in Jenni's house and he only hoped Ygoi wouldn't mind the rather sleek and trendy pale wood number. At least he had got used to the theory of a seven-pedal harp now. They had made Lethe play it to test the sound levels and although he had messed about with Ygoi's harps before, he really didn't understand how the other man could play it. It hurt his fingers just doing the sound level check.

"Which planet are you on today?" asked an amused, familiar voice.

Lethe jumped, startled out of his thoughts and stared at the man beside him. Ygoi Roemtek looked annoyingly calm for a man who was about to play live to several thousand people that evening. He also looked annoyingly neat and cool in his jeans and leather jacket with a holdall slung over one shoulder and he wore no jewellery whatsoever apart from a rather unusual wedding ring.

"You're not as tall as I remember," Lethe remarked and then thought how bitchy that sounded. He remembered it wasn't the done thing to hug another man in public, far less give him a kiss of relief that it was all over.

"Not as fat either, but I'm not complaining."

"How are the new knees?"

"Better than the old ones. How was the rehearsal?"

The two set off for the car park. "Just great. I don't reckon anyone's sussed I'm anything other than a country hick from PE Island yet. At least they keep making jokes about Canadians so I'd guess I'm OK. They've persuaded me to go more rock than country but I'm definitely leaving *Desperado* in. You OK to do the harp for more than *Fallen Heroes*?"

"I'm not supposed to be working at all. I'm not in the union."

"The what?"

"Union. Something called the Musicians' Union. Sticks up for the rights of the workers apparently."

"Against whom?"

"Tyrannical employers I suppose. Pity they don't have unions where we come from. Dirnhet sure could use one."

"Says the son of the feudal Lord..." Lethe began.

The two were taken aback to have a flash gun go off in their faces. "Lethe!" a female voice hailed them as though she knew all about him. "Well done on winning that *Talent Scout Superstar* show. You're playing live tonight here at the Arena, aren't you?"

"Yes. Who are you?"

"Caitlin Evans, freelance journalist. Who is now going to sell this picture of you to whoever will pay for it. Who's the friend?"

"Ygoi Roemtek," he introduced himself. "I..."

"Jesus! The Estonian refugee. Can you tell me what it was like being imprisoned and tortured like that? Do you speak English?"

Ygoi was about to let rip with some choice Russian now Deirdre and her father had updated his vocabulary but thought better of it. "Fluently. And, no, I've nothing to say to you."

"Why did you come to Britain? Thought it would be a soft touch? Free handouts and all the rest of it? Are you even going to do anything to pay us back, you parasite?" She was a bit miffed when neither rose to her goading. It always sold her stories better if only the celebrity would swear at her. Instead they just looked at each other, wished her a polite "Good afternoon" and went on their way. Obviously very close. Lovers, she decided.

She went over to a café on the station concourse to download her picture and get some editorial together to mail round the papers. Her fingers paused over the keys of her laptop.

Lethe Miarren, winner of Talent Scout Superstar *at Birmingham New Street today with his "friend" and songwriter Ygoi Roemtek. The crippled refugee is now walking so it's safe to assume he has taken time, funding and a hospital bed from a British person who has been waiting in agony for the same operation. Or maybe the wheelchair was just a front to get him refugee status.*

She sent the email to her usual round of tabloids hoping that Lethe Miarren's fleeting status would get her published this time. She sat and drank her plastic mug of plastic coffee and ate a Mars bar. Her laptop beeped and she saw some mail had arrived.

Thanks, Caitlin. Will take this one for five grand with more editorial. Exclusive rights. Get the full Roemtek story and you can stick a zero on the end of the figure. Get the full Miarren and you can double it. Cancel all other publications. Have arranged press pass for you for tonight's concert. Collect at stage door. Good luck.

Suddenly the coffee didn't taste quite so much like plastic. Caitlin smiled to herself as she bagged up her equipment and set off to get a taxi to the Birmingham Arena.

The white Saab got stuck in traffic and Lethe lit a cigarette. He offered one to Ygoi which was declined. "See you've taken off the face jewellery," he remarked. "Is Birmingham beyond the range of Lriam security?"

"No, but I am. My heart stopped for ninety five seconds while my knees were being done so I am now officially dead."

"Fuck me. So are you going to go back now?"

Ygoi didn't really want to go round that particular conversation again. "Doubt it. I'd rather get some sort of citizenship here, preferably one with a US visa attached and then have some sort of life with Deirdre and have another go at some kids."

"Never thought you'd get domesticated."

"Never thought I'd get thrown in a Lriam prison. So what are your plans?"

Lethe laughed. "I am going to grab life on Earth by the balls and screw it until we're both exhausted. Want to see my tattoo?" Lethe pushed up his left sleeve to show an artistic gecko on his upper arm.

Ygoi experimentally stroked the skin. "That is weird. How is it done?"

"They inject ink under the skin. Fancy having one?"

"Think I've had enough things stuck under my skin. Why are you so cheerful? I was expecting you to be throwing up with nerves."

"Tonight I may be. Right now I'm enjoying myself. You learned to drive yet?"

"Jenni's teaching me on the Land Rover. I've got dates booked for my theory and awareness but not for the practical."

The queue of traffic started to move and the Saab nosed forward. "You mean there's a test on this planet?"

"Three. And you're supposed to have a licence. Don't think a Millio cross-galaxy licence would count somehow."

"Well, fuck me. I haven't got any of that." The traffic stopped again and Lethe looked at the cab next to him. The passenger in the back seat smiled and waved. "It's that nosy cow from the station."

"Nosy what?"

"Cow. It's a turn of phrase. Don't think it's meant to insult the animal." Lethe raised his voice and bellowed at the cab. "You going to my concert tonight then?"

Caitlin opened the window, pleased he had remembered her. "Wouldn't miss it for the world."

"Come backstage and mob me afterwards?" With his left foot on the brake, Lethe stood up, leaned in through the cab window and kissed the unprotesting Caitlin hard on the mouth.

Enraged drivers behind blew their horns and Lethe laughed as he sent the Saab forwards again. His queue moved faster than that on the right so the cab was soon left behind.

"You're also supposed to wear a seat belt in a car. And you're either going to get arrested or catch some disease we've never heard of if you carry on like that," Ygoi cautioned him. "You're no better than those bloodflower eaters on Goine."

"Fuck off," Lethe said cheerfully and switched lanes without checking behind him to get to the exit lane he wanted. "I'm enjoying myself."

Ygoi envied the other man his naïve enthusiasm as the two got nearer to the Arena. They were escorted to the car park by a security guard who climbed in the back and the same man took them along to where Ygoi had to sign in a book and get given his backstage pass, thankful he had a least learned to write with a pen. Lethe strode off along the corridors he had memorised that morning while the gobsmacked Ygoi tagged along behind and tried to look everywhere at once. He literally stopped in his tracks when they got to the edge of the stage where the backing musicians were practising in a discord that would have offended his ears if he had heard it. The sheer size of the place was what struck him first. Then the banks of lights above, beside and below the platform. It looked to be half a mile wide and a mile long and looked out over an auditorium the size of a small planet. He had been to a few concerts on various planets but never, ever had he seen anything so big.

"Um, hi, you with us or still on the train?" asked a female voice at his shoulder.

Ygoi focussed his eyes on a young woman with brilliant red hair and a rather bossy expression on her face. "Hullo. Sorry, it's just a bit big."

"You think this is big? You should see the Hollywood Bowl. Right, let's get you wired up."

"What?" asked the man who was still suspicious of anything that sounded remotely like torture.

"For sound. Sorry, always forget my manners before concerts. I'm Cally, one of the sound engineers. This is your headset and mike." As she spoke she deftly clipped a small box onto Ygoi's waistband, shoved a wire up his shirt without asking first and hooked a headset over his ear. "You'll need these when the noise gets going or you won't hear the band. You can use the mike to speak to Dan on keyboards and he'll relay any messages to you the same way. On off switch on your control box. I suggest you get to your harp and try a few test transmissions with Dan so we know you're up and running. The band's all on the same frequency so you can chat with any of them. Dan will take you round and introduce you in a minute. You'll hear their chat half the time. Come on, over here." She led the dumbstruck harpist over to his instrument near the drummer. "This is your pitch. You can see how the harp is wired for sound and your mike is that one on the other side of it. Use that or shout very loud if you want to speak to Lethe, he doesn't have a headset like you guys but does have a transmitter mike so he can walk round the stage during the performance. OK, sit yourself down and get settled and we'll run some sound level tests. Headset on, please and all messages will be broadcast to you from now on." She checked the headset was secure in his ear and adjusted the tiny microphone against his cheek. "Does that thing need tuning?"

"Probably." Ygoi had never seen such a minimalist harp but it certainly had all its component parts.

Cally fiddled with the controls on the box on his waistband. "You're a bit softly spoken, I'll just pump up your volume. Use this dial if you can't hear the other guys. I suggest you leave this switched on now until we break as it looks like Lethe's ready to go. Chat to you later."

Cally whisked off through the battery of drums and immediately a voice sounded in Ygoi's ear.

"Afternoon! Glad you joined us. Hi, I'm Dan. You ready to roll?"

"Um, yes, good to go," Ygoi agreed, thinking he was having more bizarre experiences on Earth than he had ever had in his home galaxy.

"OK, Lethe wants to do *Fallen Heroes* first to get you played in so we'll take our cue from you. Give us your tempo and we'll follow."

Ygoi pulled the extraordinarily light harp onto his shoulder and checked the tuning as he noticed three very attractive ladies had lined up at the microphones. He focussed his mind on the song he had written and started on the introduction, totally forgetting to give the others the speed.

Lethe stood alone at the front of the stage and watched the harpist. He could see the looks of approval of the other musicians but he felt rather sorry for the instrumentalist. There he was stuck at the back of the stage with the headset and mike of the backing musicians while he, Lethe Miarren, former co-pilot and gangly adolescent was out at the front. He would be the one the audience screamed for, the one who was able to walk around the stage and flirt with whoever he chose in that audience. Mind you, some of those backing singers were rather cute. He moved towards the band and nearly missed his entry.

Ygoi wasn't prepared for the blast of music that came through his earpiece when everyone else got going. They had turned his gentle lament into loud rock and he didn't like it one bit. The keyboard was putting out the effects of a full orchestra of strings, the six backing singers were doing weird repeats to some of the words and the drummer was thumping a beat through the floor that literally shook the stage.

"What have they done to it?" he said aloud as the crescendo hit full decibels on the second chorus. To his amazement the whole thing ground to a halt.

"What's up?" Dan's voice asked.

Ygoi remembered what Cally had said about microphones and wished for a second he hadn't said anything. Then he was glad he had. "It's supposed to be for harp, guitar and Lethe's voice, or two voices. It's not for a fucking orchestra."

Lethe couldn't hear the broadcast conversation so he came across to see what was going on. "So we've spiced it up a bit," he defended the orchestration. "It was a bit of a dirge."

"It's supposed to be," the composer replied hotly. "For fuck's sake it's called *Fallen Heroes*. It's supposed to be a lament. You can do the lachrymal thing when it suits you. Save the hard rock for some of the others."

"You can't start a concert with a lachrymae."

"So you end with it, do it in the middle, just don't do it like that."

"You can't end the concert with it either, everyone'll go home and cut their wrists."

"They didn't when it won you that competition, did they?"

"No," Lethe had to admit and started to feel a bit trapped.

"OK, so whose idea was it to hype the song up a bit?"

"Mine," interrupted Dan. "Why are you getting so bloody worked up about it? It's only a rather run of the mill song that one Friday night audience happened to like over their curries and chips. They won't even remember what it sounded like in the first place."

Lethe waited for the explosion of temper from the fiery Ygoi Roemtek. He would have blasted someone with a Tiowing for a lesser insult than that in the old days. Then he saw the look in the other man's dark eyes and knew that with the pride and the arrogance, his temper had gone too.

"I wrote that run of the mill song," he explained politely. "That's why Lethe has got me here to play it as it should be heard and not being grunged through some computer wizardry. Now, I'm a rubbish singer but if you'll just give me two minutes I'll show you what it's supposed to sound like. Lethe, can you get ready for your bit? And try to keep in the same key as the harp this time."

Dan felt a bit embarrassed by the other man's quiet dignity and wished he had been shouted at instead. "Sorry, didn't realise. OK, quiet on stage for two minutes, please."

Lethe came and sat on the floor next to the harp and listened hard to the introduction as Ygoi played it so flawlessly. It had been a long time since the two of them had sung together and it was odd at first to hear Ygoi pick up a lower melody line that had originally gone to the guitar. The title made sense. There were two fallen heroes lamenting together and they were competing to prove who had been treated worse. Suddenly you realised that maybe it was just a drinking game, a bit of a bet, maybe it wasn't even true. Just two guys trying to out-boast each other as to who had been treated more badly and when the vocal stopped and the harp soared on without them you got the joke. It was a song for slow dancing, a lament, but you kind of thought those guys deserved it.

There was a silence on stage after the song had ended. The musicians didn't quite know what to say. It was unfashionable to describe a song as beautiful, but few of them had ever been so moved by a simple duet before.

"Told you I was a rubbish singer," Ygoi apologised. "But that should give you an idea."

Dan shook his head. "No, you're not. I've heard a lot worse than you go on to become millionaires. Can you do that duet like that live tonight? I still like the rock version but I'll concede the point just this once. Maybe we'll do the rock version as well when you do the UK tour."

Ygoi looked across at the backing singers. "Which one of them would you recommend to sing the duet?"

"Not them, bonehead," Dan almost shouted. "You!"

"What? But I can't sing."

"Don't give me that bollocks. Cally!" he summoned the assistant sound engineer. "Get Ygoi wired up to sing tonight."

The redheaded Cally shot across the stage to do his bidding which basically meant changing the box at the end of the wire and instructing the bewildered Ygoi bow to switch from chatting with the musicians to letting the audience hear his voice.

"Just don't get in a muddle," she cautioned him.

"I'm in a muddle already," he admitted.

The television crews were delighted with the writer of *Fallen Heroes*. He was quite photogenic in spite of the enigmatic scarring on his face and his English had a cute East European accent to it although it was absolutely fluent. He had an amazing rapport with the rather fatuous Lethe Miarren and those watching began to wonder if the blond pop singer wasn't stringing them along making them think he was just another airhead who happened to be able sing a bit. Texts went from the Birmingham Arena to Head Office in London and plans were changed slightly. Those in charge were a bit worried about Lethe Miarren. He had won his competition fairly but they didn't like the way nothing was known about him. It could prove rather awkward if he suddenly turned out to be a convicted drug baron. They had run police checks in Canada and the UK but had drawn a blank. Now, it seemed, there was a man who could get through that wall of reserve. The two were known to have been carer and invalid but the invalid could walk and play the harp now, he didn't need a carer and it was obvious the two had known each other for a long time. They talked of things and people that made no sense to anyone else. The Canadian and the Estonian knew each other at a deeper level and if anyone was going to expose the truth about the new pop star it was his long term friend.

Lethe and Ygoi went to the former's dressing room for lunch and the TV crew let them go alone.

"Probably think we're a couple of gays," Lethe remarked idly as he shut the door behind them.

I think the truth might shock them more. Got any ice?"

"Try the fridge. Why?"

"My hands hurt after that session just now."

Lethe lit a cigarette and lay down on a large sofa. "You do know everyone wants me to fail in this job, don't you?"

Ygoi was busy with the ice bucket. "No, I don't. Why would they want that?"

"Makes better viewing apparently. The whole idea of this was to send out talent scouts to spot people, you know, street artists, mostly young people, music students and so on and set them up on a pedestal so they would fall off it. They didn't expect someone my age to win. Then suddenly you get thrown in with TV crews, recording studios, people are throwing money at you, everyone wants to sponsor you. I've got a Rolex watch out of it, see, and all I have to do is wear it on stage tonight. And I'll tell you one thing, these watches are fucking uncomfortable over a Millio tag. I've got to wear the darned thing on my right arm. Anything to drink in the fridge? Smirnoff Ice if there is any."

"Loads," Ygoi threw a bottle across and Lethe knocked the top off with his hand and the table.

He drank half the bottle in one go and began to feel better. "I hate this life," he announced suddenly and sat up on the sofa to watch his friend pour himself a glass of sparkling water. "Every single fucking thing I do is monitored and they are just waiting for me to make a mistake or otherwise fuck up in general. First they said the album wouldn't sell, which is bollocks as I know the advance orders are above half a million already and the thing isn't even released until after this gig as they want to put on *Fallen Heroes* as a live track. They tell me what to wear, what to eat, where to drink, what to drive and every single fucking thing about my life is told to me by someone else. I have lost control and I don't know how to cope with it. If I quit now then I owe people money and it means they've won."

Ygoi had also once lost control of his life. They had shut him in the darkness and skewered him with metal. He had lived crippled and stinking of excrement for so long the clothes he wore had stuck to his skin. He went across to the window and looked out at Birmingham. The size of it was bewildering to a man who came from a galaxy where cities did not exist. The noise and smell of it were frightening to someone used to the silence of solar energy.

"Drinking yourself into oblivion isn't the answer."

"It helps."

"In the short term. You're in a prison just like I was except I was tortured with pain and dark and you are being tortured with gifts and expectations. Do you want to succeed in this business?"

"Yes. I like the singing and that but I just want all those fuckers out of my life."

"They'll go. You've got the gig in America as part of your initial win. Is that the end of it?"

"I don't think they know. They honestly don't think I'm going to survive so the end, so far as they can see, is the day I quit."

Ygoi looked at the ring he wore. "I didn't quit. Don't know why I didn't. Anyone else would have." He thoughtfully drank some of the water. "There is an organisation on Earth called Amnesty International. They fight for people imprisoned and tortured and I've told James that I want it set up so a tenth of what I earn goes to them."

Lethe finished off his drink and went to the fridge to get another. "What's your point?" he grumbled. He had forgotten just how bright Ygoi was and he had lost the plot a bit here.

"Fight back. You won't have to climb into shit-ships or scavenge coins with your teeth but you go out there and you fight for what you can get. If you go out on that stage tonight and rock the pants off your audience then they will be your Amnesty International. If you can get the support of the people you'll be too strong for the TV company and they can't beat you. Go and do the same in the States and you'll have them behind you too. Grab any chance you're offered from live gigs to TV shows. And if you want me two paces behind you with that harp on my shoulder then I'll do it for you. I owe you big time and I'd bet all I've got that no Earth system can beat the two of us."

Lethe felt a bit better now Ygoi was starting to take charge. "Pity you can't be my agent."

"I wouldn't have a clue where to start. Maybe Jenni could help, wasn't she something to do with magazines when we first knew her?"

"Nah, she was a dancer of some sort, wasn't she?"

"You sure? I thought she'd been a model or something. Tell you one thing, she makes a mean wedding ring for you when you need one."

Lethe just snorted and helped himself to a third drink. "Yeah, right. Like I could trust anyone I met now. All they'll be interested in is seeing if sleeping with me can help their own careers."

Ygoi was rather saddened to think that Lethe Miarren should have become so cynical and he wished he could think of a way to help.

TEN

What Ygoi was not expecting was the heat on stage. When the musicians met up in the wings ready for the concert the lights had been on for some time and the arena itself was full and standing. The support act was just finishing and the heat coming off the stage hit him like a wall. He stood between Dan and Kevin the drummer, both of whom were taller than he was, and watched the end of the act. It was a group of four girls who all looked very young, who were incredibly athletic and who couldn't really sing in tune to save their lives but got away with it because they were very pretty and exuded such a lot of energy and enthusiasm. The other musicians weren't saying much, their minds full of the concert they were going to do and the song order which they hoped Lethe would remember. Dan had a list of the songs stuck to his keyboard just in case.

"You OK?" Dan's voice sounded through the set in Ygoi's ear and he jumped.

"Fine."

"You look a bit pale."

"It's hot in here. I'll be fine once we get going."

"Well don't faint on me. I had a bass guitarist do that once when I was playing at Knebworth. Very embarrassing."

The girls came rushing off stage, whooping and shrieking with excitement that their session was over and pleased with how they had done. Their instrumentalists followed them, they were as young and inexperienced as the singers and looked rather enviously and the old stagers in the wings. There were six instrumentalists and six backing singers all dressed in black and looking very professional.

"Go!" bawled the voice of the stage manager in the ears of the waiting musicians and they got a shout of applause when they walked on.

Lethe was on the other side of the stage and he watched his musicians sort themselves out with a calm nonchalance that hid their nervousness. He watched the backing singers line themselves up at their microphones and the instrumentalists chatting through their headsets. There was a bit of warm-up fun between the drums and the keyboard while the harpist checked his tuning and he got a round of applause when he finally got the truculent instrument to nose into pitch. So he gave them a blast of Abba's *Chiquitita* which the bass guitarist picked up on and all the instrumentalists jammed for a bit which the audience loved. Funny, Lethe thought, five people from Earth and an alien from Sunara could just sit down and play together like that. Said something for the music he supposed.

The stage manager gave him a nudge from behind and Lethe Miarren walked out into the sweltering heat of the stage and the audience roared. He was glad he was in his tattiest jeans and a sleeveless T shirt. Ygoi had called him a slob for going on stage with no shoes on but he was wearing his Rolex to keep the sponsors happy. He had a list of ten songs to get through and remembered what Ygoi had said to him about getting this audience to be his Amnesty International. So he chatted to them before he started. Made jokes about Canadians and then found out there was a bunch of them in the audience so he got them to sing the Canadian national anthem and cracked such a filthy joke about Mounties that he had got from the drummer, there was nearly a riot. Whatever the audience had been expecting from the country hick from PE Island it wasn't that he should have such a deliciously wicked sense of humour. His voice they had already heard with its subtle country rock feel, his guitar playing they soon found out was so good he could have played a classical concerto if he had wanted to and although he was nearly twice the age of the girls who had been on before his stamina was incredible.

It took nearly two hours to get through nine of the ten songs and he saved *Fallen Heroes* for last. The new songs he performed had been greeted with shouts and cheers so he knew the album would sell when it was released. He could feel the power of the crowd and it was exhilarating. It was like being drunk while fully conscious. It was like eating half a dozen bloodflowers from Goine and still being able to stand. He was intoxicated with the excitement, so tired he could hardly walk and the sweat was pouring off him so much he had to take his T shirt off to wipe his guitar strings. He had made a mental note to take a towel on stage with him next time until he realised he got more reaction from the audience when he went half naked. He walked across to the harp, and the drummer handed across the chair that had been at the back of the stage all during the performance. The stage lights went out except for two merciless spotlights that beat down on the heads of two men used to the heat of twin suns.

Lethe saw Ygoi perform the switch on his control box so his voice would be heard by the audience and he gave the weary harpist the most encouraging smile he could muster.

While Lethe incited the audience to greater decibels, Ygoi flexed his aching hands and was thankful this was the last song. He thought his former co-pilot was being a bit daring by stripping to the waist as it wasn't the done thing to bare flesh in public in the Millio galaxy unless you worked underground in the mines of Dirnhet as the heat of the suns would have burned the skin off you in half an hour.

Lethe caught the glance of his compatriot and waved the audience into comparative silence. Ygoi's tired fingers played a glaring wrong note in the introduction but nobody seemed to mind as the song that had captivated a Friday night audience was heard live in the Birmingham Arena as it was intended to be sung. A lament by two men, the harmonies sometimes so close the notes jarred and throughout the ethereal ripple of the harp accompaniment gave the music that odd, dreamlike quality that had made it stand out in a national television competition. As there had been each time, there was the most peculiar silence after the final note of the harp had floated across the auditorium and Ygoi thankfully switched his control box back to his headset and vowed he would never again sing in public. He hated himself for that wrong note and he was so thankful the ordeal was over his hands were shaking. He pushed the harp off his shoulder and Lethe suddenly seemed to wake up and bounded off his chair. Only then did the audience release the feelings they had pent up while the song was being performed and they whistled and stamped and cheered until the musicians on stage began to think the noise would never stop.

Lethe was triumphant. There was no way now those TV crews could touch him. This was power and he was the one who controlled it. He looked over his shoulder and saw the crew in the wings filming his performance. The camera on its dolly had nearly tripped him up several times as it whizzed round the stage following his every move and he knew excerpts from this concert were going to be broadcast as part of an update the following evening.

Those in the wings knew they had lost the power too. They had underestimated Lethe Miarren and something had to be done about it. They couldn't control this phenomenon. There was something about this man. Something they couldn't identify. Something that meant he wasn't going to crack like an ordinary mortal. Somehow he wasn't fazed by all this. The problem was there was nothing known about him. He just seemed to have turned up in the Cathedral square in Exeter busking in the spring sunshine. The remit of the programme had been to find no-hopers. Someone the crew could record maybe getting it right at first, being swept along on an uncontrollable tide and then going down in a blaze of drink and despair. And the blond country rock singer had seemed to suit the brief in every way. Good looking, a bit shy, and totally unable to cope. He had been a wonderful stereotype at first and had crashed the trendy pop scene beautifully, getting smashed out of his skull at clubs nearly every night and not being too fussy who he took to his bed.

Then the, literally, dark figure of Ygoi Roemtek had come into things and now he seemed to be more than a temporarily crippled Estonian. He wore a wedding ring and someone on the TV research team had speedily tracked down records of a very recent marriage to a US citizen called Deirdre Hunsecker. She was known to be a Yale scholar in the UK on a three-year visa according to the American Embassy who confirmed that Ygoi Roemtek had applied for a temporary visa to go to the USA to accompany his wife home for Thanksgiving with a view to getting a more permanent visa in the future. Unfortunately Mr Roemtek had no papers to prove his nationality and there was a bit of a problem with that one.

It had been a busy day for the television team but the concert had been worth every second of it. They had some wonderful moments for the next *Talent Scout Superstar* update and would be able to screen the whole concert at a later date. Because there was no doubt about it, Lethe Miarren was not going to fail. The programmes had been intended to show how hard the life of a pop icon was, not how easy it could be to whip up an audience of thousands and make each one feel like a friend. They had unleashed a demon and the demon had to be controlled. Frantic messages were relayed from the crew in Birmingham to the company in London and drastic steps were taken. It just made the late evening news broadcasts – the latest pop star, Lethe Miarren had been dropped by his agent. No reason was given but the hick from PE Island was now out on his own. Everyone said he wouldn't survive.

Lethe was still furious as he drove his white Saab from the Arena to the hotel where he and Ygoi were scheduled to meet up with the Ravenswood House party. He had a vague idea he had been unpardonably rude to some young woman at the stage door but Ygoi had stopped to apologise on his behalf which had annoyed him even more and the two had a spectacular quarrel on the short journey. Lethe was rather relieved to find Ygoi hadn't had the temper completely tortured out of him, but the atmosphere between them was still filthy when they reached the hotel only to find the paparazzi had got there first. There weren't very many but they had all heard about Lethe's agent and wanted to know what he was going to do about it.

"Get another one," he growled at them and nearly fell over a tiny woman who looked vaguely familiar. He was about to tell her to fuck off out of his way but she slapped him hard on the arm which stopped him in his tracks.

"Don't you push me around, you fucking bastard," she yelled at him. "I've had enough of you for one day. First you're all smiles at the station, then you snog me in the taxi and then you tell me to fuck off at the stage door. Well, fuck you, Lethe Miarren, I don't care if they offer me a million pounds for your story, you're not worth it!" She was about to go rampaging off but Lethe, inexplicably turned on by her rage, grabbed her arm.

"Whoa. Hold on a minute," he requested. "I'm sorry if I've offended you, really. Can I buy you a drink, at least? You won't get my story but I never meant to be rude."

Caitlin Evans let herself get jostled right up close to Lethe Miarren and she looked into his gorgeous blue eyes. "Drink's fine," she agreed and realised he was pushing a door card discreetly into her hand.

"Room 1214, go order what you want," he muttered in her ear.

Caitlin wriggled out of the crowd and was gone.

The two men reached the sanctuary of the lift. "Did you just do what I think you did?" Ygoi asked Lethe as the lift whisked them upwards.

"Sure did. You've got sex on demand for the night and I kind of wanted it too."

"I married mine."

Lethe just laughed and felt a lot better knowing there was going to be a hot woman in his bed that night. "And tomorrow I start looking for another agent. How hard can that be?"

Ygoi knocked on the door of room 1219. "Ask Jenni. I'm sure it was magazines she was in and she's got less to do now I'm mobile and Deirdre's gone back to her studying."

Whatever Lethe was going to say remained unspoken as Deirdre came blasting out of the room, wrapped herself round her husband and kissed him long and hard on the lips. "Come on, you," she breathed in his ear. "I want to see you upright and we're just next door. Say nightie night to that lot."

"See you tomorrow," he called to the people in the room and let his wife tow him off by the wrist.

Lethe went in on his own, thankful the party wouldn't be prolonged. "Thanks for coming," he said to Jenni and James. "Did you enjoy the show?"

"Absolutely brilliant," she assured him. "You look totally worn out. Go and get some sleep and we'll see you in here for breakfast. Time enough to tell you our news then."

"Sure, see you then," he agreed and shot off to his own room to find out what was going on there.

Lethe Miarren lit himself a cigarette and gently kissed the woman who lay in his arms in bed. "Want to stay the night?" he asked. "Or do you have a home to go to?"

She helped herself to a cigarette from the box on the bedside table and lit hers from his. "I'd love to stay. You're not really just some Canadian country hick are you?"

"Why does everyone assume people from PE Island have straw in their hair. We are quite sophisticated, you know."

"But it's been proved you weren't even born there."

"True," he conceded. "But it's the place I think of as home."

"Is that where you met Ygoi?"

Lethe had guessed she would try to get a story out of him and was thankful their biographies had been worked out. "Him? No, he's never been to Canada in his life. We met in Sweden. My dad's job moved around a lot in those days. He was just seventeen and I was fourteen. I remember being quite envious as he was already shaving and I still had spots and sticky-out knees."

Caitlin had to smile. These men were all the same, they'd tell you all their secrets if only you shagged them hard enough. "And what was he doing in Sweden?"

"Looking up his mother's family. They come from somewhere up near the Arctic Circle."

"Holiday?"

"Not really. She'd died when he was quite young and his dad was in some kind of trouble with the old

Soviet police. I think they'd just got out over the border through Finland. His dad was sent back and died in the labour camps but Ygoi got away from them somehow or the other and just drifted around most of Europe. We kind of kept in touch with letters when one of us had an address."

"So was it the Soviets who had him tortured? Like his father?"

"No, the Soviet Union fell years ago. Ygoi was imprisoned much more recently."

"Where?"

"Can't say."

"Can't or won't?"

"OK, won't."

"I don't believe you."

Lethe stubbed out his cigarette and sat up in the bed, dislodging her from his chest. "Don't believe what?"

"I believe you met him that long ago. I think you're right he was in prison quite recently but I don't believe any of that crap about escaping via Finland or any of that. It sounds like an old black and white film plot."

Lethe tapped into the memory part of his brain but knew he had told the story that had been agreed. "That's what he told me. If he wants to tell lies that's up to him."

"Do you believe it?"

"Yes."

"So can I sell his story and get my money? I'll share it with you."

Just for a split second Lethe thought of his dwindling finances and was tempted. "I can't really help you. I've told you all I do know. He was born in the part of the old Soviet Union we now know as Estonia, his father was Russian, his mother was Swedish. We first met nearly twenty years ago, kept in touch, lost touch and then next time I saw him he'd been in prison and beaten up."

"But where did you meet up with him again?" Caitlin persisted. "What country in the world has such an appalling human rights record that they would do that to someone?"

"Do what? One of your brethren said Ygoi had been tortured for his religious beliefs, which we both know isn't true as he has no religion, and suddenly it seems everyone knows all about it."

"He'd been fucking knee-capped. We saw him in the wheelchair during *Talent Scout Superstar* and his hands were all kind of mashed up too. I suppose he got free health care here even though he is a convict in his own country."

Lethe didn't like her manner "Actually he got private health care."

"And you paid for it, did you?"

Lethe saw where this one was going. "Not saying."

"Hang on, you're a friend of that bloke with the double barrelled name who works in the Home Office. Oh my God. He's pulled some strings for you, hasn't he? You're no more Canadian than I am. Just who the fuck are you, mister?"

Lethe panicked. This one wasn't going to be put off. "I'm the guy who has just fucked you half senseless and if you breathe or print one word of what I said then you will find out exactly what happened to Ygoi as the same will happen to you. Understood?"

His tone was cold but Caitlin Evans had been threatened before. "Fuck off," she said rudely and reached for her clothes. "You don't scare me, Mister Whoever-You-Are. I'll find out your story and I'll sell it for ten fucking million pounds. Just you see if I don't."

Sir James and Lady Jenni Kirkwood-Barnes were enjoying a leisurely breakfast the day after Lethe Miarren's concert when someone knocked on their hotel room door and a barrage of sneezing came from the corridor.

"Goodness, sounds like someone's got a stinking cold," Jenni remarked as she opened the door and found three people outside. "Ah-ha. A mass invasion. Your hot date gone, Lethe?"

"Yes she has, and with a flea in her ear as your Mrs McDougall puts it so well."

"Never mind, I'm sure there'll be others. Ygoi, have you got a cold?"

The sneezing stopped for a few moments. "I don't know. Have I?"

James gave, the snuffling man a box of tissues. "Right, sit down you lot. I have something I want to say to you all." The three sat in an obedient row on the end of the bed and James cuddled his wife to his side. "Now, I like to think this is due to fair weather and a following wind, but Jenni tells me I have to thanks the old wives of Nurtasia for the fact we are expecting our first child in the new year. This is something we have hoped for for a long time and we both wanted you all to be the first to know."

Deirdre shot to her feet and gave the astonished couple an enthusiastic American hug. "That is so great! Well done, you guys. I hope it all goes well and that you have twins."

"What a funny thing to say," Jenni laughed and returned the hug. "You're sure you don't mind, after your recent hopes?"

"That wasn't a hope, that was a scare. Apparently it's usually twins after the Nurtasia treatment. Or triplets."

"What?" Jenni demanded. "You didn't tell me that bit."

Ygoi finished with the tissues and gave her a hug and a kiss on the cheek. "Thought it might put you off."

Lethe got more reluctantly off the bed and gave Jenni a hug too. "Does that mean I can't ask you to be my agent?" he asked.

"What?" she gasped again and wished he had mentioned it first.

"Those bastards at the television company have sacked my agent. I was going to ask you to do it."

"Are you serious?"

"Perfectly. And the first thing you have to do is dig Ygoi out of the load of shit I've just landed him in."

"Nothing could be worse than the load of shit I threw myself in. Come on, tell us what you've done."

Lethe helped himself to some coffee. "She was asking questions. Some paper or another has offered her a small fortune if she can find out the truth about us." He smiled rather ironically. "Never thought I'd have a price on my head. So I told her the official story about the USSR and going via Finland and she didn't believe a word of it."

"Would she believe it if I told it to her?" Ygoi asked and started sneezing again.

Lethe shrugged. "Maybe."

"First rule of diplomatic war," James told him. "Get the enemy onto your side if you can. Do you have a number for this woman?"

"She gave me her mobile before we had our row."

"Then ring it," James advised. "Take her to lunch, to dinner tonight or whatever you need to do. Get her on your side. Take her somewhere expensive and formal and don't sleep with her again or she'll get you pillow talking as she did last night. Don't give her Ygoi on a plate just yet either. You are the main prize at the moment and your stories will hold good. The old USSR went down in such a mess it's hardly surprising one Estonian hasn't got any papers."

"And that's another thing. I think you're going in the shit too because she knows you work at the Home Office and she's going to accuse you of issuing false papers."

To his surprise and relief, James roared with laughter. "My dear chap, it seems she is as naïve of the workings of the Civil Service as you are yourself. She will meet an official wall of silence let me assure you. I, like Caesar's wife, am above suspicion." He saw the blank looks on the faces of the two extra-terrestrials. "Shakespeare? Oh, never mind. You have the more pressing need of an agent to sort out first. Jenni, my love, do you want the job?"

"You're joking. What do I know about being an agent?"

"No, hear me out. You are an intelligent, well-connected woman who is slowly being bored out of her mind in a house which is run too well by others. We can easily set you up with an office in one of the rooms…."

"But I'm having a baby," she protested and tried to sound as though she didn't really want to work as an agent while her mind was about ten steps ahead and already had Lethe booked into work for the next five years. She looked up at her husband and they exchanged a smile. He knew perfectly well what was in her mind but they were over their crisis now. United by their old love for each other and a new love for the life they had created.

"Great idea!" Deirdre enthused, unable to keep quiet any longer. "You can call it Gecko Management, you know, 'nothing we can't climb' kind of thing. I'll see if I can get you some contacts in the US because if Lethe can crack the US market he'll really have it made. There's a huge country scene out there and so long as he stays Canadian he won't get the same resistance as someone from England."

The two women were about to get down to some serious business when the husband of one of them interrupted. "No. You have a PhD to finish, Deirdre, and your parents would never forgive me if you didn't."

"Don't you go all chauvinistic on me. I'm not like one of your women tied to her husband all day and not allowed to work."

"Do you honestly think I'd dare try to tell you what to do? I'm just asking that you finish your studying first. If it helps, I'll help Jenni run the agency for you until you've got your doctorate."

"Done!" Deirdre exclaimed.

"OK, Lethe," Jenni instructed. "Now I am officially your agent, you get that woman on the phone and buy her lunch then I want to have an official meeting with you to discuss what your original agent was working on. Don't suppose I'd be allowed to contact him, would I?"

"You can try. I've got his number somewhere. I know he's booked me on a chat show in London tonight."

"I'll ring him. You call your girlfriend." Jenni looked at her husband. "But if your journalist friend is going to start digging the dirt then there's something I want to tell you about me before she does. Unless you worked it out when you were here last time."

Caitlin Evans felt slightly nervous as she walked into the foyer of the Ritz hotel in London. She had put on her best dress, had done her hair up and brought her freelance journalist's equipment not sure whether she was going to war or meeting a friend. Lethe hadn't said much when he rang her but seemed glad to hear she was going to be in London and had offered to buy her tea at the Ritz. She cursed herself for leaving her phone in her bag as two big time celebrities went past with each other. They hadn't been seen out together in public before. Then she heard the mutterings and even the two already well known turned to watch the young man who walked so confidently into the posh hotel it was hard to believe he was a hick from PE Island.

Lethe had accepted the advice of his new agent and was impeccably, if casually, dressed. He had washed the habitual gel out of his hair and it flopped in ragged blond layers to his shoulders with his fringe now irritatingly in his eyes. He wore his Rolex watch, a chain wound round his other wrist and a discreet signet ring on his right little finger. His clothes were Gucci, even if he had bought them in an exchange shop in Exeter, and his aftershave was Chanel. He thought Caitlin looked really cute and wondered if she was even five foot tall. He saw the height of her heels and guessed not. Quite aware of the attention he had attracted he greeted his date with a casual arm round the waist and a kiss on the cheek.

"Hi, glad you could make it. Come on, I've booked a table."

Caitlin was bemused by this easy charm but guessed Lethe Miarren had come down from his concert-induced high and would probably be more rational today.

"Did you sell the story?" he asked once they were settled at their table.

He seemed completely unaffected by the opulence of the surroundings but Caitlin tried to look everywhere at once and spotted one or two other 'names' at various tables.

"You only gave me half a story but, yes, I've got some people interested. And before we finish here I'll get the other half out of you."

His smile sent her all peculiar. "Trust me, you won't. Even though you are sassy and cute and hot in bed." He offered his hand. "Friends?"

She took the hand without knowing why. "Fine by me. Now give me a story I can sell so I can afford to eat tonight. I'm a freelancer and if I don't sell stories or photos, I don't get paid."

He hadn't expected her to be so hard. "I got a new agent."

Caitlin sniffed. "I know all about her. She's the wife of James Kirkwood-Barnes and she used to be a pole dancer and stripper. I remember the fuss about those two when they got together. She'd done nude work for *Playboy* and all sorts. I think gossip just stopped short of calling her a call-girl. There was all sorts in the papers, what with his job and everything. They reckoned she could be passing on state secrets in the bedroom and the Home Secretary nearly had to resign over it. Then it turned out her dad was an Admiral or something stupid like that and they had no grounds to suspect her of anything. The most unlikely couple but they seem to have stuck it out, although everyone said they never would."

"Well, now she's cleaned up her act, but still knows people in the business, and she's my agent. If you want to rake up her past that's up to you but I think she can ride out the storm." Lethe was just thankful he had learned the truth from Jenni before he heard it like that. It seemed his new agent was a darned sight better equipped to deal with the media than he was. They didn't have newspapers or TV where he came from and if Caitlin was a typical example of its ethics he was kind of glad.

"She rode it out ten years ago," Caitlin admitted wryly. "There's no new ground on that one. So what's she got lined up for you? You're going on TV tonight, and no doubt won't tell them where you're really from either."

"Correct."

"Is Ygoi going to be on it with you?"

"No, he's got a stinking cold and he'll be helping Jenni out with the agency until Deirdre's finished her PhD."

"His wife, right?"

"How do you know all these things?" Lethe asked amazed.

"I'm a journalist. It's my job. Want to know some gossip about some of the other people here now?"

"Go on then."

So they leaned close together over the table and Caitlin told him some of the more scurrilous things she knew. He was quite visibly shocked by most of it and she thought maybe he really was a good Catholic boy from PE Island. Then she remembered some of the love games they had played and she wasn't so sure.

"You got a room booked here then?" she asked at the end of her revelations.

"No, should I have? I've got a perfectly good flat just off the Pentonville Road to sleep in tonight."

Caitlin didn't like the way he said that. "Aren't I coming with you?"

"No. I offered to buy you tea to say sorry for the way I treated you yesterday but that's it so far as I'm concerned." He let the disappointment register then added brightly, "Unless you'd like to come and see the chat show tonight? They've sent me a couple of tickets and there's no-one else I could ask. Ygoi was going to come but he's really not at all well."

"Got a cold, you said."

Lethe nodded. "He's staying at the flat for a bit. It's Deirdre's really but she's in the middle of some time in the States for her PhD."

"I'd like to see this flat one day."

"Maybe. You wouldn't like it too much right now with all Ygoi's germs in it. Don't reckon they breed them as tough in Estonia as they do on PE Island."

"I should have thought they bred them tougher."

They didn't chat much during their meal. Caitlin found it hard to believe that this impeccable gentleman had unleashed such savage passion she had never known sex like it. She jumped in her chair as she realised where his foot was going. Lethe Miarren wasn't wearing any socks and he was about to do something indecent with his toes.

"What the fuck are you doing? This is the Ritz for fuck's sake."

"Eat your tea," he told her quietly and got inside her knickers.

Caitlin Evans wore trousers to go to the TV studio that evening. She had never, ever been so deliciously embarrassed in her life trying to control herself in a public restaurant while a man did that to her. She went through the routine bag search and ticket check and went to find her seat which turned out to be in the front row. Sitting in the seat next to her was a rather thin man whose face was half hidden by unruly dark hair that had flopped forward and he seemed to be reading Shakespeare. Guessing he was some kind of student, Caitlin sat down and looked round the studio. The man next to her sneezed.

"Bless you," she said without thinking.

"Thank you," he replied in slightly accented English.

She pushed aside the hair and saw the scarred face with the not-quite-closed holes in the side of the nose. "Thought you had a cold."

"I have. But I wasn't going to miss this one on a free ticket." Ygoi closed his book and smiled at her then. "Pleased to meet you, Caitlin. Lethe told me you might be coming."

The two cordially shook hands and Caitlin didn't quite know where to start.

"Been a journalist long?" he asked pleasantly.

"Since my marriage broke up."

"Kids?"

"Got a girl of five. She's with my mum at the moment."

"Happened to me too. My son must be sixteen by now. Lives with his mother and her new husband."

"In Estonia?"

"Prague. It's a long story."

"You must have married young."

"Too young. You too?"

"Not really. I was twenty eight when Emily was born."

"You only look about sixteen now."

Caitlin felt herself blush and was annoyed about it. "It's because I'm small."

His smile was sad. "People always tell me they thought I was taller."

"How's your wife's PhD coming on?"

"Fine. She's in the States for a while to catch up."

"You going to join her?"

"Maybe. Depends on what Lethe wants to do with me."

"Were you really seventeen when you first met?"

Ygoi remembered the interrogations on Lriam and knew this woman was nowhere near their standards. He opened his book again and bowed his head. "You have been offered money for my story, Caitlin. I'm not giving it to you for free."

"I know someone who'll pay half a million for it."

He just turned the page of *Romeo and Juliet* and didn't answer.

Caitlin looked at his strange wedding ring and wasn't sure how to get through his reserve. He wasn't shy; he was kind, sympathetic and had learned her secret faster than anyone else she had met recently. She still wasn't sure why she had told him about Emily. His English was flawless, but with that gorgeous accent that added to his mystery. Ygoi Roemtek was a complete and total enigma and she wasn't sure any more that she wanted the puzzled solved.

The interviewer was a young, gay man who obviously had the hots for his guest and was not quite professional enough not to let this intrude on the show. As soon as the audience noise had settled and Lethe was seated at a safe distance, the interview began with a casual:

"Well, congratulations on winning *Talent Scout Superstar*. And on your show in Birmingham. Being broadcast straight after this show in its entirety. How are you feeling now?"

"Exhausted," came the honest reply. "But I've a few days off before the next round of things and Ygoi is writing songs for the next album already."

"Yes, your harp player. Odd sort of instrument for a pop singer to have as backing."

Lethe had seen the list of questions and knew the answers he had to give but the interviewer was making him nervous. Although he was used to the attitudes between men in his home galaxy, he knew no man on Earth would act like that unless he wanted full sex. And when he got nervous he tended to forget things. "It's like a piano except it's on its side," he replied and knew that wasn't what he was supposed to say.

The interviewer got a message over his earpiece to stick to the script. "They've classified your music as country rock, would you agree with that?"

Lethe desperately tried to access the memory part of his brain and he wished Ygoi could come and rescue him. "Yes, I suppose."

The interviewer cast helpless eyes towards the production team offstage. This one was going to be a struggle. He got a message in his earpiece to cool it a bit as he was making this one nervous, so he sat back in his chair and resisted the urge to touch this rather beautiful man. "So who were the singers you listened to as a child? Presumably George Hamilton and his famous *Canadian Pacific*? There can't be many other songs which mention Prince Edward Island?"

Lethe relaxed as the other man physically moved away and his memory clicked in. "I wasn't actually on PE Island all that long. I've always liked folk music and used to listen to whatever was being played wherever we were living at the time."

The interviewer let his breath out. They were back on track. "You've lived in lots of places I gather. When did you first start singing?"

"As a child. We didn't have a television or anything so we used to make up our own music. Most people I knew then played some instrument or another and most sang. I chose the guitar mainly because nobody else in my family wanted it. And it's the kind of thing you can take with you when you move. No point in anyone in my family playing a harp. We were a bit of a bunch of nomads."

"Unusual not to have a TV. How would you describe your childhood?"

Lethe Miarren turned out to have a rather boring and conventional family background. His parents were still alive somewhere 'in the wilds of Canada', he was an only child but had got through a succession of pet cats as he moved about so much when young. The stage manager got a bit bored with all this and looked around the audience to see if they were still awake. It was then that he saw something interesting in the front row and relayed a message to the interviewer.

Completely unfazed and hiding his lack of interest beautifully, the interviewer shamelessly left the script and dived straight into the dangerous waters Lethe's new agent had said were forbidden for this broadcast.

"Then you met up with this guy who could play the harp. Somewhere in Sweden, right?"

It was almost possible to see the guards being put up by the blond man in the chair. "Yes," he admitted cautiously and wondered what was going on. There seemed to be some sort of flurry backstage and two stage hands shot off as though their behinds were on fire. A hand on his thigh soon brought his attention back to the other man on set with him.

"The start of a long and beautiful friendship?"

"Not like you mean," Lethe squeaked and moved the offending hand. "Ygoi's mother was Swedish, he was there with his father looking for her family to tell them she'd died. He wasn't there on a pleasure cruise."

That wasn't the expected answer. "Oh, I'm sorry. I didn't realise. But the two of you obviously hit it off, musically at least, and you stayed in touch?"

"Yes, it wasn't easy as he was living in what was then the USSR."

"And you met up again after he defected?"

"If you like."

"Can we have the house lights up, please?" was the apparently unconnected request. "We've got a surprise guest in our midst." And a cure for the interminable Miarren ordinariness, the interviewer thought to himself.

Ygoi suddenly worked it out and looked for an escape route but two studio hands were closing in and his only chance would be to climb over the heads of the people sitting behind him. "Fuck it," he said, which rather surprised Caitlin who thought it was all part of the act.

"Ladies and gentlemen, please put your hands together for the other half of *Fallen Heroes*, Ygoi Roemtek."

Ygoi sighed with annoyance but dutifully got to his feet so the cameras could catch him being wired up for the second time in two days then he shook the hair out of his eyes and walked under the glare of the lights to the appreciative barracking of a rather bored audience.

ELEVEN

Gecko Artists Management called its first meeting the day after Lethe Miarren's first TV interview. Gecko didn't have an office so Jenni, Lethe and Ygoi sat around the living room of Deirdre's flat and drank coffee. Lethe got a bit grumpy when Jenni wouldn't let him have a cigarette near her unborn child but he gave in to her wishes.

"Right," Jenni began. "First of all that was a complete pig's ear you two made of the show last night. You were flirting with each other like a couple of old queens in a public toilet and that may be acceptable where you come from but please don't do it here unless you want everyone to believe you're a couple."

"That fucking guy got his hand in my underwear," Lethe complained. "So we were winding him up by pretending to be together."

"When?"

"When the monitors were all showing that clip from the concert."

Jenni looked at Ygoi. "True," he corroborated. "I saw him do it. He was very subtle with it, don't think the audience saw anything but I was right next to them at the time."

"That is gross. And against the law. Do you want to do anything about it?"

The two men exchanged a slightly sheepish look. "We did," Lethe replied.

"What did you do?" Jenni asked with a vision of police constables knocking on the door any minute.

"We got him all hot and excited then I distracted him and Ygoi shot him in the balls with a Tiowing set slightly higher than necessary. Don't worry, won't do him any lasting damage. He'll just think he's got a dose of cramp in a funny place for a few days."

Jenni was rather shocked by that and knew she ought to be cross with them but it really was too funny for words. They had this wonderful system of punishment that would save police forces a lot of time if only it could be made to work on Earth. "What am I going to do with you two?" she asked and sighed theatrically. "First of all, if two men kiss each other on this planet they have already reached the stage of carnal knowledge or aren't far off it. We are not so liberal with our affections as you are. And besides which, you can't just go round shooting people."

"We don't unless they deserve it," Ygoi pointed out. "So which Embassy has been ringing up the Foreign Office all morning? The Russians because we were rude about the USSR, the Swedes because they want to deny my mother ever coming from there, or the Finns for their crap border controls?"

"None so far as I know," Jenni told him, marvelling at how quickly he had grasped Earth politics. "Anyway, to business. I've got all your dates from your old agent who has no idea why he was fired either but he tended to back up your theory that the whole point of the programme is to make you fail. And many more shows like last night's and you will. You just can't afford to improvise on your stories. OK so you two have an amazing rapport that we would probably call telepathy. I'm just thanking God you didn't snog each other in front of the cameras because I wouldn't put it past you. You are both incredibly bright which means you can second guess each other and get away with winging it to a degree that I would never dare try. So this morning we are going to write your biographies with such fine detail that you could sell them to the first publisher you get tomorrow and there won't be any loopholes in either of them. Where are at with the delectable Miss Evans, Lethe?"

"We went out after the show last night. I did as you told me and wouldn't go to bed with her but had a very proper cup of coffee with her at her flat and met her daughter. She's called Emily and she's five and she was quite cute really."

"So do we classify Caitlin as friend or enemy?"

"Neither. She'd sell Emily if the price was high enough. But she's agreed to back off for a bit because she got a juicy story off some footballer or another at the club we were at and she's going to sell that instead."

"Well done, you. Keep in her good books, we may want to use a press agent in the near future." Jenni paused to answer her mobile. She didn't say very much but she looked rather worried. "That was James. He's sending a taxi for you, Ygoi, and you're to meet him at the Swedish embassy."

"When?"

"Right now."

"Fuck it. How did he sound?"

"Completely baffled."

The taxi came and Lethe went down the stairs with his friend so he could have a cigarette outside.

"Trouble, do you think?" Lethe asked as he took a welcome inhalation of nicotine.

"I'm trying not to think anything. Were we particularly rude about the Swedes last night?"

"Don't think so. In fact I thought we were quite polite about them saying your mother was Swedish and she was a dear little thing who taught you to play the harp."

"No, that was my father who used to teach at the Moscow Conservatoire."

"Was it? Oh, fuck it, I haven't got a clue any more. Why couldn't you have been a Canadian too?"

"Do I sound like a Canadian?"

"Guess not. There's your cab. Good luck."

Lethe finished his cigarette then went back upstairs to the flat. "He's gone. Have you really no idea what it's about?"

"No. I don't think James had either. Oh, God. I hope you haven't upset anybody."

Lethe was also getting to grips with Earth politics. "Surely if we'd upset the Swedes they would demand to see your Foreign Secretary, not some guy from the Home Office and a guy whose mother allegedly came from somewhere north of the Arctic circle."

"True. Shall we try to do some business or just give up and go shopping?"

"Shopping."

"God, you're worse than any woman,"

"Probably, but they don't have shops like this where I come from."

The two were only out for about an hour and couldn't really concentrate on what they were doing. Nobody bothered the latest pop star as he stocked up his wardrobe in the company of an older brunette woman. They went back to the flat to find James and Ygoi on the doorstep.

"And where have you two been?" James asked. "We get here for a celebratory cup of tea and there's no answer."

"Shopping." Jenni opened the door of the flat and they all went in. "What are we celebrating?"

Ygoi took a small book from the pocket of his leather jacket and gave it to her. "I'm no longer a refugee."

Lethe bunched close to Jenni as she flicked open the passport issued that day at the Swedish Embassy in London to Ygoi Roemtek, born in Tallinn but granted citizenship of Sweden, and by default the European Union, because of the nationality of his mother. It had his photograph and signature in it and had already been appended with a visa giving the bearer the right to enter the United States as many times as he wished and it was valid for three years.

"Fucking brilliant!" Lethe pronounced and gave Ygoi a hug and a kiss on the cheek which quite startled the others until they remembered it was normal behaviour in the Millio galaxy.

Ygoi felt oddly choked up inside and had to blow his nose even though his first cold had gone as suddenly as it had arrived. "And James has bought me a ticket to New York, flying out this afternoon."

"Right then," announced the efficient agent. "Just time for a quick cup of tea then we'd best get you to the airport. Lethe, be an angel and run back to the shops to get Ygoi some sort of suitcase. We'll pack the stuff you've just bought and he'll have to get anything else he needs in America. Have you told Deirdre?"

"Oh, no," James said with a delighted smile. "That's the whole point."

Deirdre Hunsecker, who hadn't changed her name on marriage, had a head full of Irish vowel sounds and the twang of Arkansas as she let herself into her parents' house. She looked at her watch and calculated it wasn't too late to ring Ravenswood House now. She had been a bit upset when she had rung yesterday and Jenni had told her Ygoi had gone to bed with a terrible sore throat as he just couldn't shift his cold and couldn't possibly come and talk to her on the phone. She had rung his mobile just in case but that was switched off.

She could hear her parents talking in the kitchen and went to see if there was any iced coffee left to drink.

"Hi, honey," her mother greeted her. "You've got a visitor."

Deirdre shrieked with delight when she saw who the visitor was and would have dropped her precious laptop on the floor if her father hadn't caught it first. She hugged her husband and literally wept with happiness even though she had seen him two days ago. To have him in her home territory was just perfect.

"How did you get here?" she asked, wondering for one frightening moment if he had popped across in Lethe's spaceship.

He showed her a passport. "You now have a Swedish husband," he told her. "Apparently I have the right to be Swedish as that is where my mother came from."

She took the passport from him and studied it carefully. "And this is a real, genuine Swedish passport?"

"Issued at the Swedish embassy in London after the Ambassador saw Lethe and me on that chat show and learned I had a Swedish mother. Visa supplied by the US embassy the same day. But there's a catch."

"Uh-huh, isn't there always."

"I'm here for five days and I've got to fix up ten appointments for Lethe to start his US career in the autumn."

"Jesus. You're going to be busy."

"Not all the time," he reminded her and kissed her.

Deirdre's parents had to admit their son-in-law worked hard. He used his mobile to phone and to send emails and managed to book himself a horrendous schedule of appointments that kept him out of the house all day and thus neatly kept him away from any professor who held a Chair in Scandinavian Languages at Harvard. His father-in-law took him to a Mets ball game one evening with Deirdre and found the whole thing quite exhausting. His daughter already understood the rules, the visitor with the Swedish passport soon picked it up and the two of them were among the noisiest in the crowd. Frank felt as though he was out with a couple of children and was quite worn out by the time they got home. Mrs Hunsecker took charge of them for the last few hours her son-in-law had in New York and took the pair of them shopping. At her insistence, Ygoi Roemtek was delivered back to JFK airport with a new haircut which had been a frightening experience as his habitual long, curly hair had been razored off his neck and his ears exposed for the first time he could remember. He was so tired out from his spell in the USA he got on the plane and slept the whole seven hours to London.

Jenni met her assistant at Exeter St David's and thought how good he looked these days and his trendy, short haircut had turned his looks into something quite stunning. He had drifted towards a vegetarian diet as first milk had crept in and then he had discovered the delights of cheese and he was finally starting to put a decent bit of weight on. He wasn't as tall as Lethe but he certainly had presence, and the most gorgeous dark eyes, Jenni thought, now she could see them.

"Am I pleased to see you," he told her and threw two suitcases into the back of the Land Rover. "How's the baby?"

"Fine. Not been a day's trouble. How was America? You look well on it."

"Great. Like the new haircut? It was Deirdre's mother's idea."

"It's a lot shorter than I'm used to seeing. Suits you." Jenni gave in to the temptation to kiss that newly exposed neck, and the two climbed into the car. "How did you get on?"

"Better than I'd hoped. Met a guy at a ball game and he's a big shot in a record company there. I gave him one of the CDs and he wants Lethe out there to do some promotional work. Got him some interviews lined up but most of the US market wants to wait until he's done his bit in out there as part of the original competition prize. We'd do best to push the west coast and then move across to the east coast as they're a bit more conservative there and may not like the idea of a Canadian country singer as much as the more liberal west coast."

The Land Rover left Exeter and set out along the country roads that Ygoi had learned to think of as home. The weather was getting hotter and the two in the car decided to turn off the air conditioning and open the windows just to let a breeze blow through. They were still discussing the American market when they were halted by an accident in front of them. It wasn't a bad shunt. A red car seemed to have side-swiped a white van and both vehicles were slewed across the road while their drivers had a furious argument as to whose fault it was. They heard the engine of the Land Rover and the bald man in the overalls bad temperedly moved his white van a bit further off the road calling the driver of the red car all sorts of names as he did so.

It was a woman driving the red car and she walked up to the Land Rover on the passenger side and companionably leaned on the open window.

"Sorry, we've had a bit of a crunch. Can you get through?"

"Yes, I think so, thank you," Jenni replied. "Anyone hurt?"

"No, just the cars. Can you tell me the time?"

Ygoi looked at the dashboard clock as he didn't own a watch. "Half past three."

"Thanks," the woman said then suddenly her left hand slipped off the window sill and touched that of the man in the passenger seat. It was the work of a split instant and could have been an accident. "Sorry," she said and looked slightly embarrassed. "Anyway, if you're sure you can get through I'll go back to sorting out White Van Man there. Sorry to have held you up."

Jenni negotiated the Land Rover past the accident and the car soon picked up speed. It was then that she looked at her passenger who hadn't resumed their discussion and saw how his face was pale and his hands were shaking.

"Don't you feel well?" she asked.

"No, truth to tell I feel a bit sick."

"Want me to stop for a minute?"

"Yes please."

Jenni pulled in to a passing space on the narrow country road. "Jesus you look awful. Are you running a temperature or have you just got jet lag?"

Ygoi steadied his breathing. "That woman at the accident. She has a tag in her wrist. I felt it when she touched my hand. She's scanned my wrist tag with something she was holding in her hand. I need to get to Lethe's studio to make sure I haven't been reactivated."

"Bloody hell. So where's she from?"

"She has to be from my galaxy. I almost recognised her but you know how sometimes you think you know someone but don't really? I've seen the fat guy somewhere too, but I don't remember him being so old or so fat. You heard how she was speaking. She's been here long enough to pick up the slang and the idioms. Could have landed here the day after we did and been watching us the whole time. Could have got here last week. We've got to warn Lethe to stay away as his tag is still active."

"Let's check you out before we phone Lethe. You could just have felt the lump of a watch buckle on her wrist and she could have had a snotty tissue in her hand. Don't get paranoid yet."

Ygoi desperately wanted to believe her. He had had a wonderful few days in the States; he had citizenship, he had a wife, a fantastic sex life and the prospect of a career as a musician. He didn't want to go back to the Millio galaxy. And if that woman was from there she had almost certainly come to take him, or Lethe, or both of them, back. He tried to kid himself it had been a watch buckle and a snotty tissue.

Jenni realised she wouldn't get any more conversation out of her passenger. She didn't bother to stop and park the Land Rover in the stable yard but drove it straight across the parkland to the studio and just about had time to switch the engine off before she joined Ygoi at the door of the studio.

He took a deep breath and held up his left wrist against a tiny dark square beside the door. "Fuck it," he said as the door opened. He strode down the corridor so fast the heels of his American boots crashed on the floor and Jenni had to trot to catch up, hoping his new knees could cope with the pace. He offered his wrist to the scanner of the door to the control room. "Fuck it," he said again as that door opened too. He sat in one of the chairs and passed his wrist across the blank square in the panel that Jenni had noticed before. Panels slid back in front of him and the large screen Jenni remembered from his old ship rose up from the back of the console. Ygoi held his wrist over a second scanner and after a few seconds a display of glittering yellow writing appeared on the screen. "Fuck it, fuck it, fuck it."

This, Jenni thought, was more like she would expect from a spaceship. Dozens of controls, dials, switches and digital gauges that made a helicopter flight deck look like a child's toy. And above it that screen which she remembered was called the videoradionic and it displayed information generated by the on-board computer.

"Not good news?" she hazarded.

"Sit," he instructed her and she hurriedly sat in the co-pilot's seat. "See that writing up there? That's my life history. If I were still deactivated, there would be no record accessible through the tag."

Jenni looked and saw the name of Ygoi Roemtek, birth planet Goine, usual domicile planet Sunara, registered space craft details now obsolete, cross-galaxy licence revoked, imprisoned on Lriam for tree syrup smuggling, standard procedures applied. Escaped from prison, out of galaxy, current destination unknown. Birth tag deactivated at death. Record to be archived 03134668. There were the details of his ex-wife, the name of his child and all sorts of things she didn't understand but assumed charted his life and work for the past thirty five years. She didn't understand the numbering system either but guessed it was something to do with dates.

"You're dead. It says so."

"Just give it a minute. This doesn't happen very often. Just occasionally people get going again after what you would call a cardiac arrest. And never after such a lapse of time as I've had."

"What are the numbers?"

"Dates. The days are only eighteen of your hours long so we have more of them and we have fifteen months to a year. Our years are the same as yours if you count them in hours or days. Our calendar is erratic because we don't count from any messiah so our years are calculated from about where the original settlers thought they were when they got there, backdated beyond your Christianity, and with a couple of inaccuracies as they didn't know how long the journey had been. There was a war over the dating system a few hundred years ago. We're just starting the year 4569 now." The computer beeped and a new line of red writing appeared. *Updating. Please wait.*

Jenni found herself staring at the screen and praying. She reached across and held Ygoi's hand so hard she was hurting him but he didn't even notice.

Reactivated 28014569. Lriam security actions completed. Free citizen of all galaxies. Cross-galaxy licence revalidated. Current domicile unknown.

"Good or bad?" Jenni asked.

Ygoi let out his breath with a sigh of relief and reclaimed his squashed hand. "Not as bad as I'd thought. At least the security beams have been turned off. They've probably never had one of theirs reactivated before and the computer's algorithms created an oddly humane precedent of giving some poor sod a second chance. We need to get Lethe down here now to check his record."

Lethe was starting to get a bit bored with being a pop star. He had quite envied Ygoi being able to fly off to America for a few days and roamed the London flat wishing he'd swallowed his pride and gone down to Devon with Jenni. James was staying at the flat as well as he preferred it to his London club which meant Lethe felt a bit inhibited about bringing women home. He only had to go out to a bar or a club and at least six people would try to get him to take them to bed. He'd accepted quite a few of them but now he had insects crawling round in his pubic hair and didn't know what to do about them. They didn't have things like this where he came from and the itching was sending him mad as well as taking his skin off. Thoroughly fed up, he hurled a few clothes into a holdall, left James a note and presently roared away from the kerb in his Saab.

He had just cleared a jam at Junction 12 on the M25 and picked up some decent speed on the M3 when his mobile rang. As one hand was occupied with having a scratch and the other was on the wheel, he stopped scratching long enough to press the dashboard button to take the call.

"Hi," Ygoi greeted him. "Where are you?"
"On the M3 heading west. How was America?"
"Good. You on your way here?"
"Sure am. Ygoi, have you ever had fleas?"
"Several times. Not recently."
"I've got fucking fleas crawling all over my dick. Don't you laugh like that, it's not funny. Must have picked them up off one of the women. Stop laughing, you bastard!" Lethe cut the call off and bad-temperedly floored the accelerator, not noticing the police car lurking on a slip road.

Jenni hadn't seen Ygoi giggle until his eyes ran before. She couldn't help but join in although she had no idea what was so funny.

"What?" she pleaded as her sides started to ache.
"He's got fleas on his dick. I told him he'd catch something the way he's been sleeping around."

Two people slumped over the control panel of a spaceship and laughed until they wept.

Finally Ygoi regained some of his senses and wiped his streaming eyes on his sleeve. "He's on his way down here now. Is there any treatment we can get him? Why am I laughing? I had fleas enough in prison and they're not funny. It's just the location I guess. Let's go to the kitchen and I'll make us some tea."

Jenni tucked a hand through Ygoi's arm and the two went back along the corridor at a slightly lower rate of knots than they had the last time. Ygoi swiped his wrist across a panel on the inside of the entry door as they passed and the door closed silently.

"Don't shut the gardener in," Jenni told him and the two started giggling again. "Come on, let's have a cup of tea then you can drive us back to Exeter and we'll go into Boots. Have you got the guts to ask for some treatment for crabs?"

"For what?"

"Crabs, we call it. Pubic lice if you want to be polite."

"Sure, doesn't bother me. I'll tell them it's for you."

"You would too, wouldn't you?"

"Yup."

The two had their tea then got back into the Land Rover and Jenni instructed Ygoi in how to drive it off-road. They did a detour round some of the rougher terrain of the parkland then set off for Exeter. There was no sign of the white van or the red car, somehow they hadn't thought there would be. Ygoi always enjoyed going to Exeter. He had come to love the cathedral, even if he did have problems with the concept of God, as the architecture never failed to impress him and it had a nice feel to it.

To Jenni's admiration, Ygoi was completely unfazed in Boots and they got some special shampoo for Lethe although the two young girls behind the counter where obviously wondering why two sensible-looking thirtysomethings wearing wedding rings were buying crab shampoo. Jenni and Ygoi knew Lethe wouldn't be arriving for a while so they didn't hurry and Ygoi drove back to Ravenswood House in a calm June evening. Jenni had rung the house and told Mrs McDougall not to cook any supper for them and to take the rest of the evening off.

"You're too good to that grumpy old bat," Ygoi told her.

"She's all right. She just can't get on too well with vegetarian cooking. Don't take it personally. Anyway, I thought we could cook something in the studio and Lethe can get his lice in his bath rather than mine." A sudden thought occurred to her. "Oh my God. He's sharing the flat with James and if he's left any little buggers in the bathroom then James will probably get them too. Good job we got two bottles of the stuff."

Ygoi changed gears for the last steep hill before Ravenswood. "Don't," he requested. But it was too late and the two were giggling all over again.

"Don't know what you think is so fucking funny," was the greeting from the man leaning on his white Saab and smoking a cigarette when the Land Rover pulled up next to him.

"Climb on in," Ygoi told him, "and we'll tell you. What's put you in such a mood?"

Lethe trod out his cigarette and got into the back seat of the Land Rover. He had to admit, grudgingly, that Ygoi could handle that bus alright but he wasn't feeling magnanimous enough to say so. "What happened to your hair?" he asked next, thinking how well it suited the other man.

"Mother-in-law's idea. Darned sight easier to deal with." Ygoi glanced in the mirror and saw the scowl on Lethe's face. "So? What's up?"

"Got stopped for speeding by the fucking police on the motorway. I've got ten days to take my documents to Exeter fucking police station. I haven't got any fucking documents."

"Then, my love," Jenni told him, "you will find yourself up before the magistrate, you will be fined and you will be banned from driving until you have a licence and insurance. I'm afraid that, and your dose of crabs, is a consequence of your reckless lifestyle."

"Fuck off," Lethe said and looked out of the window at the parklands. At that precise moment he hated the pair of them and wanted to get in his spaceship and fly back to the Millio galaxy. "Why are we here?" he asked as the Land Rover stopped at the very spaceship he had been thinking of.

"You may have slightly worse problems than dick fleas," Ygoi told him. "Allow me."

Lethe watched the other man scan his wrist tag over the door sensor and the door opened. "Oh fuck," was the best he could offer. "How did that happen? You've been deactivated. It should only be me who can open this now."

The three went in and Ygoi shut the door behind them before both he and Lethe scanned their tags and Lethe keyed in a code on a pad below the sensor. A red light flashed once as a warning.

"We're OK," Lethe deduced. "Two tags and one untagged."

"What was that?" Jenni asked.

"Scanning for life forms," Ygoi explained. "We haven't shut the gardener in this time. I'd guess Lethe's fleas are too small."

"Who reactivated you?" Lethe asked as they went along to the control room.

"A woman driving a red car. It's not too bad. I'm a free citizen so there won't be any more Lriam beams shining on me. We just want to check your status to be sure."

Lethe shrugged. "I haven't committed any crime. Except driving without a licence and insurance," he admitted wryly. "Fucking nuisance. I'll have to take the fucking test now." He sat at the controls and held his wrist over the scanner.

Jenni and Ygoi squashed themselves into the other chair and watched the details as they were written on the videoradionic. Born and raised in Sunara, one wife executed for adultery, six years as apprentice pilot to Ygoi Roemtek, cross-galaxy pilot licence achieved and a whole list of the jobs he had done. Registration of spacecraft, out of galaxy, current domicile unknown, wanted on Lriam for abduction.

There was a silence in the control room. Ygoi gently extracted himself from the chair and typed the challenge into the keyboard.

Lethe Miarren had broken the rules by taking a Lriam prisoner out of galaxy without killing him first. All-galaxy alert and reward in high category for living capture only.

Lethe lit a cigarette and Jenni didn't say anything.

"You are so in the shit," Ygoi told his former co-pilot sympathetically. "And it's all my fault."

"I couldn't leave you to fucking die!" Lethe shrieked at him and ran from the control room.

Jenni was about to go after him but Ygoi stopped her. "Let him go. It's how he copes when he's scared. I'll go and sort him out in a minute."

"What happens now?" she asked and her voice shook.

"Well, I'm guessing that the woman we met saw us go and followed us and alerted Lriam security before she went out of range. How else would she know what Lethe had done? You can see we're 'domicile unknown' and no bounty hunter is going to waste time going out of galaxy to look for him as we could be anywhere in seven galaxies. A few might try their luck in Tundara galaxy I suppose but they're not going to come here without a very good tip-off. And if she's a bounty hunter and knows we're going to Home galaxy although she may risk it to get the prize she's not going to share it with anyone. OK, so it's an all-galaxy alert and the reward will be pretty lucrative but they'll wait for him. A ship like this can only carry food and water for about three years. And then he'll have to dock somewhere in the Millio galaxy to get his fuelling system serviced and that's when they'll get him."

"Is there nothing can be done?"

"Only by deactivating his tag so he is officially dead too. Could you get David to stop his heart for ninety five seconds like he did mine?"

"Probably. But isn't that a bit drastic? It might not start again."

Ygoi idly tinkered on the keyboard and got the computer to translate all Lethe's data into a language Jenni didn't recognise. "We have no direct communication with the Millio galaxy. If the woman we saw wants to get help she's got to fly back to do it and I'd guess she won't risk that in case Lethe clears off to a different galaxy and she loses him for good. She's done pretty well to get this close and I'd guess she roughly located this ship between the time the Lriam beams broke the anti-tracking and your guy Darren got it going again. She's now looking for it on foot which is good because your estate wall means we can't be seen from public land and she can't get in as a tourist without paying money at the gate. She's scanned me into her computer by now so she knows where I am. She's only got to read the papers to know that Lethe is mostly in London. Has Ravenswood been mentioned by name?"

"Yes. Do you remember the article in the Sunday paper the day Lethe got his car?"

"Which someone had left at the gate."

"Her?"

"Most probably/"

"Oh, God. Someone took a rod of trid from David's hospital, do you remember?"

"I was trying not to think about that." Ygoi was thoughtful for a while. "Right. Got it. I'd guess White Van Man is part of it and they've been staging that accident thing for a while now and she's been scanning any man of roughly my or Lethe's description she comes across. Today was her lucky day. Because her scanner told her she'd found somebody, she went back to her ship to find out who. And because she was off the road Lethe would have got through without her stopping him. Or the mood he was in he would probably have driven straight through the middle without stopping."

"What will she do?"

"She's a bounty hunter who saw a cross-galaxy pilot chuck a Lriam ex-prisoner in the back of his transporter and she thought she'd tag along in case there was some money in it. She'll be armed to the teeth, as you say here, and I've no doubt she's formed that rod of trid into smaller rods by now and she'll have the gun to heat and shoot them. The pain beams are transmitted from Lriam, she won't be able to contact them to redirect the ones that were following me now they're turned off so at least Lethe's brain won't get fried if she catches him and shoots trid into him. I'd guess she's got to go for orthodox kidnap and abduction and take him back to Lriam for punishment and her payment."

"How can we stop her?"

"Get to her first and kill her. Before she can leave this planet. Her ship will be twice as fast as this freight carrier anyway and once she's got Lethe off the planet I can't follow her as I've still got the wires in my brain that will blow my head apart as soon as I pass Jupiter. Which I will probably reach about the time she is on the outskirts of Millio."

"Only if she tells Lriam to turn the beams on you."

"She will have pierced Lethe with trid by the time they pass your moon. She will get Lriam to turn the beams on him as soon as she can. Probably fairly low level but as soon as they send out a blast in his direction I will be caught in them as well. And the nearer we get to Millio the stronger the beams are and even Earth gold won't be able to protect me that close to the source."

"Are the rest of us in danger?"

Ygoi sighed and turned off the screen display. "I don't know, is the honest reply. You might be useful as a bargaining tool to get Lethe to give himself up but I'd have thought most likely not. We from the Millio galaxy have no quarrel with people in yours and we're not really into wars as we don't have enough spare people to fight them. You know about our crazy systems of direct punishment, she's got no reason to hurt any of you. She's really got no reason to hurt me unless I get in the way of her mission. I can't think any more. I'll go and give Lethe his crab shampoo then we'll have some food."

Ygoi found Lethe sitting on the toilet, fully clothed and staring into the middle distance. His eyes were red and puffy and he was still sniffing a bit. Ygoi sat on the bath beside him and gave him a hug and a kiss on the forehead.

"I can't even have a shit," he lamented. "I'll get fleas down this toilet too."

"Here, take a shower and wash your fleas off with this stuff. I'll go and cook supper."

Lethe raised his head and briefly returned the kiss, grateful for his friend's efficiency and common sense. "Thanks. Never thought I'd see the day when the great Ygoi Roemtek would wait on me," he said bitterly.

"Get used to it. I've appointed myself your bodyguard until we track down the woman and her red car."

"Any ideas who or where?" Lethe asked as the two got to their feet and he took his shirt off already feeling slightly consoled.

"I have a feeling I know them but can't place them. Talk about it over supper and, no, I'm not cooking meat for you."

Lethe took the bottle of shampoo. "Piss off, Shit-face," he said fondly.

Caitlin Evans had had a lovely day taking her daughter to the zoo. She had been paid handsomely for her footballer story and she was, for once, at peace with the world. Even her dose of crabs had finally cleared up. She was just giving Emily her tea when her mobile rang and the screen told her the caller was Lethe M.

"Well, hi, wasn't expecting to hear from you again," she greeted the caller.

"Hi, want to come to the magistrate's court with me?"

This sounded promising. "What have you done?"

"Driving without a licence. Tomorrow I'm going to Exeter police station to confess and I guess I'll be up before the magistrate some time next week. You can sell the police station story tomorrow morning, ring Exeter to confirm if you like. And I want a press agent to cover my UK tour. You don't have to sleep with me if you don't want to. Not sure what you could do with Emily."

"She can go and stay with her gran. No problem."

"Good. I'll give you directions to Ravenswood and let you know when the hearing is. Can you do one thing for me on your way down? If you see a white van and a red car in a collision, see where the woman takes the car to afterwards?"

"Are you crazy?"

"No, but I've been told I'm at high risk of abduction and they're part of it. I guess I'll be more vulnerable out on the road than I am here."

Caitlin could see an exclusive dancing before her eyes. "You're on. Have you told the police?"

"Not yet, it's only a rumour but I'd be a fool to ignore it. See you soon."

He hung up and Caitlin smiled at her daughter. "Well, Em, fancy a few days with granny and grandad?"

"Yes, please!" cried the child who often found her mother a bit peculiar.

Jenni and Ygoi had listened in shamelessly to Lethe's half of the conversation as they sat round the kitchen table in the studio after their evening meal. Jenni had to admit to herself that Ygoi's cooking wasn't quite up to Lethe's standard but perfectly acceptable in a vegan kind of way.

"Another recruit to the army?" Jenni asked when Lethe put his phone down.

"She can't wait. And she's on for the tour."

"Even better. So, what are you two going to do now?"

"Raid the roof hold," Lethe told her.

Jenni watched as the two men pulled themselves up into the roof hold by the strength of their arms.

"Want to come up too?" Lethe asked her.

She held up her arms and they hauled her in. "Good God," she exclaimed, using her husband's oath. "What's all this?"

"Food mostly," Lethe told her. "It's all dried so it'll keep for years. If you go right to the back you'll find the water tank. These are the guns I keep here. You'd better have one too if you're part of the bodyguard,"

"I can't carry a gun."

"Of course you can," Ygoi assured her. "Take one of the little ones and I'll show you how to set it low then you can go and do some target practice in the garden."

Ygoi sat patiently beside her in the hold door with their legs dangling down into the corridor and showed her a disc about the size of a two-pound coin. "This will be the best one for you. Look, you set it like this. At this end of the scale it will stun a butterfly for ten seconds, at the other end it will kill a cat. It won't kill a person so you can't turn into a murderer but the top end of the scale would be good to stun someone for about five minutes."

Jenni watched as Ygoi's expert hands moved over the disc and the lights on it flashed and sparkled.

"This is how you target it, don't look at the thing you're shooting at, look at the image here and once you've got what you want just press the button once. That will lock the energy bolt and next time you press the button it will hit what you've got in the image at the strength you've set. The beam comes out here so don't point it the wrong way or you'll shoot your baby. If you haven't got time to program it, turn the scale up to maximum, point the raised dot at what you want to hit and press the trigger button twice. OK? Here, put it in your pocket and I'll take you out for some practice this evening."

Jenni did as he asked and was amazed at how heavy the disc felt in her hand. "Don't let me shoot the baby, will you?"

He patted her belly. "I shall look after your baby as though it's my own."

Lethe sat down on his other side. "Shown her the baby gun?"

"Yes, but we're not going to call it that."

"Oh, right, OK. I've got a spare Tiowing 4, can you handle it?" Lethe handed his friend what looked, to Jenni, more like a conventional handgun. It wasn't very big, it had a scale on it like the one she had been given but she couldn't see the screen.

"How do you know what you're shooting at?" she asked.

Ygoi sighted along the barrel. "You don't. You aim this one by eye but it's not what you might call subtle. Lethe, this is ridiculous. I could blow up the house with something this size."

"Can't handle it?" Lethe jibed and rather missed the old Ygoi who would not only have enthusiastically accepted the Tiowing 4, he would probably have gone out and shot up a couple of old spaceships with it just because he could.

"Of course I could handle it. I'm looking to blow up one woman and maybe a fat bald guy as well, not half of Exeter. Do they still make the Assassin?"

"You could never handle one of them. There are only about ten people in all seven galaxies who are licenced to carry one of them."

"Yes, and I was one of the ten. Have you got one?"

"Yes," Lethe admitted grumpily. "I bought it a couple of years ago and got my registration to apply for level one training but never got round to doing the course."

"Can I borrow it, please?"

"If you're still licenced."

Ygoi held out his hand and Lethe grudgingly gave him a metal object that looked something like a starfish but with so many controls on it Jenni couldn't make head nor tail of it. Ygoi gave back the Tiowing and stuck the Assassin on the waistband of his trousers by no means of support Jenni could see.

He saw her puzzled look. "Harnessed static. Down you come. Got something to show you."

The three dropped out of the hold, Lethe secured the roof and they went back to the control room where Ygoi again scanned his wrist and got his details on the screen. He then scanned the Assassin which beeped and lit up with an impressive array of lights for a few seconds then went darkly silent again. "There you go," he told Lethe. "Security clearance code JZ20X, you put it in."

Lethe typed in the code, Ygoi scanned his wrist again and the screen cleared blank then started putting up green writing.

Jenni looked at the writing but it didn't mean much to her. "What does it say?"

"This bastard has been licenced to use the Assassin since he was eighteen. He's got level seven on it. Nobody gets level seven on an Assassin."

Ygoi shrugged and cleared the screen.

"No wonder you could outshoot anyone else if you were using an Assassin and they were all stuck on Tiowings. You absolute bastard. That was no way a fair fight."

"What does an Assassin do?" Jenni asked and thought how silly that sounded.

"It can do anything from, how did he put it? Stun a butterfly for ten seconds to blow up half of Exeter. Including the cathedral. But you've got to be licenced and registered to use it. You saw how he had to scan his tag on it. If I did that it wouldn't even become active."

Jenni looked at the man who was checking over the weapon he had taken off his trousers and she saw again the Ygoi Roemtek of ten years ago. She couldn't help but miss the rather quiet, gentle man in the wheelchair.

He saw her look at him and smiled in that nice way he had these days. "It's OK, I'm not the mad, bad and dangerous guy I was once. You can't come out of Lriam prison in a shit ship and go back to what you were."

Jenni pulled both men into a hug and kissed them on the cheek. "Just look after yourselves. Right, who's going to wash up?"

TWELVE

Ygoi didn't want to go to Exeter police station to see Lethe charged with driving without a licence and insurance. Personally he thought Lethe deserved it then he got a bit depressed because once he would have thought Lethe's actions were daring and clever and now he just thought it was irresponsible so that must mean he was getting old. Feeling rather staid and middle-aged, he went out into the garden where Jim and two of his helpers were weeding the herbaceous borders and some morning tourists were looking at the gardens and waiting for the house to open at midday. Ygoi sat on one of the benches and watched the gardeners at work for a while. His head ached from thinking so much and he still felt he hadn't reached any conclusions.

Lethe's only hope, so far as he could see, was the annihilation of the woman driving the red car. The problem was he didn't know where she was. He tilted his head back to let the weak Earth sun shine on his face and was thankful for the Earth habit of wearing sleeveless T shirts and chopped-off jeans to make shorts. People wandering by were complaining of the heat but it rather suited the man used to the twin suns of a different galaxy. The conversation of two of the apprentices impinged on his mind after a while and he realised one of them was Darren who had inadvertently mended the anti-tracking devices in the spaceship.

Darren wasn't even thinking criminal thoughts when he realised the foreign bloke on the bench was talking to him.

"So how do you hotwire cars?"

"Dunno what you're talking about," Darren tried.

"Yes you do. You're the one who mended the air conditioning in Lethe's studio. Jenni tells me you know how to hotwire cars. I'm just curious, that's all."

Darren looked at the bloke with his dark hair and his eyes the colour of a black man's and his skin turning a dusky shade of brown in the sun. He looked foreign alright, he had what looked like fight scars on his face that showed up more now the rest of him was getting tanned and he had scars on his knees from the operations he had had to get him out of the wheelchair. Darren guessed he could trust him.

"Depends on the car. Some are dead easy. Something like the one Mrs KB drives is harder as they've built in all these things to stop it. And it's got immobilisers and things too."

"It's got what?" Ygoi asked and Darren knew he wasn't kidding.

"Stops you driving it away without a key."

"But isn't that what hotwiring is all about? You'll have to excuse me, I've only recently had anything to do with cars and they're a bit of a puzzle to me."

Darren quite liked this bloke. He wasn't talking down to him, wasn't treating him like an idiot, didn't appear to be anything to do with the law and really seemed to want to learn. Darren sat beside him on the bench and muttered,

"Want me to show you?"

The idea of learning to hotwire cars rather appealed to the man who had been feeling so middle-aged. "OK."

"Pick you up at the gates at ten tonight? Can you drive?"

"Not very well and I only have a provisional licence."

Darren sniffed. "See yah." He went off to get back to his weeding and Ygoi resumed his sunbathing feeling much cheered.

He didn't get long to bask before Lethe stopped beside him. "Fancy a swim?"

Ygoi sighed and opened one lazy eye. "What?"

"Jenni's had the pool engineer round and the pool's now ready to use. She's gone off there already."

"I was just enjoying the sun. Why would I want to get wet?"

"Up to you," Lethe agreed and went on his way.

Ygoi went to see what was going on at the swimming pool. He had never been very fond of swimming although it was something everyone did in the Millio galaxy, primarily as a relief from the heat of the suns, but he had never been very good at it. He was quite content to resume his basking in the sun in the privacy of the pool area, lying face down and stark naked on a towel. He idly watched Jenni and Lethe trawling their lengths for a while.

"How did you get on with the police?" he asked Lethe at the end of one length,

"OK. I just went in with the bit of paper the police on the motorway had given me and the guy at the desk said 'Where are your papers, then?' and I told him I hadn't got any. So I got charged with driving without a licence and without insurance and the magistrate wants to see me at ten o'clock tomorrow morning. You want to come?"

"Not really. I'll be out tonight and don't know what time I'll be home."

"Going anywhere in particular?"

"Darren's going to teach me to hotwire cars."

Jenni flopped onto the side of the pool. "Don't you dare. You'd get more than a fine if you get caught stealing cars."

"I don't want to steal anything. I'm just curious to know how to start the engine without the key. Thieving is against the law in our galaxy too."

Lethe knew what that stubborn look meant and didn't say anything but Jenni didn't have his insight.

"You'd still be done as an accessory and it wouldn't just be a fine. You'd go to prison."

Ygoi didn't want to hear that. He just wanted to do something mad and reckless once more in his life and get away with it. "Fuck off," he said rudely and stalked off back to the house, wrapping the towel round as he went.

"What's up with him?" Jenni asked Lethe.

"Feeling his age. He was miserable for a week when he hit thirty. Can't be far off his thirty sixth now, it's our third day, fourteenth month. His passport says fifteenth of November so that was some fucking quick maths he did. But then he always could. Race you for two lengths?"

"No chance," Jenni challenged as she slipped back into the water.

It was past dusk by the time Ygoi got to the gates of Ravenswood House for his appointment but the others were already there. Darren was driving a gold Vectra and there was another white man in the front and two black men in the back. These two shuffled up a bit to let Ygoi in and introduced themselves as Wayne and Nathan and the one in the front said his name was Alan. Darren explained they were just going for a few drinks first then they would get on with the cars. By the time they reached the pub they had found out Ygoi didn't do drugs and he hadn't got either a credit card or a tattoo. The man from another planet felt as though he had crossed yet another galaxy as he met the other side of life in Exeter where people supported their tobacco and worse addictions with their benefits and petty crime. They decided he was weird but harmless and forgave him because he was nearly as old as their dads and obviously a foreigner. One of the crowd had heard of Estonia and they thought Sweden was a place full of Volvo cars and blonde girls with big tits.

The quartet who had adopted Ygoi for the evening sat round a table in the pub and got through so many pints of beer he wondered if they would be sober enough to drive any sort of car, even a legally owned one. Then he worked out they just didn't care.

Alan was the most drunk of the lot of them. "Oi, fucking gay boy," he challenged Ygoi. "What's wrong with British beer?"

"Nothing, I just don't like it." He really didn't want to have to explain that even the smell of the beer reminded him too much of Sunaran ale and that was a drink he never wanted to taste again.

"Don't like it," Alan mimicked. "Fucking poof don't drink fucking beer. Don't tell me, yours is a fucking prosecco like all the other girls."

The others giggled a bit nervously and admired Alan's nerve, goading a stranger like that.

"He's not a fucking poof," Darren defended their guest. "He's got a fucking wife with legs up to her arse and tits like this. She's a bit of fucking all right, she is."

Ygoi thought Darren's concept of the slender Deirdre's breasts was somewhat exaggerated, but he didn't say anything.

Alan leaned drunkenly across the table. "Drink something, fucking gay boy or I'll pour it down your fucking neck until you fucking choke on it."

Ygoi didn't like his tone. "You buy me a bottle of vodka and I'll drink it for you. But you bring it here sealed. No spiking it."

The others shouted their approval of that idea. They'd never heard of anyone drinking a whole bottle before but they weren't going to pay pub prices. They went down the offie and bought a bottle of the cheapest vodka in the shop then went back to Wayne's place to watch the foreign guy get sick. So they sat round the table in the kitchen and Wayne's big brother and his dad came to watch too. And then that fucking foreign guy drank down the vodka from the bottle as though it was water, then he smashed the empty bottle on the table to prove there was nothing left in it and held out hands as steady as any brain surgeon.

"Fancy hotwiring some cars?" he asked and his quiet voice with its funny accent wasn't the slightest bit slurred.

"Fuck me," Alan conceded. "Ain't seen nothing like that before. Where the fuck did you say you come from, mister?"

"Estonia. We drink home brewed vodka for fun. Pure alcohol. Not cat's piss like this."

"You're all right, mate," Alan decided. "Go on, Wayne, get your dad to give him a tattoo."

"But I don't want..." Ygoi started then stopped when the blade of a flick knife touched his throat.

"Stop it, Alan," Wayne's dad warned. "Put the blade away."

"Fuck off. Get your fucking needles out or I'll cut this guy then I'll start on your precious fucking Wayne."

Ygoi could feel the Assassin against his ribs under his shirt but he knew that if he made any move towards it one of the others would tear the shirt off him to get to it and if they weren't careful half the houses in the street would get blown to smithereens.

Alan took the knife back an inch. "Right, now you get it, don't you. Oh, what the fuck." He stuck the knife in the innocent Nathan's hand and pinned it to the table. "Tattoo the fucking wanker."

Ygoi had met this before. Mindless cruelty. The firing of white hot metal into a man's body, the transmission of pain beams, the mashing up of the hands and all without a word being said. The others were obviously frightened witless of Alan and he watched Nathan and Wayne wrestle the knife out of the hand. He had a good idea how much that hurt and wasn't surprised to hear the things Nathan was saying. Revenge could come later, right now it was up to him to stop anyone else getting hurt. "Do your tattoo," he said to Wayne's dad. "But I choose what it is and where it goes."

Alan was satisfied. Wayne's dad worked, legitimately, in a studio at the back of his house and Wayne's dad was an artist. By the time Ygoi Roemtek learned how to steal cars he had an exquisitely drawn black panther prowling down his right forearm. It was four o'clock in the morning when the Vectra got back to Ravenswood House. Wayne and Nathan had been left at Exeter General hospital so the latter could take his hand to A and E and Ygoi had also learned how to do doughnuts, whirling stolen cars round Exeter until their tyres smoked.

"See you later then," Darren said to Ygoi as he stopped the car at the gates.

"You can't drive home, you're pissed." Ygoi told him.

"Fuck off, mister. The filth won't be out at this time of the morning. The night shift all goes to bed when the sun gets up."

"Darren, out of the car. Let Alan drive it home. You can sleep in the kitchen for what's left of the night."

"And get Mrs fucking McDougall on at me? No fucking chance. I'll kip in the greenhouse. See you tomorrow, mate," he said to Alan as he got out of the car. "Burn the fucking wreck out somewhere, won't you?"

Alan just laughed as he got in the driver's seat and revved the engine. "Got your number, wanker," he said to Ygoi. "I'll get Wayne's dad to tattoo your fucking dick next time or else I'll cut it off you. And then I can rape your fucking wife for you. Bet she's really hot when she puts up a fight."

Darren was tired and drunk but he watched Alan race the car away and thought he saw Ygoi take something out from inside his shirt. He spun it in his right hand and held his hand out palm downwards towards the retreating car. The morning sun made it look as though the panther on the arm flexed its muscles under its wrapping of cling film and suddenly the Vectra slewed across the road into a tree as its back tyres burst. Ygoi spun the thing in his hand again and Darren could have sworn there was a crackling noise and a bolt of white light shot from under Yogi's fingers then the Vectra turned into a fireball.

Darren nearly shit himself. He looked at the man standing next to him and saw him idly scratch his ribs as though he had never taken anything out from under his shirt and the whole thing had been in his imagination. Perhaps he had imagined it. It had all happened so fast. Except there was a burning car down the road and there was no way Alan could have got out of it.

"What the fuck was that?" Darren breathed. "Have you got a fucking gun?"

"I think your mate Alan was too drunk to drive," Ygoi remarked pleasantly. "If you've got your mobile with you, I suggest you ring the fire brigade."

Gecko Artists Management called another meeting in the afternoon. There had been a bit of a fuss that morning as Darren had been too upset to work as his mate had been blown up in front of him last night and he had nearly been in the car with him. He spun some story about Ygoi Roemtek shooting white light at the car as it drove away but his alcohol to blood ratio was so high when they tested it, the police didn't give too much credence to his statement. Alan Baxter was well known to the Devon Constabulary and nobody on the force shed a tear for the small time drug dealer and full-time thug and thief. The Vectra had been stolen earlier that evening and by the time the fire brigade had got there the fire had been so intense there was nothing left of car or driver. Ygoi Roemtek also had a ridiculously high alcohol to blood ratio but he didn't seem the slightest bit affected by it when he gave his statement to the police and told them Alan Baxter had been drinking all evening, and he had seen the Vectra shoot across the road as though the man at the wheel had lost control and it had exploded on impact with a tree. Both witnesses claimed to have spent a harmless night drinking and both denied all knowledge that the Vectra was stolen, saying Alan had provided the car.

Jenni didn't want to know the details and kept the meeting strictly business. "Right, now you two have had your brush with the Devon police can we keep it all straight and legal? OK, to business. Do you want to cancel your UK tour?"

Lethe had been thinking about that. "No. We know the instructions are to get me to Lriam alive for punishment so the bounty hunter's not going to shoot me dead. She's not likely to do anything while I'm actually on stage, she can't get near me in the tour bus and she'll have to be fucking clever to get at me in the hotels and such with a TV crew filming every move. I'll have Caitlin in my bed every night and she tells me she's a light sleeper as she's used to keeping an ear out for Emily. And now Ygoi's got the Assassin I'll be OK so long as he's around."

Jenni looked at the man sitting opposite her at the table in the morning room. She wanted to know and didn't want to know the truth of what had happened to the stolen Vectra and the man inside it. The police were satisfied it was an accident. Ygoi had said it was an accident. It was only Darren who said there was anything funny going on and that had been just before he passed out from the effects of the drink and the fright.

Ygoi was desperate to deflect Jenni's mind from the track it was on. He put his right hand on the table and the other two saw the panther on his arm. "Like my tattoo? I got a bit envious of your lizards."

Jenni took his hand and studied the drawing, glad to have been distracted. She wasn't quite sure why Ygoi would have gone back on his word about tattoos but couldn't really believe it was a simple case of envy. "That is gorgeous," she complimented. "Who did it?"

"Wayne's dad. He's got a proper studio in his house. Either I had this done or some poor sod called Nathan got his hands cut off."

Jenni peered more closely. "You can even see its eyes and its teeth. God, he's even managed to give it green eyes. That is really amazing."

Lethe felt quite put out. "You didn't go on about my lizard like that." He took Ygoi's hand to see for himself. "Mind you, that's a fucking brilliant cat. Reckon he'd do one for me?"

"It's a panther."

"Yeah, right, looks like a cat to me. Anyway, tour's still on and I'm off to catch up on my swimming. Either of you two coming?"

"I'll come and sit in the sun," Ygoi offered. "As I'm the official bodyguard. Think I need to sleep half the day to work off the vodka. I just can't take the drink any more."

"You're supposed to be helping me to run an agency," Jenni reminded him rather heartlessly. "I'm sure Lethe will be fine on his own for an hour or so while I give you your work for the day." She felt more like a parent than a friend as she watched Lethe leave the room then engaged the sulky dark glare of Ygoi Roemtek.

Jenni was beginning to understand their rather basic concept of crime and punishment. He thought that being chained to the laptop for the morning was going to be her way of punishing him because she still had doubts about Alan's accident. She looked at him and remembered the sad, gentle man in the wheelchair who had been punished more than any man ever deserved to be. It had been an accident. A simple, horrible accident and nothing more.

"Take this folder and your phone down to the pool and just double check everything's in order for the photoshoot coming here. Then you can get on to the list of venues for the tour and check on harp availability, unless you're going to buy one as you said you might. Oh, and contact the Musicians' Union and get yourself in it now you're an EU citizen. Go on, hop it." Ygoi got to his feet and took the papers from her. "Just tell me one thing. If Lethe had driven without a licence in your galaxy what would you have done with him?"

"Depends. If you steal a transporter to drive it the owner can shoot you but that's for the theft. You can't get a spaceship until you have a licence which you have to get by serving an apprenticeship as Lethe did with me."

Jenni was silent for a while, just looking at the man holding the folders of papers against his chest and tried to think of how to ask the question. She jumped as he leaned down to her and gently lifted her face by the chin.

"And nobody, absolutely nobody, ever threatens to rape my wife, or you, and gets away with it."

He gave her a soft kiss on the lips then left her alone in the morning room.

The hot weather broke in a spectacular thunderstorm a short while later and James got drenched dashing from his car to the front door when he got home for a long weekend. His wife met him in the hall and they exchanged a kiss.

"And how's my son and heir?" he asked and gave her an extra hug.

"Hard to believe. I've not had a moment's sickness or anything like that. In fact, if the doctor hadn't confirmed it I wouldn't have believed it."

"You're getting fatter," he murmured and the two started snogging in the hallway. He backed away as she tugged at his waistband. "Probably best not." He wasn't quite sure what to say after the bad patch they had been through. He had never been unfaithful in all their years of marriage, even when his wife had been so cold towards him. He hoped she would understand. To his astonishment, Jenni suddenly grinned hugely and kissed his nose.

"Don't worry, my love, I know all about it. You've picked up Lethe's crabs in the bath. He brought them home with him. Don't worry, we've got the shampoo on standby and he's keeping his strictly in the studio. God knows what they've done to his water recycling."

"Thank God for that. I was too ashamed to go into Boots and get some."

Jenni took him by the hand and led him towards the stairs. "Come on, I'll even rub it in for you."

"Where are the Basingstoke hippies?" James asked as the two went slowly upstairs hand in hand.

"Sulking somewhere, they've not been having a good time recently and they hate the wet weather."

"Well, I'll speak to them later." James paused on the stairs and kissed his wife. "I hated all those months when I felt we were drifting apart. Ours is an odd relationship I grant you, but I'm glad we're back on course."

"Me too," Jenni smiled. "Maybe our fallen heroes have brought us some magic from the stars."

"Romantic," he teased.

"I try to be. Wait until you hear what the pair of them have been up to recently."

James and Jenni found their guests in the drawing room which should have closed to visitors for the day but there was an impromptu concert going on and the last few, rain-sodden tourists had been allowed to linger to listen. The bass of the harp was thundering through the floorboards while the guitar took up the higher melody. It was dance music, it was a celebration and it could almost make you believe the sun had come out again.

The meagre audience whooped and clapped when the music ended.

"You two ever play ceilidhs?" one of the men watching asked. "Definitely a bit of the Irish in that one."

"Can't say we ever have," Lethe admitted and wondered what on Earth the man was talking about.

"Come down to Bodhran Barney's on a Thursday night, bring your guitar. Sure and they'll love you.

Don't know about the harp though. They've got a Gaelic harp, can you play one of them?"

The two were struggling a bit with the man's Irish accent.

"Never tried."

"Ach, well, bring that bus with you in a lorry. There'll be lots of people to help you get it out the other end."

The room warden remembered he had a job to do. "So sorry, ladies and gents, but the house is officially closed now so I must ask you to move on."

"Bodhran Barney's, Thursday!" the Irishman called over his shoulder as he and the others were escorted by the warden.

The two from another galaxy turned to the natives for a translation. "What is he talking about?"

"It's an Irish pub in Exeter," Jenni explained. "I've heard say the music is really good. You'll have to borrow the sheep lorry if you want to take the harp. Anyway, come along to the morning room for a cup of tea."

James was a little puzzled to see Ygoi remove a metal starfish from the frame of the harp and stick it above the back pocket of his jeans but he guessed he would find out soon enough. He walked beside Ygoi as Lethe and Jenny went on ahead.

"Jenni tells me you have joined the ranks of the barbarians."

"Huh?"

"A tattoo?"

Ygoi held out his arm. "Only a little one."

James thought it wasn't that little and didn't take his hand to study the work. "Quite remarkable. I gather it wasn't entirely your idea."

Ygoi cut out the next few minutes of conversation. "She thinks I blew up that car yesterday, right?"

James wasn't sorry not to have to find a delicate way of asking. "Did you?"

"It was an accident."

"Not revenge for a perceived or actual threat?"

"It was an accident. Nothing to do with me."

"And you would say that in a court of law?"

"Yes."

"Then I am satisfied."

"Do you believe me?"

"No."

The two walked on, each understanding the other.

The next day the humidity levels soared and the two from another galaxy, where the fierce suns burned off any excess moisture, could hardly drag themselves from their beds.

Jenni and James looked at the two of them sitting so lethargically at the breakfast table and felt rather sorry for them.

"I've decided to take early retirement," James told them.

They just looked blankly at him. Coming from a galaxy where overwork finished you off quite young they really didn't have a clue what he was talking about.

"Stopping work," he offered.

"So who pays for the house then?" Ygoi asked, trying to understand yet another odd idea.

"I get a pension," James began and then wished he hadn't as he then had to spend the next ten minutes explaining exactly what that was. Then there was the concept of the money he and his five brothers had inherited on the death of their father.

While the minefields of Inheritance Tax were still being negotiated the crew arrived for the photoshoot. To their great delight Lethe Miarren was looking amazingly gorgeous at that hour of the morning. When you saw him close up his ragged blond curls were thick and shiny, his eyes the most incredible shade of summer-sky blue and his lashes and brows mercifully dark which would save them a fortune in make up. The other three rather heartlessly left him to his fate as they couldn't see he would be abducted by anyone with all that lot fussing round him. James went to his study to plan his early retirement while Jenni and Ygoi stayed in the morning room which had, by default, turned into the office of Gecko Artists Management. There was a lot of post that morning which Jenni left Ygoi to deal with while she got on with finishing off the letters that had come in yesterday.

Ygoi didn't mind being the assistant in an agency. Every pilot in the Millio galaxy knew how to operate computers way in advance of Earth technology and once Jenni had explained to him how letters were done she had more or less left him to get on with it.

Jenni looked at her assistant and wondered how it felt to have come down from cross-galaxy pilot and all round hero to being the typist in an agency set up to promote your own former apprentice. She watched as he took one of the incoming calls and dealt perfectly politely with someone who wanted to book Lethe to open a fete somewhere or another on a day when he already had a booking. They took the calls in rotation and the next one was hers. A young string quartet looking for an agent. Jenni hadn't intended to do anything other than look after Lethe's interests but somehow word was getting out about Gecko and several people had rung her up trying to hire her services.

She put the call on hold. "What do you reckon? Shall we expand our client base?"

"Up to you. Soon as Deirdre's finished her PhD I'm out of here. I'm sure she'd like to be kept busy. Then you can sign me on as one of your clients too."

Jenni took on the string quartet.

"Fuck me," Ygoi next exclaimed in the silence.

"Is that an invitation?" Jenni asked amusedly.

"If you like. Got my Musicians' Union card. That was quick."

"Congratulations. When is Deirdre coming back?"

"Two days before the tour starts. Don't expect to see me outside the bedroom for those two days."

Mrs McDougall interrupted the workers with morning coffee and a recorded delivery envelope addressed to Lethe.

Jenni poured the coffee and handed the package to Ygoi to open.

"You really can fuck me this time if you want to," he told her and shoved a temporary Canadian passport under her nose. "He's got his nationality. Just got to go to the Embassy in London to get the real thing."

Jenni grabbed the papers from him and scanned them. "About time too," she decided. "Do you want to go and give him the good news?"

He looked out of the window to where the suffering Lethe was being artistically posed near the fishpond. "Too hot."

"Go on, you big wuss. Go and see if they want a coffee break."

Ygoi reluctantly ambled out into the humid sunshine where Lethe was having his hair and make up sorted out for the next shot.

"Want a coffee break?" he asked.

The man in charge of the shoot turned to accept the offer and looked at the speaker. "Who are you?"

"I'm Ygoi. Sometime harpist and most time assistant agent."

"Now, you are gorgeous."

Ygoi knew this one wanted more than a friendly kiss given the chance and he physically backed away. Lethe started grinning, he had had half a morning of being propositioned by this man. "What?"

"You are as dark as he is fair. I want the two of you together. I need you indoors really with some good lighting. Steve!" he summoned the photographer. "Find me a dusty barn somewhere."

Jenni missed her assistant and came out to discover what was going on. She walked into the middle of a heated disagreement but when she was told what it was all about, backed the man in charge. "Go on, one photo won't kill you and we can use it on the album cover if it's any good. Try the home barn if you want inside. It's quite plain." She wasn't really surprised to find Ygoi so shy. It must have come hard to a formerly sexually attractive man to know you were now underweight and scarred like a tomcat. But she thought he was still a looker and hoped somehow this would boost his self esteem.

The fair Lethe and the dark Ygoi were stripped to the waist and sat one behind the other on a hay bale in the home barn. Lethe's arm with its lizard reached up across his chest to hold Ygoi's wrist with its panther which was reaching down over his shoulder and their faces were half shadowed with the light just catching the rings in Ygoi' ear. The raw eroticism of it was a turn on for all those watching and Jenni cheated by taking a picture herself using the camera in her mobile. Fortunately for her, nobody saw her do it except the subjects of the photo and they both just knew it was going to get sent across to New York at the first opportunity. Without either saying a word, Lethe tightened his grip as if trying to stop his chest being groped and tilted his head back just enough for his throat to be exposed as though expecting it to be kissed. Ygoi didn't oblige as Lethe's hair was tickling his nose and he sneezed just after Steve clicked the shutter.

"Hold it," Steve commanded them. "Head a bit further back please, Lethe and you, tilt your head forward."

It was hot and humid in the barn, there were two studio lights trained on the sweltering models and a tiny trickle of sweat ran down from Lethe's temple.

Jenni jumped as an arm slid round her waist from behind but then she looked down and recognised her husband's hand.

"Good grief," he exclaimed in disgust. "Just what are those two doing over there?"

Jenni knew exactly. "Winding up the guy in charge to see if he explodes. I'll bet you a tenner they'd go as far as snogging each other."

James, as a happily heterosexual man, didn't want to believe it. "No. They're both perfectly straight men. Ygoi's married and Lethe is sowing so many wild oats he could harvest half of Kansas."

Jenni was confident of success after her talks with those two about Millio galaxy sexuality. "Bet you?"

"Done."

They watched as Steve stopped to change the battery in his camera and to run back through some of the images he had already saved so the two knew they weren't about to be photographed. Lethe nestled his head back onto Ygoi's shoulder, he closed his eyes and Jenni's mobile took another surreptitious shot as she won her tenner. She felt James stirring uneasily beside her and seriously thought he was going to be sick. There came a kind of falsetto squeak from the man in charge and he rushed outside. Ygoi looked at Lethe's watch that had been out of shot.

"Twelve minutes. I win."

"No you don't. I said it would take a snog. Pay up."

Lethe saw the look James was giving them. "It's all right, it's only acting. You haven't got to start locking your bedroom door. I was fed up with that guy coming on to me so we're just getting our own back. I do seem to attract them," he mused but not really bothered about it. He slapped Ygoi on the thigh. "Fancy doing it again when he's over that?"

"Not likely. You smoke too much and you taste disgusting. I'm not doing that again." Ygoi took the towel one of the make up ladies handed him and wiped some of the sweat off his face and neck. "And I don't want him out there thinking he can be next in the queue."

The object of their bet tottered back in again. "Perhaps we should stop for the break that was offered?"

"I'll ask Mrs McDougall to bring you some coffee," Jenni offered.

Ygoi walked back to the house with Jenni and James, scrubbing his tongue with the towel and occasionally spitting as he went.

"How can anybody smoke those things?" he asked.

"They're not so bad if you smoke them yourself," Jenni told him. "I smoked for years."

Ygoi pulled his shirt back on and hung the towel round his neck obviously not convinced. "And you let me see that one you took before you send it to Deirdre, please," he requested.

"What one?" Jenni asked innocently.

Ygoi tried to get the phone from her hand but she laughingly held it out of his reach. He made another grab at her top and then the two of them were tussling like a pair of children over the phone in her hand. James watched benevolently as his wife and another man got rather engrossed in what they were doing and was quite surprised when Jenni was the eventual winner by which time the pair of them were wheezing with laughter. Jenni mantled herself over the phone so Ygoi couldn't get to it but he was tickling her ribs by this time and she really couldn't concentrate on what she was doing. She couldn't see too well either as she had to keep jerking the phone away from Ygoi as he wasn't going to give up, but eventually she managed to key in a contact with her thumb and sent the picture across the Atlantic.

"Gone. And now I'm going to save that one just for the fun of it."

"And Steve will sue you for the copyright."

"God, you've been working with me too long. He stopped taking picture while you were still looking at the camera so that's my shot."

Ygoi resigned himself to some merciless teasing from his wife and watched as Jenni showed the image to her husband.

"Well, what do you reckon?" she asked him, realising she just may have sent the wrong photo to the innocent wife of one of the models.

James looked at the picture on the screen. "It's, um, a very striking image," was the best he could manage. "Much as I don't find homo-eroticism my thing. How much did you wager Lethe?"

"Five pounds."

"Cheapskates," Jenni laughed. "James bet me a tenner you wouldn't snog each other. Which reminds me, pay up."

"Pay you in kind?" James asked hopefully.

"In your dreams."

Deirdre Hunsecker was sitting in the university library when her computer told her some mail had arrived for her from Jenni's mobile. Wondering why Jenni was mailing her she opened the attachment and physically jumped in her seat. She heard a footstep behind her and hastily slammed shut the lid of her laptop.

"Since when did homo-erotic art have anything to do with linguistics?" asked the amused voice of her professor.

Deirdre felt her blushes spread down from her face to her chest as her professor gently raised the lid of the laptop again and had a closer look at the blond head sunk onto the sun-bronzed shoulder of a dark-haired man just before their lips met and at the lower edge of the image were the tattoos of the lizard and the panther and the holding of hands against the bare chest of the blond man.

"Cool picture. Do you know these guys?"

Deirdre really didn't want to own up but knew she had to. "Um, the dark one is my husband."

The professor leaned down and planted her elbows on the desk to see the picture better. She looked up and saw a colleague a few desks away. "Miriam," she called quietly, so as not to disturb the other readers. "Come tell me what you think of this. It's a photo of Deirdre's husband."

Miriam came across expecting to see some guy in a checked shirt outside a house somewhere in England.

"My God. That is perfection of erotic art." She planted her elbows on the desk on Deirdre's other side and the two professors studied the picture while the wife of one of the models wished the floor would give way so she could sink beneath it.

"See here," Miriam enthused. "We've got the elusiveness of the gecko and the calm stalking of the panther. It's incredibly symbolic that it should be the dark man and the panther taking control like that."

"Yes," agreed the other woman. "But look at the hands. The blond man is holding back the power of the darkness."

"True, but why is he accepting the kiss unless he is willing to be ravished by the darkness, And you can see he is accepting it from the way his head is lying. Look at the way his hair curls into the other man's neck. It's as though a vestal virgin were lying with her hair strewn on a pillow wating for her seducer. He has closed his eyes and is exposing his throat to the ravages of the panther. Deirdre, will you ring your husband and ask his permission for this photo to be printed off? I'd like to use it in one of my lectures later today. Just go outside now and use your cell phone. We'll need to get a copy mailed across to the guys in the print shop to tidy it up a bit as this quality won't take too big an enlargement."

Deirdre didn't like to refuse. She rang the landline for Ravenswood House and Jenni answered it.

"Hi, Deirdre. Why aren't you hard at work?"

"I was. Then you sent me a rude photo and now two professors have hailed it as a triumph of erotic art and want permission to print it."

"Hang on. Which one did you get in the end? Are the two of them sitting side by side or are they actually kissing each other?"

"Um, the second one."

Jenni knew then she had definitely sent the wrong one. She had meant to send the previous shot which hadn't been nearly so explicit. Oh, well, too late now. She'd just have to bluff it out. "It's a good photo, isn't it?"

"Jenni, it is the hottest thing I've seen since Ygoi came over for those few days and had his hair cut off. Is he around?"

"Listening in on the other side of the morning room. Deirdre, it was me who took that photo and I gladly give you permission for you to do what you like with it."

Deirdre could hear some very profane protests from her husband.

"It's my photo. You're just the unpaid model. It's only for a couple of sad old professors to dribble over." Jenni barracked back across the room. "Publish and be damned, as they say. It was just our Basingstoke hippies and their idea of punishing some poor sod who came on to them. When are you coming home?"

"Pretty darned soon from the sound of what he's calling you."

Jenni laughed. "He's harmless. Tell your professors I hope they enjoy it."

Deirdre went back to the library where there were now some half a dozen people round her laptop. "I spoke to Jenni, she took the photo, and she said you're welcome to it." An idea occurred to her. "She said it's called *Fallen Heroes*."

Miriam sighed. "Yes, now it all makes sense. All that intense imagery, the panther and the gecko, light and dark. Just perfect. OK, mail it across to the print guys, I'll give you the address."

The print guys tidied up the ragged edges of the original picture and turned it black and white. They printed it large on glossy paper as well as creating a digital copy and Professor Miriam Cohen gave a lecture about it to her group of Modern Art students and allowed one linguistics PhD student to sit in as well. One of the students told her father about it and he rang the university. Twenty four hours later the photographer had been paid one heck of a lot of dollars for it and the picture was hanging in a private gallery. Within two days it was being produced as a postcard and a poster and had gone viral on the internet. When the identities of the two models were eventually released by the photographer, Gecko Artists Management was swamped by requests from America for Lethe Miarren and Ygoi Roemtek to do everything from music recitals to strip shows and speculation was rife as to what the exact relationship was between those two.

Deirdre asked to take a break from her PhD and flew back to England to be with her husband before he set off as backing harpist on Lethe Miarren's UK tour and cheerfully strangled Jenni before he went. She arrived at Ravenswood House in the morning and was hurled straight into the maelstrom of the debate around the breakfast table without even being allowed to kiss her husband.

"I've been offered an indecent amount of money for the full body shot," Jenni greeted her. "What do you reckon?"

"Go for it," Deirdre recommended and finally got a lovely kiss from Ygoi as she sat next to him. "But I want to be photographer's assistant for the shoot."

"Are you sure you don't mind?" Jenni asked. "I mean these two hippies couldn't care less who sees their body parts but then they weren't brought up with all our inhibitions. But I don't think I'd be too happy if James posed naked with another bloke."

"And nor would I," James remarked. "And I have no wish to be photographer's assistant but I will help you with the hiring of equipment if it helps."

"Do you know how to take photos like that?" Deirdre asked.

"I've been on the receiving end in my young and foolish days. I bet if you ask James properly he'll tell you just how many copies of *Playboy* he kept."

Deirdre looked at James but he just smiled and quite clearly wasn't going to tell.

Deirdre appointed herself hair and make up artist for the photo session while Jenni got on with the lights in the home barn. The two models just thought the whole thing was faintly ludicrous but if it earned Jenni enough money for her husband to be able to retire, which was what the both wanted before the baby came, then the two from the other galaxy felt they owed her that much. They both meekly let Deirdre style their hair but had called her all sorts of names when she had used the wax on them a few days earlier.

"Right, come on the pair of you," Jenni instructed and had to remind herself she was just the photographer, and a married one at that, when she saw her models groomed and exfoliated to perfection. "Just get yourselves as you were before and keep your trousers on for now. We'll worry about your legs before we get you stripped off completely."

The two got settled on a hay bale and Ygoi put his arm over Lethe's shoulder so he could take the other man's weight. "Did you clean your teeth this morning?"

Lethe stuck his tongue out to show the Polo mint he was sucking. "And I've not had a fag since breakfast."

"Cut the chat," the photographer ordered. "Concentrate on what you're doing. Deirdre, come and pull some legs into position for me and stuff some straw in his mouth if he doesn't behave."

The two men fell off the hay bale twice before the photographer admitted defeat and got them on the floor instead. She got the shot she wanted, the lighting was perfect, there were enough spare hands and ankles to create shadows where she needed them and hide the fact the models were wearing rolled-up jeans to save their behinds from the rough wooden floor. The image was definitely more erotic art than pornography and the two were wedged firmly in position by a hay bale covered in black cloth rammed hard against Ygoi's back. There was just one last thing bothering her.

"Ygoi, would you take your wedding ring off, please?"

"Why?" grumbled the man who was starting to get a backache.

"Spoils the line of your hands."

Deirdre took the ring from her husband's finger and tucked it securely inside her bra. "I'll keep it warm for you."

With the last detail perfected and thankful the ring was loose enough not to have left a white band against the tanned finger, Jenni checked the image on the back of the camera. "OK, get snogging."

Deirdre sat on another hay bale and held one hand over the ring against her breast as she watched her husband kiss another man. The camera made whirring and clicking sounds several times.

"Right, stop before you start enjoying yourselves!" Jenni shouted at the models.

Ygoi turned his head and spat out a Polo mint. "How can you eat those things?"

"Would you rather I smoked?"

"Go on, piss off," was the instruction and Ygoi pushed the other man off him. "Give me a pull, I think I've got stuck."

Deirdre handed her husband his shirt. "Do you know what I'd do if I were you," she said to Jenni. "While you've got the lights and everything all set up

I'd take a whole load of photos and maybe make a calendar or something with them. Or even sell the lot at megabucks each. Have you sold the rights?"

"I get to use it to promote the UK tour and the US tour when it happens. Apart from that I've sold the rights to the original head-shot, but I still get credit as the photographer." Jenni looked at her two models, one was buttoning up a checked shirt and the other had just gone outside to light a cigarette away from the highly flammable hay. "How about it, you two? Fancy doing a calendar? Not forgetting we only have twelve months in our year."

The two looked at each other. It was a small thing to do for the woman who had done so much for them.

"Five minutes," Lethe asked. "So I can finish my fag and go and clean my teeth again."

"Just have the fag. I don't want any more snog shots."

Ygoi sat next to Deirdre on the hay bale, thankful he had his jeans between his skin and the prickly hay. "You OK?"

"Bit hot," she said and he knew what she meant.

He kissed her gently. "You're not going to blow mints into my mouth too, are you?"

"Not this time," she smiled. "Now go and sit on your own hay bale before you get all excited. That's not allowed in photographs." She stroked tender fingers over the panther on his arm and remembered how she hadn't known whether to be angry or sad when he had told her the full story of how he had come to go back on all he had said about tattoos. "It's going to be a beautiful photo."

"I'd rather it had been you."

"Me too."

"Finished," Lethe's voice announced briskly.

"Good," Jenni replied as her mind raced to think of what to do for twelve images. The problem was going to be cutting down the finished shots to a choice of twelve. She saw Ygoi get to his feet and start to unbutton the shirt. Oh, no. You get over here under the lights and give the shirt to Lethe for a few shots. I can do a lot with a shirt and a body like yours. Lethe, you bring over that T shirt you had on at breakfast and give it to Deirdre to tear some holes in it. Come on, you two, hurry up, I've only rented these lights for a day."

The two did as they were told but couldn't help wondering what had happened to the rather bored housewife with nothing to do all day.

THIRTEEN

"And is that really you?" Dan asked. "Or is it a couple of body doubles with your heads stuck on?"

"No, that's really us," Ygoi agreed.

"And you actually kissed that bloke?"

"Fucker tongued a Polo mint into my mouth while we did it."

Dan laughed, satisfied it was all a publicity stunt. But what a publicity stunt. The two stood at the front of the stage with their backs to the empty auditorium and looked at the two huge posters hanging at the back of the stage. The monochrome image of the full body shot of the two men had become quite notorious already and there it was, enlarged to fit a stage, with the words *Fallen Heroes UK Tour* emblazoned on it in gold. They were in Wembley, it was the first gig of Lethe Miarren's UK tour and the star was in another room somewhere giving a press conference and assuring an over-zealous music critic that the concept of *Fallen Heroes* was not directly inspired by Bowie's *Man Who Fell to Earth*. There was no TV crew with him any more. Lethe Miarren didn't need the prop of being the winner of *Talent Scout Superstar*. He had outgrown that tag and was booked into work for the next four years. So the TV company had dumped him and proclaimed the whole thing an outstanding success and gone on to find the second person to be the winner of the contest. But they were going to make damn sure the next one didn't get away from them as the first one had.

"You ever been to a ceilidh?" Ygoi asked Dan next.

"Not for years. I used to play the pipes a bit but earned more of a living doing this pop stuff. Have you?"

"Did one in Exeter last Thursday. Fucking brilliant. I've adapted a couple of numbers for when we do Dublin and Belfast. Can you still play the pipes?"

"Probably. I'll have to go home and get them between here and Cambridge. Instrumentals?"

"Yup. Gives Lethe a chance to show off his guitar playing. Can we get a bodhran player?"

"Get Kevin on to it. If it's got a skin stretched over it and a stick to bang it with he can play it."

Ygoi put his head on one side and studied the photo more critically. They didn't have photography where he came from but he could see the appeal of it. It had been more fun when he and Deirdre had tried out the calendar positions in the intimacy of their bed afterwards. He looked at the ring back on his finger and had a thought. "Do you think I'll be expected to snog Lethe on stage?"

"Twice nightly."

"But then everyone will thing we're a couple. Which we're not."

"Serves you right for posing for mucky photos like that. Let's get off the stage. can hear sounds of audience approaching."

Lethe waited happily off stage while watching his backing band get ready. It was the same six instrumentalists and same six singers he had had in Birmingham but this was the start of the three-week tour and he was going to spend nineteen out of twenty one evenings on stage, twenty one out of twenty one nights in bed with Caitlin Evans and there had been no more suggestions of bounty hunters from Lriam coming to get him. He watched Ygoi checking the tuning of the pale harp he had had made from his royalty money. It was an impressive piece of instrument and when the bass register got pumped through the amplifiers the sound was incredible. But Ygoi wasn't rocking the floorboards, he was chatting through his headset to Dan on the keyboards about something that was amusing the others no end. It was all a long way from a stinking Sunaran drinking house. He watched the expert fingers of the harpist ripple over the strings and remembered.

"Go!" someone hissed behind him and Lethe walked onto the stage in the glare of the lights and the roar of the audience was a narcotic to his mind. He picked up his guitar from its stand and started his chat with the audience while he checked the tuning. He could see the huge monitors at the sides of the stage, those tantalisingly erotic posters beside them and he wondered if the audience was expecting him to snog Ygoi on stage. Lethe looked at his backing band and gave Kevin his cue for the drumming. The first song belted out into the air of Wembley and was nearly drowned out by the screams of the audience.

They first played the Irish medley in Cambridge and had it perfected by the time they reached Dublin and Belfast. Ygoi had never quite got to grips with the Gaelic harp so he stuck with his orchestral harp but the pipes, bodhran and guitar had their sound levels boosted to compensate and the quartet rocked half of Ireland while the other backing musicians got carried away and danced round the stage. The second night in Belfast most of the audience got up and danced too.

From Belfast they travelled to Scotland and had their first day off of the tour. It was a cold, drizzly day in Thurso and they only had a little while there before catching the ferry to Orkney to play one night in Kirkwall. It had been an odd booking but one of the original TV production crew had an aunt living in Kirkwall who complained that they were always expected to travel to the mainland for everything so Lethe Miarren's UK tour was going to Kirkwall. The ferry journey was rough and nobody was sorry to check in to the one hotel for the night.

Ygoi was restless, which annoyed him because he was also very tired, but in the early hours of the morning he gave up hope of sleep and left Deirdre asleep in their bed. He looked at her fondly with her long hair all over the place and a smile on her lips as her closed eyes darted about in the realms of some pleasant dream or another. It was still late summer in Orkney and already the sky was a bit light as he left the hotel. The night porter was convinced he was off to listen to the dawn singing of the birds and Ygoi didn't contradict him. He walked down the main street as far as the impressive bulk of St Magnus' pink cathedral and then sat idly on the cathedral wall for a while. There was a red car parked on the other side of the street but he told himself not to get paranoid about red cars. Behind the car was a blue car, then a green one, and behind that was a white van. With a dent all along one side.

Someone sat beside him on the wall. "Saw you from the window," Lethe remarked. "Can't you sleep either?"

"No, which is kind of annoying as I'm really tired."

Lethe lit a cigarette. "What's the matter? Had a row with Deirdre?"

"There's a red car over there."

"Yup. And two more over there."

"Not the right sort, unlike that one there. And there's a white van with a dent in it. Of just the right sort."

"Oh, shit. You armed?"

"Always. Problem is there are loads of red cars and white vans. I can't go round shooting them all up just in case."

"Take a couple of tyres off each?"

"They'd only get them mended before they did anything. Don't suppose you've seen anyone in the audience? She's quite small, pointy face, dark hair all chopped off at one level. If the guy is in it with her he's probably about James' age, fat, no hair."

"You think they're following the tour?"

"Very likely. They're just more exposed here as it's such a small place. You're hard to reach at Ravenswood so I'd guess you're more vulnerable out here on the road. Want to cancel the tour?"

"No. I've never had so much fun in my life."

"I can tell."

Lethe looked at the battered van on the other side of the road. "Did you blow up that car the other night?"

"Yes."

"Did you mean to?"

Ygoi looked at the now famous, and much imitated panther on his arm. "Yes."

"So you can still handle an Assassin then?"

"Bit out of practice. I hit that car with a dose that would have taken out a small train."

"Bit hard to practise round here with everyone watching."

They looked round the deserted streets.

"Could go down to the harbour." Lethe looked behind them. "Or up into the hills. Pity we haven't got a car."

Ygoi nodded towards the blue one. "There's that one."

"That's not ours."

"We're only going to borrow it."

"Fuck me, you really did learn how to steal cars."

"Yup."

Lethe was rather envious of Ygoi's talents as he calmly broke into the car and got the engine started. Assassins, it turned out, were very good at cutting holes in car windows so doors could be unlocked. They took the blue car up into the hills and looked out across to the other islands. Lethe was still trying to work out the point of having gears in a car and just watched as Ygoi spun the Assassin in his hand and sent the bolts of power out across the landscape to land harmlessly in the sea.

"Want a go?" he asked Lethe. "You've got the registration and I'm qualified to teach you."

Lethe dubiously took the starfish and got his first lesson. Handling an Assassin was as complicated as he had feared but he turned out to have a surprisingly patient teacher and he did finally manage to knock a starling off a branch to where it sat on the ground looking a bit confused before flying off rather drunkenly.

He gave the Assassin back. "How long did it take you to get to level seven?"

"Few years. I had one of the best teachers in the galaxies."

"Who?"

"The guy I co-piloted for. He knew I was only sixteen when he took me on but he was desperate for some help. His wife had just had a baby girl and they wanted the extra money."

"Which is how you got your licence at seventeen. And qualified on the Assassin at eighteen."

Ygoi gave into temptation and blew up and old, ruined croft. "Yup. I didn't go cross-galaxy for a couple more years and we used to meet up every so often. He'd got me to level seven by the time I was twenty one but then I went cross-galaxy and we just didn't meet up again. He was at level twelve. I think he still holds the record. If he's still alive. Must be getting on a bit now. Don't know how old he would be. He was starting to lose his hair when I knew him and going rather to fat. His wife was tiny. Skinny thing with dark hair and blue eyes and rather a pointy face, but she died when the kid was about two."

Blue eyes looked into brown as they realised who he had described and Ygoi wondered how he hadn't recognised the girl. Probably because he hadn't seen her for best part of fifteen years and in another galaxy. He hadn't really got a good look at the man and realised that must have been deliberate.

"Your fucking teacher is the one out to get me? With his daughter who he has probably trained to level ninety five by now? And I've got you at fucking level seven? And we've got one fucking Assassin I bought second hand and they've got two which they've probably had custom made. Can that thing you've got go beyond level seven?"

"Let's hope we don't have to find out. Come on, I'll take you back to civilisation."

"Is there such a thing on this island?"

Ygoi didn't answer but he felt a lot less confident of being able to look after Lethe as they went back to Kirkwall and left the blue car where they had found it. Its owner was deeply puzzled when he went to it a few hours later. It was very muddy, there was a neat round hole in the driver's window and there were twenty miles he didn't remember on the clock. Apart from that, nothing about it had been touched.

Deirdre was rather worried to wake up and find herself alone in the bed. It wasn't like Ygoi to sneak off and it wasn't like her to sleep so soundly he didn't disturb her. Her phone display told her it was half past five and she sat up, pulling the duvet round her as the room was chill. To her relief, Ygoi came into the room just as she was wondering what to do next.

"What's the matter?" she asked.

So he sat on the side of the bed and told her. "Now," he concluded, "don't think I'm being all, what was it you said, chauvinistic about this but I really think you should go home to Devon."

"I'll be fucked before I do," Deirdre challenged, having no intention of going more than a few feet away from her beloved.

"Well, yes, if you like."

"No, I mean I'm not going."

"I have just explained to you it's no ordinary bounty hunter out there. It's my tutor. You might be impressed with what I can do but he's the one who taught me it all."

"No. Every student progresses on from what the teacher tells them. I know a hell of a lot more about regional accents in Britain than my professor does but I could still say she taught me everything. We just feel like that. You've learned one hell of a lot since that guy signed you off to your own ship fifteen years ago. Where is Lethe now?"

"Gone back to Caitlin."

"Is he going to tell her?"

"No, she still thinks he's a Canadian. She knows he's been threatened with abduction but that's all."

"Do you have anything other than the Assassin with you?"

"Lethe's old Tiowing. He carries it when he can but he does keep stripping his shirts off on stage."

"The Estonian dart gun," Deirdre remembered.

"That's the one."

"Could you teach me to use it?"

"Sure, it's not difficult. We should have given you the baby gun rather than Jenni, but we just didn't think they'd go for him out on tour."

"They haven't yet. Come on, we're both wide awake anyway. Let's go and shoot up some trees."

"There aren't any trees. I think someone's already shot them. Remind me after the show tonight and I'll borrow the Tiowing off him for you."

After their disturbed night, Ygoi and Deirdre were late down to breakfast and most other diners had gone. Dan was still munching his way through a kipper which smelled rather offensive to a vegetarian nose, and an elderly couple were discussing different types of gull over their boiled eggs.

"Try the porridge," Deirdre suggested to her husband. "Get your strength up."

"What's porridge?"

"Oats and milk. Or maybe just oats and water."

Ygoi soon found out he liked porridge. Deirdre knew her husband didn't mind if she ate meat in front of him so she had bacon and eggs and the two half-listened to the conversation on gulls as they were too tired to make up something of their own.

The hotel manager interrupted their silence. "I'm so sorry to disturb you but there is a gentleman at the front desk who says he is an acquaintance of yours and wonders if you could spare him a few minutes. I wouldn't normally dream of bothering you like this but he was quite insistent you would see him and told me to tell you that you had last met in the Sahara. At least I think that's what he said."

Ygoi guessed who it was but didn't understand why. "Yes, fine. I'd like to meet him again."

The manager went away and Ygoi took the Assassin out from under his jacket and put it on the table next to his bowl of porridge.

"Your teacher?" Deirdre asked and watched the fat man cross the dining room.

"May I join you?" the man asked and his voice had a definite Irish lilt to it.

"Please do."

The man helped himself to a spare chair and sat at the table. "I'm not here to harm you."

"Prove it."

A second Assassin was placed on the table and even Deirdre could see the second one made Lethe's number look like a five year old's toy. Ygoi looked at it but didn't trust himself to speak.

"Take it," the fat man offered. "Give me yours."

"What?"

"I saw Lethe Miarren throw you into the back of his transporter as though he was taking you somewhere to finish you off. I followed and saw him take you into his ship so I knew he had other plans for you. I alerted Heesha and asked her to join me just to see what happened to the pair of you. We followed you here. It was Heesha who told the Lriam authorities Lethe had gone super galaxy and got the abduction charge against him. She is my daughter, but I'll warn you now she is evil. Takes after her mother. I have tried and tried to ger her to call off this quest and go back home and leave you in peace. They've mended you here and I'd never have thought Lethe would turn into what he has. I saw him when you first hired him, remember?"

"Vividly. You told me I'd hired a child to do a man's work."

"Was I right?"

"Kind of. He's learned a lot."

The fat man smiled. "He had a good teacher."

"Not half as good as the one I had."

"True. And now I'm going to teach you again. The fat man checked Deirdre's left wrist. "Who is this?"

"My wife. She belongs in this galaxy."

"So do you now. Come on, wife, whatever your name is. I'll teach you too. Lethe will be OK for the next couple of hours."

"How do you know?"

"Because I slipped Heesha some drops in her tea this morning so she won't wake up until lunch time. Come on. Have you got a car?"

"No."

"Then we'll take her car. Here are the keys. You need to learn to ride a motorbike. Much quicker. Let's go."

The fat man scanned Ygoi's tag on the new Assassin and the weapons were exchanged. Ygoi felt rather nervous of the new starfish stuck on his ribs. He had got quite fond of the old one. The red car was still parked outside the cathedral and the fat man told Ygoi the route to take. They left the mainland and headed out on the road towards South Ronaldsay. The landscape was deserted when the fat man told Ygoi to pull off the road and gave him back his old Assassin.

"Nobody will find us here. Show me how you teach your wife to use the Assassin."

"I can't log her on it. She's not tagged."

The fat man sighed and plonked the dark starfish in Deirdre's hand. "If you pick up someone else's Assassin and the lights are on you can use it. If it is sleeping like this one, press the two blue buttons here on limb four. See?"

Deirdre did as he had told her and pressed the blue buttons. She watched as the lights on the weapon sparkled and flashed as though running through a little warm-up routine then it sat in her hand with a single amber light glowing in its centre like a malevolent eye.

Ygoi felt oddly embarrassed as he repeated for Deirdre the lesson he had given Lethe in the early hours of the morning but she was quicker to pick up the principles than the man born in the galaxy where these things were made. Deirdre couldn't believe that the starfish in her hand had just stunned a passing skua. It was a peculiar way of shooting something for a woman used to seeing pistols being shot and she wasn't sure her fingers could grip the thing for long with her hand held like that.

"Safest way," the fat man told her when she asked. "That way if you get it wrong all you will lose is your hand." He shook his right hand out of its sleeves. "As I did."

Ygoi looked at the blasted fingers and knew this man was no sort of a threat now. "What happened?"

"There is a technique to permanently disable an Assassin. I was teaching Heesha and made a mistake. Let me see you use the new model."

Deirdre watched in awe as her husband spun the starfish and sent bolts of energy of several colours crackling out from between his fingers where they shot out across the Orcadian cliffs and hissed harmlessly into the sea. Only the puffs of steam as the water boiled on impact showed where the bolts had landed.

"I'd say you've sunk to level five. And be careful. Twice you nearly lost your thumb. And then how will you play your harp?"

"With my teeth," Ygoi growled. He thought he'd done quite well with the Assassin, especially as it was a new model.

"Now you are going to sulk. One tiny word of criticism and you sulk." He caught Deirdre's smile and decided he quite liked this new wife of Ygoi. "You've had the sulk treatment too?"

"Several times."

"He'll get over it." The fat man gave Ygoi an encouraging hug and a kiss on the cheek. "Heesha can operate an Assassin at level twelve. I'm going to put you straight in at fifteen."

"There's no such level."

"There is. Now concentrate, don't argue and you will get to keep all your fingers."

Deirdre knew she would never again see anything like the pyrotechnics that spat from between Ygoi's fingers as he got his lesson. "What is the capability of that thing?" she asked at one point as red and white bolts shot out simultaneously.

"At full power it could destroy the mainland of these islands and every living thing on it."

"And the one Heesha is using?"

"Heesha has never seen this one. Hers is like this old one here which I am now going to teach you to destroy. She also has a Tiowing 6 and the trid gun to shoot the rods in you before you reach Lriam so you will be in range of the beams earlier."

"I still have wires in my head. She won't need a trid gun on me."

"You are not the prize. She has no reason to hurt you. Now, this is the last lesson I am ever going to give you, so learn it well."

"Where's your ship?" Ygoi asked as he stuck the new Assassin under his jacket and took the old one back.

"I really don't know. Somewhere in the hills. Not here. You're safe here." The fat man turned aside and coughed until he hacked up bloody mucus from his lungs. "I also shot myself in the chest when I shot my fingers," he explained. He wiped the blood from his mouth with a sleeve. "Set it at stun 2. Good. Turn it up to red 12, green 8, spin it up to at least 495. Now slap it on something hard and hold it until you see six red lights in the limb matrix 9. Use this rock. It'll hurt but don't let go or you will lose your arm, never mind your hand." He leaned against the red car. "See the lights yet?"

"No."

"Hurting?"

"Not as much as having my hands mashed up into cages. Lights showing."

"Now throw it against something solid. The car will do."

"Get out of the way then."

"I'll be OK and you're far enough away. Just throw it. Flick it sideways and keep your fingers clear."

Ygoi threw the Assassin at the car. There was a collision of metal, the Assassin sent out a display like the biggest Catherine wheel Deirdre had ever seen then car and fat man went up in a sheet of white flame and the Assassin clattered to the ground; a pretty, useless starfish.

"Bloody hell!" Deirdre exclaimed and looked round but there was nothing to see. The heat of the explosion had been so fierce there was nothing left to burn. Flesh and machinery reduced to particles so tiny they had dispersed on the wind. "Where did he go?"

Ygoi picked up the Assassin and gave it to her. "Put this in your bag. It's harmless, as he said, but not the kind of thing to leave on the roadside. And I think I can hear a bus coming." He cuddled his wife who seemed to be in an advanced state of shock. "Come on, it's what he wanted. You heard what he said. It's Heesha we've got to worry about."

The bus full of birdwatchers stopped and the driver opened the door so he could call across to them. "You two want a lift back to Kirkwall? You're miles out and the weather's closing in so we're going back anyway."

"Yes, thank you," Ygoi replied and steered the silent Deirdre up the steps into the warmth of the bus. "Didn't realise how far we'd walked and it was going to be a long hike back."

"Easily done," the driver laughed. "Couple of places down near the back for you. Won't be long. Although if we catch those skuas again we may make a quick stop if the weather lets us."

Lethe was waiting for them at the hotel reception. "Where have you two been?" he demanded, sounding quite put out.

"Out. Come up to our room and we'll tell you," was all Ygoi said before he was called over by the receptionist.

"Package for you, Mr Roemtek," she said politely. "Funnily enough it was left by the gentleman you went out with but he said not to give it to you until you got back."

"What gentleman?" Lethe asked as Ygoi took his parcel and the three went upstairs.

"Where's Caitlin?"

"Buggered off with some guy from *The Daily Telegraph*. I don't expect to see her again this trip. Unless I really do get abducted and then she'll sell the story of our nights together to whoever will pay her the most."

Deirdre was starting to get over the shock. She tucked one hand through his arm and tried to console him. "She may surprise you yet. I thought you two got on real well together."

"So did I," he said bitterly. "But I can't offer her a permanent job on an established paper."

Ygoi opened the package once the three were in the bedroom. He wasn't sure what he was expecting but it wasn't to see an Assassin in the palm of his hand. "I'd guess this is for you," he said to Deirdre and gave it to her. "As he gave you a lesson this morning. I daresay he'd have left a note but probably didn't get round to learning to write like we did."

Lethe perched on the windowsill and would have lit a cigarette but Ygoi pointed at the very prominently displayed *NO SMOKING* sign on the dressing table. "Just what is going on?"

Ygoi whisked cigarettes and matches away from the man who was about to defy hotel policy. "I met an old friend and look what he gave me."

Lethe looked. "Fuck me. What is that?"

"The latest model and I've just had a lesson at level fifteen."

"No such level."

"That's what I said. Then he tricked me into blowing him up so the war is now between you and his daughter Heesha."

"Heesha Teitger?"

"Yes. Do you know her?"

"Know her? She was my first fuck. We were two in a group who'd been eating bloodflowers on Goine. She was rubbish at it too."

"What are bloodflowers?" Deirdre asked, not sure if she liked the name.

"Something like the ones you call poppies," Ygoi explained. "Goine is a tiny planet, I was born there.

They grow all these bloodflowers for people to go and eat themselves sick on. First they make you drunk and then you start imagining you're seeing and hearing things that aren't there. That's the warning. If you carry on past that stage you start to bleed inside and then you die. That's why they're called bloodflowers."

"You mean there's one particular planet where you all go to get stoned?"

Lethe didn't think before he spoke. "It's the one planet where morals aren't policed. That's how I could get to have sex with a girl I wasn't committed to and the residents are all whores. Men and women. The women keep getting pregnant and they eat the bloodflowers to abort them."

Deirdre saw the hurt look in Ygoi's eyes and Lethe realised what he had said. "Sorry, didn't mean to imply your mother was one of them."

"I never knew her. I'd guess she didn't eat enough flowers so I got born and tagged and then when I was two days old she skinned my dick which is what all Goine mothers do to their baby boys, nobody knows why. Then she sold me to a committed couple from Dirnhet who hadn't had children of their own. There's quite a market in unwanted Goine babies as our population is falling so fast. Turns out the one who picked me is the last feudal Lord of Dirnhet," he concluded bitterly. He looked at his wife and friend and knew none of that mattered any more. "And I bet Heesha Teitger won't let you fuck her this time."

"I think you're probably right. So are you going to teach me to level fifteen on that thing then?"

"I'll take the pair of you out after the concert tonight and teach you both level five on the old one.

Which is probably all you'll be able to handle for a while."

The tour left Orkney the next day and Ygoi felt oddly homesick for a few hours as though he had left part of himself behind. There was something about those islands with their ancient stones that had touched something in what he guessed those who believed would call his soul. Except where he came from nobody believed in souls. So he wasn't quite sure what it had touched. Just something from somewhere in his mind. The group headed south to Inverness and Edinburgh and finished up one hot and sultry evening on the outskirts of Gateshead. The concert venue was an outdoor one and the musicians were all getting tired by this time. It was only the enthusiasm of the audiences that kept them going. That and knowing they were into the third week and that they would soon all be going home.

Caitlin Evans didn't go back to Lethe Miarren's bed. She let him screw her after the concerts but she did it in his dressing room and then she went off to spend the night with the new man she had met. Lethe hated himself for doing it but he was always on such a high when he came off stage he was a bit afraid he might have another go at Deirdre. And as she had the Assassin and as she had had the same lessons he had with it, he wasn't going to risk it.

The sound equipment failed during the concert at Gateshead and it was stopped part way through.

Lethe joined the backing band while the electricians tried to salvage the sound well enough for the concert to continue.

"Left my fags in my room," he told Ygoi. "Think I'll go and have one while we've got a few minutes."

"Got one to spare?" Dan asked.

"Sure. Coming for the break, Shit-face?"

"If you like."

"Why do you call him that?" Dan asked as the three men left the stage just as the electricians pulled out the wrong plug and the lights went out too.

Lethe swore as he tripped over a cable but then the emergency lights kicked in and the three found their way to the room and the cigarettes.

Yogi helped himself to a bottle of water from the fridge and went out into the corridor, leaving the other two to their cigarettes and that was where Deirdre found him.

"Hi," she greeted him and slid her arms round his waist before she kissed him.

"Hush, I'm still wired up to the rest of the group," he told her as the barracking sounded in his ear. He switched the headset off.

Deirdre pinched a swig of his water. "Be another ten minutes they reckon. A storm's hit the local sub station or something."

Lethe came to join them. "Storm's hit the what?"

"Sub station."

"Dan's just having a pee. We might as well go back and do something in the darkness. Your harp's loud enough to be heard and so are the drums and probably Dan's pipes can carry a good way so I'd guess we can do something to entertain until we get the amplifiers back. Tell you one thing, it's fucking dark in these corridors."

Ygoi had to smile. "Not when you've been shut in the dark for as long as I have. This is quite nice."

Deirdre picked herself up from the floor and realised Ygoi was just staggering to his feet beside her. "Lethe told you it was dark," she laughed and tucked a hand through his arm. "Sorry, did I knock you over too?"

Ygoi looked along the corridor. "Where is Lethe?" He switched the headset back on. "Dan?" he asked. "You got Lethe with you?"

"I'm shut in his bloody toilet. Come and get me out!"

Ygoi looked at Deirdre's watch but it had stopped. "Fuck it. Heesha's got him. Dan, Lethe's been abducted. I'm going to go and look for him." He heard a thundering noise in the earpiece and Dan popped out of Lethe's room.

"That's kicked their bloody door down. I've been hollering for five minutes and nobody heard me. Where is Lethe?"

"He was under threat of kidnap. They've just taken him. Can you call the police and alert them to a white van?"

"Sure thing. Keep your headset going. You're good for a couple of miles. There are some police here anyway for crowd control so shouldn't take a minute. Go!"

Ygoi headed for the exit and Deirdre went with him. They got out through a fire exit into the car park where pools of overhead light stabbed the encroaching darkness.

"Which way?" Deirdre asked as the two scanned the cars hoping against hope to see a white van.

Ygoi's eyes were better in the dark and he saw a ghostly shape flitting towards the way out. "There. Lethe must have put up a fight if they've only got that far." He chose a black Honda and broke into it. "Come on, they'll be heading for the hills. Where the fuck are the hills?"

Deirdre had done her Northumberland dialect only recently. "Rothbury." She took the Assassin from her bag and cut the chain which tied a BMW motorbike to a railing. The rider had secured his helmet the same way and Deirdre calmly helped herself. "Hotwire me, please," she asked,

"I didn't know…" Ygoi began as he worked out the principles of bike engines and the BMW roared into life.

Deirdre kissed him hard and pulled on the helmet. "There's a lot you don't know. See you in Rothbury. Follow me."

The two stolen vehicles went out of the car park just as the police cars came in. The engineers tracked down the cause of the power failure. It wasn't a storm in the sub station. Someone, they didn't know how, had cut the cables.

FOURTEEN

Lethe wanted to giggle when Deirdre tripped over in the dim corridor and pulled Ygoi down with her but the smile died on his face when a forgotten voice spoke behind him.

"I've just hit your friends with my weapon set on stun. If you don't turn round and walk with me I'll up the strength to fatal."

Lethe turned and looked into the cold blue eyes of the first woman he had ever had sex with. "Heesha," he remembered and decided to try the diplomatic approach. "Been a long time since Goine."

She spun the Assassin in her hand and sent a bolt of energy through his shoulder. "Walk."

The shot hadn't done much more than sting, but Lethe wasn't going to risk a stronger blast. He delayed further by lighting a cigarette and ambling slowly. He looked back at Ygoi and Deirdre lying in a heap. "Are you sure you haven't killed them?"

"Yes. I do know how to handle this weapon."

"I just want to make sure."

"Get moving."

"Or what? You'll shoot me dead? You only get the reward for living capture."

"Or I'll shoot you in the place it hurts most. They're not dead. I've got no reason to kill them. It's only you I want. Now, go." She pushed Lethe hard in the back.

Guessing his first woman wasn't going to be much of a conversationalist, Lethe obediently walked in front of her along the gloomy corridors in the weak spots of light from the emergency lighting.

"I'm due back on stage as soon as they've fixed the electrics."

"They won't fix them that quickly. I've cut the cables. In fact I'd say you've given your last concert."

"Were you enjoying the tour?"

She slapped him hard on the head. "Walk. And just shut up."

The slap had hurt and Lethe wanted nothing more than to beat the smirk off her face and then turn her own Assassin on her. What was the use in him being trained to level five if Deirdre had got the thing in her bag? They went out into the car park and the hot summer air struck the bare arms of the man who had gone on stage in a sleeveless T shirt. It wasn't quite dark but the lights were on in the car park. He wished there would be someone there doing nefarious things to motor vehicles, or even a security patrol, but the car park was deserted. His captor poked him in the back with the Assassin and shoved him towards the white van he had seen before. She opened the rear doors.

"In."

He wasn't going to get in that thing that stank of some animal or another but a bolt of energy in the back of his left leg changed that. He lost all sensation in the leg below the knee and half fell into the back of the van. Heesha grabbed his legs, tipped him unceremoniously in and blasted him with enough power to knock him unconscious. She locked the back of the van and then scrambled into the driver's seat before heading out of the car park.

Lethe woke up to find the stink of animal was making his eyes and his nose run but he had nothing to wipe up the snot with except his T shirt, so he used that. He sat up groggily and then got knocked down again as the van hurtled round a roundabout. He sat up more cautiously this time and sneezed. There was a wire mesh between him and the driver's area so he could see that they were driving through a fairly large town. It was stiflingly hot in the back of the van as though it had been sitting in the sun all day and he ran a hand through his hair to get it off his face. He looked round his surroundings and checked the back door just in case he could have thrown himself out onto the road. He knew he couldn't do that without injury but would far rather have risked broken legs than being shut in a van with Heesha and her Assassin. Level twelve. He hadn't even known level twelve existed. He crawled up to the wire mesh and looked out through the windscreen.

"Where are you going?"

"Shut up or I'll hit you with another shot."

Lethe sat on his legs and just watched the streets of the town. He had to hang on to the mesh when Heesha swung the van round a few more roundabouts and then saw a sign for the A696 to Otterburn and Rothbury. He thought of the landscape he had seen from the tour bus as they had driven there that morning. Hilly, beautiful and almost as desolate as the Orkneys. She could take him out into those hills and nobody would find them. Lethe wiped his nose again.

"Can you open a window? It stinks in here."

Heesha fired the Assassin over her shoulder and Lethe hit the floor again.

Next time he looked out of the mesh they were out of the town and he tried to remember what he had been thinking of. Heesha's last bolt had slugged him in the stomach and he didn't feel too good. He crawled away from the wire partition and was sick at the back of the van. Now it stank of animal and vomit. He went back to the wire, mostly to get away from the stink and thudded back against the side of the van. He closed his eyes as the waves of nausea kept coming and going. The sweat was sticking his hair to his neck and running down his back. There was no air coming into the van and he started to get a headache.

"Open the window, please," he pleaded with his captor.

She pulled the van off the road into a lay-by and Lethe could see the Otterburn road was still quite busy. "Put the side of your head against the wire," was all she said.

Lethe thought that was a funny way to get some air into his lungs but he shuffled a little closer,

"Nearer than that." Heesha's fingers got through the wire, locked into Lethe's hair and the left side of his head crashed into the partition.

Out of the corner of his eye he saw her take something out of the glove box then he literally screamed with pain as she shot two rods of white hot trid through his ear.

"The next one goes in your eye," she promised him. "Now, just shut up. It's not far to go now and we'll soon have you locked up on Lriam."

Lethe sat in the middle of the van with one hand over his ear. The rods were too hot to touch and the pain stung tears to his eyes. He looked at the back of his captor as she swung the van back onto the road and wished he could kill her. Was that how Ygoi had felt when they had shot the bolts through him, Lethe wondered. A calm, murderous desire for revenge? A motorbike swerved in front and Heesha gave the rider a blast on the horn. The motorbike went on ahead and Lethe saw the long blonde tail of hair hanging down from underneath the helmet. Funny, Deirdre had had her hair in a plait just like that last time he had seen her. He wondered if she had woken up yet.

Ygoi drove the Honda out of the car park and wondered how Deirdre knew her way round Gateshead. Then he remembered she had studied the Northumberland dialect just before she had gone to Devon. There was that folk song she had taught them, *The Hills of Rothbury*, that some old guy had sung to her. Funny sort of a tune. He kept his eyes on the motorbike ahead and was full of admiration for his wife. They didn't breed them this feisty in the Millio galaxy. This was a woman who operated as his equal not as some child-rearing educator patiently waiting for a husband to earn them a decent living. He couldn't imagine Deirdre with children somehow. He braked beside her at a red light and saw she was saying something to him.

He opened the window. "What?"

"We're heading out on the Rothbury road. Follow the signs for Otterburn if you lose me. We'll have to hang a right somewhere to get up into the hills. I haven't got the tyres to go off road and the van won't be able to either. If you get the chance get off the road and take short cuts, that thing will take you anywhere. You'll see the hills fairly soon after we clear Newcastle."

The lights went green, Deirdre let in the clutch and was gone.

They were just negotiating some roundabouts when Dan's voice sounded in Ygoi's headset and made him jump. He had forgotten all about it.

"Hi, Ygoi, you still in range? Where are you?"

"Just going round some roundabouts in Newcastle."

"How did you get there?"

"Stole a car and a motorbike. Call the police off us, will you? We're going to bring them back."

A different voice boomed in his ear. One who didn't realise you only needed to speak quite softly into the microphones. "Ygoi? This is Mike Duncan of the Northumberland police. Identify your vehicles, please."

"BMW motorbike and a black Honda four-wheel drive. We're heading out on the Otterburn road."

There was a pause. "OK, we've had two people reporting those vehicles stolen from the car park. I'll warn uniform not to pursue. You're on a very short waveband and you're about to go out of range. What I want you to do is retune your headset until you hear your song *Fallen Heroes* then identify yourself with the title of the top CD in the rack in front of you. I have the information from the owner and it will verify your identity."

Ygoi took the Assassin out from against his ribs and stuck it on the dashboard so he didn't accidentally knock it off with his elbow as he fiddled to adjust the dial on the control box behind his back. He got all sorts of hisses and crackles before he heard some familiar harp music. He just managed to avoid running down a cyclist and the man's foul language was loud enough to be heard through the closed windows. Ygoi took the top CD off the rack and had to admire the irony.

"Hullo," he said uncertainly into the microphone.

"Is what you're looking for *Tranquil Moods*?"

The harp music stopped. "It is," came Mike Duncan's voice. "Well done. Now tell me what you can about this kidnapper?"

Ygoi knew the absolute truth couldn't be told, even if it was necessary. "The woman's name is Heesha Teitger. She's a bit of a nut case who's had a thing about Lethe since they were teenagers. She's only using the van as a temporary measure and she's got a faster vehicle hidden somewhere. We think it's in the Rothbury hills."

"Damn," muttered the man who didn't realise how sensitive the microphones were. "Could be anywhere." He raised his voice a little. "Is she armed?"

"Yes."

"OK, I'll mobilise uniform and firearms and we'll get some roadblocks set up but it's a pretty wild area up there. Have you got any idea what this faster vehicle might be like?"

"Absolutely no idea," was the truthful reply. Probably metallic, looking a bit blue in the dusk as its sides would be an alloy of trid. He would guess about the size of a single decker bus but could be any shape really. Although current fashions in Sunara favoured low and sleek lines rather than the square chunky shape of his old ship. He wished he could have had that again. He could have found and destroyed that bus of Heesha's in five minutes flat. The Honda started complaining and Ygoi guiltily put it into fifth gear as Deirdre opened the throttle on her bike and roared off into the gloom.

"We're clear of Newcastle now," he reported to the policeman. "Just hit the…" he caught sight of a road sign, "A696. I think my wife is about to break your speed limits." The speedometer of the Honda started nudging the hundred. "Yup, well over the speed limits. Fuck me, how fast does that bike go? I'm on a hundred and ten and can't catch her."

There was another pause. "About a hundred and eighty five I've just been told by its owner. The owner of your car says he doesn't know, he's not been above forty in it."

Ygoi had this image of a calm policeman talking into a microphone while the owners of the stolen vehicles fretted in the background. Vaguely he realised they must have closed the concert down as soon as they knew Lethe had been abducted and got people to claim their cars somehow to flush out any possible stolen ones. He came up fast behind a caravan doing fifty and had to stamp on the brakes. The motorbike was way ahead now and he was stuck behind this caravan. Cursing fluently, he changed the Honda down into as low a gear as he dared and rocketed past the caravan with the engine howling, just dodging back in time and getting flashed at by the infuriated driver coming the other way. He raced back through the gears and hurled the suffering car round a bend. The back wheels felt as though they were scrabbling on the road a bit but he could see the motorbike ahead.

"I can see the bike again now," he reported to the policeman.

"Traffic have just had reports of the pair of you, they're leaving Newcastle now and will try to catch you up. When they get to you, pull over and let them take over the chase. It's their job, not yours. We've scrambled the helicopter to look for the white van too and you should get a visual on it any minute."

Before he saw the helicopter, Ygoi saw the hills of Rothbury. Deirdre had gone on ahead again, able to dodge past the cars on her more nimble bike. He drew up behind a chain of vehicles toiling behind a late-running tractor and wished he had learned to ride a motorbike. The slow speed gave him a chance to look round and he saw something odd up on one of the hills. Something slightly blue in the encroaching dusk. Something only eyes tortured in the dark could have seen at those low light levels.

"Stuck behind a tractor," he told the policeman. "I'm taking short cuts. Apologise to the farmers for me." He swung the Honda off the road much to the surprise of the other motorists in the queue, and set off across the fields towards the hills.

The policeman sounded slightly amused. "The owner says can you be careful, please. It's only ever gone between his house and the shops before. Keep your headset going, the helicopter will pick you up soon."

The Honda crossed a ditch with a bit of a lurch and a crunch and started scrambling up the foothills. "Tell him I'll buy it off him if I don't wreck it." Ygoi kept his eyes on the distant objective and those stuck on the A696 watched the black car disappear into the twilight and wondered why the idiot didn't put his lights on.

Lethe watched as the motorcycle began to slow down in front of the van then realised at the last second the driver of the white van didn't care if she hit some lunatic on a motorbike in front of her.

Deirdre had been expecting the white van to swerve to avoid her but saw it thundering up behind her in her mirrors and opened the bike's throttle again to get out of the way. She wished she had the weight of the Honda Ygoi was driving and wondered for a second if he had managed to get past the tractor yet. She couldn't push the van off the road, she couldn't set herself up as a target to be avoided and she didn't want to set herself up as a target to be hit. The bike, on the other hand, was certainly insured and could be quite a useful road block. The road they were on now was climbing into the hills and was very narrow. She pushed the bike on a bit faster and instinctively braked as the road unexpectedly turned sharp right.

Lethe felt as though he was holding his breath as he looked at the tail light of the motorbike in front. Who else would be out on this deserted country road at that hour of night? They must have driven with their tails on fire to catch up. And where the fuck was Ygoi? Perhaps the shot of energy had been too much for a man with wires of trid in his brain and he was dead on the floor in the back corridor of that theatre.

Heesha was calling the motorcyclist all sorts of names as the motorbike slowed and speeded up again. The white van followed the bike up the road into the hills and then the road switched viciously right. There came a crunching, banging sound and the van lurched off the road and tumbled down into a water-filled ditch at the side of the road.

Lethe was thrown all round the inside of the van and was totally disorientated when the doors were opened and Heesha hauled him out.

"We've hit the motorbike. We'll have to walk."

Lethe pulled his arm free. "Where's the rider?"

"Over there."

Lethe staggered giddily over to the body lying in the road and recognised the voice that was swearing more profanely than any woman he had ever heard before.

"Deirdre? Where does it hurt?"

"My fucking legs," she lamented. "I felt the bike start to go and tried to get off. Landed on my arse and now I can't get up. Can you take the helmet off, please? It's OK. I know my neck's not hurt."

Lethe knelt beside her in the road and helped her to take the crash helmet off. "I can't leave you in the middle of the road," he told her. "Can I move you?"

"No. My cell phone's in my bag. Ring for the ambulance. Christ it hurts. How the hell Ygoi ever put up with pain like this I'll never know."

"Where is he?"

"Out there somewhere in a black four wheel drive. I'd guess he's gone cross-country as the road was clogged with a tractor."

Lethe went over to the motorbike, cheered to think Ygoi was charging around the countryside somewhere looking for them. He crouched down beside the wrecked bike and found the bag. It was in the middle of a tangle of exhaust system and the phone was smashed to pieces.

Heesha pushed him roughly in the back. "Get back in the van," she told him.

"The fuck I will. It's half full of water."

She shot another energy bolt into his guts. "Do as you're told. Who is that woman?!

Lethe threw up at the roadside. "Ygoi's wife. You can shoot me as much as you like. If you stun me you can't carry me as I'm too heavy. If you kill me you won't get any money. And if you kill her then I'm sticking with her until Ygoi finds us so the same applies."

"Look at her legs. She's going to die anyway. I'll just finish her off for you. And I've told you which bits I'll shoot if I have to. What's that in your hand. You picked something up."

"No I didn't." Lethe just managed to throw the metal starfish towards Deirdre before Heesha's booted foot crushed down on his hand. He grabbed her leg with his other hand and felled her onto the ruins of the motorbike. Just too late he realised that was a foolish thing to do to a woman who had a primed Assassin in her hand.

The valiant black Honda climbed up the hillside until even its four wheel drive couldn't cope with the contours. Ygoi could still just about see the spaceship near the top of another hill in the distance. To those not expecting to see it, it was like a rather large caravan of an odd shape. But he knew what spaceships from the Millio galaxy looked like and, to the trained eye, they didn't look anything like caravans. The low light cheated his sense of distance but he guessed he couldn't get to that spaceship across country any faster than the white van would get there on the road. He climbed up on the roof of the car to get a better view. That was definitely a spaceship and the noise he could hear in the distance was the police helicopter. And it probably wouldn't be a good idea for the crew of a police helicopter to catch sight of a spaceship. He got back into the car and primed the Assassin before getting back on the roof.

The helicopter pilot and his companion were desperately scanning the countryside below and wishing they had heat-seeking equipment on board. "Let's get this straight," the pilot remarked. "We are looking for a dark haired man, wearing black clothes, driving a black car up an unlit hill in the dark. And we're not allowed to turn our lights on until we see him in case we scare away the main man who at least has the sense to be driving a white van?"

"That's about it."

"Needle in a bloody haystack. Keep looking."

"Something over there. Looks a bit like fireworks."

"Sod me, I think you're right." The pilot banked the helicopter towards the tiny flickers of light on the hillside.

Ygoi heard the helicopter getting closer and knew he had to make a decision. Should he just blow up the spaceship and hope Lethe wasn't on it, or fire enough stun power into it to knock out any life forms then try to get over there before the police did. He did some calculations in his head and was almost certain there was no way the van could have got that far so quickly. They would have to walk the last bit anyway. He spun the Assassin one last time and held out his hand. Blue and green crackled out from between his fingers, there was a split second of delay then the roar of the explosion on the next hillside.

The helicopter pilot brought his aircraft to a steady hover. There had been a sudden, blinding shaft of white light shooting up from the ground about a mile straight in front of them. Then it was all gone. There was no fire, no heat. Just darkness again. But the darkness seemed all the darker after that column of light.

"What the bloody hell was that/" he asked.

"Don't know. But I think we should get the fuck out of here."

"Think you're right."

Ygoi got back into the car and heard the helicopter going away again. He stuck the Assassin on the dashboard. "Well," he reported to the policeman, "they won't be taking the fast getaway vehicle now."

"We've had a report from the helicopter crew of what seemed to be an explosion on the hillside."

"That was it."

"How?"

"Petrol bombed it," Ygoi improvised desperately. "I'm now going to look for the van."

"OK. We've just had a message from the pilot to say there's no point in him continuing the search and they've requested another crew to go out with heat-seeking equipment. We'll soon find them. We've got uniform out looking as well but you're on your own until they meet up with you. We'll discuss any criminal charges against you when all this is over."

Ygoi turned the Honda and headed off towards a road he had seen on the way up. It was dark now but his tortured eyes hardly noticed as he steered the black car across the hillside.

Lethe had never known a headache like it. His right eye hurt, his nose felt as though someone had lit a fire in it and half his bottom teeth seemed to be loose in his jaw. He just managed to raise his head and realised he had been cushioned on Deirdre's chest.

"Sorry," he said thickly and a tooth fell out.

She put a steadying hand on his head. "Keep still for a bit. Heesha's gone off. I think she's going to try and find another car."

"My head."

"Hush. Try not to think about it."

"What did she do?"

"She hit the side of your face with the Assassin. It's all right, she hasn't spoiled your looks. I think she missed her aim a bit."

Lethe had another go at getting his head off Deirdre and looked around. "It's dark."

"Very nearly," she agreed. "But the moon will be up soon."

"What moon?" he turned his head. "Oh, that moon." He put one hand over his left eye and realised what had happened. "Has she shot my eye out?"

"No, honestly. You look absolutely fine. Not even a bruise."

"I don't care what the fuck I look like. I can't see anything out of one eye."

"Maybe it'll wear off."

"Maybe." Lethe lurched to his knees. "How are you feeling?"

"Doesn't seem to hurt so much but I'm getting a bit cold."

Lethe wished he wore more clothes on stage. "I've got nothing to give you. Hang on, I think there was a blanket or something in the front of the van." He stood up and fell down again. "This is like being drunk," he declared and suddenly wanted to laugh from sheer hysteria. Everything about him hurt, he was blind in one eye and now it seemed he couldn't walk. He looked down at his feet. Apart from the fact he had no shoes he couldn't see any reason why he shouldn't be able to walk. He tried again. Something tugged at his left ankle and he staggered but didn't fall. "She's tied me to the fucking motorbike. Can you reach the Assassin?"

Deirdre handed it across and watched as Lethe failed to prime it.

"She's also stamped on my hand. Can you do it? Looks like she's used some sort of wire."

Deirdre got herself on her elbows and yelped at the pain in her hips. "Oh, God. This isn't good."

Lethe managed to hold her in his arms and she literally ground her teeth and forced herself to remember her lessons. The Assassin sent out a weak blue light and Lethe was free. Deirdre thudded down onto her back again and Lethe hobbled over to the ruined van. He managed to tug the door open with his left hand and found some old hessian sacks on top of a dog blanket on the passenger seat. It wasn't much but it was better than nothing and at least they weren't wet.

"Best I could do," he told her as he carefully covered her with the smelly sacks and the blanket.

"They're fine. Really. Be on all the catwalks next season," she told him and shivered. She closed her eyes. She was really getting very tired and cold and it would be good to sleep for a while. She felt Lethe cradle her gently and his body was warm and comforting against her.

Suddenly the night sky flared with a column of white light that seared into the darkness for a second or two, then it was gone and Deirdre was roused from her stupor.

"What was that?"

"If we are very, very lucky the only means of getting me to Lriam is now parked in Jenni's garden in Devon and that was your husband blowing up Heesha's spaceship with his Assassin." Something smacked him on the back of the head and he reeled.

"Who has got an Assassin?"

"Ygoi has. Your father gave it to him. Where's the new car then?"

"There's nothing round here. Let's go. Leave her there. She'll be dead soon."

"I'm not leaving her. Your spaceship has just been blown up so now what the fuck are you going to go with us?"

Heesha hit him on the side of the head and he was now convinced his top teeth were loose too. "I'm going to wait for the next car to come here then I'm going to take it and we're going to go all the way to Devon to get yours."

"You'll never do it. Half the police forces in England will be looking for us."

Heesha looked at the stubborn man in front of her. She knew she couldn't win in a physical brawl and she couldn't drag him if she stunned him. And she had a feeling he would rather lose his own life than leave this woman to die. "Bring her with us then."

"You can't move her." Lethe had to keep turning his head to see where Heesha was and he was now getting a neck ache.

"So I can't move her, you won't leave her, so we can wait until she dies. It won't be long. I'm sure your husband will find us eventually and then I'll have his car."

Lethe let the implication of three-way commitment go. He looked down at the woman in his arms and realised she had gone limp and cold. "Oh, fuck it. Deirdre, wake up! Don't you dare die on me until your hero gets here to rescue you."

She mumbled something and reluctantly opened her eyes. "Oh, God, thought I was dreaming. Why don't my legs hurt any more?"

"I expect you're just a bit cold. Come on, cuddle up to me and I'll keep you warm."

Heesha got bored. She stuck the Assassin on her waistband and got the trid gun out of her pocket. "May as well start to get you ready for Lriam," she told Lethe. "You'll be there soon enough." She grabbed his hair with one hand, jerked his head back and shot a bolt through his nose. She got some satisfaction in hearing him swear but he didn't dare let go of the woman he held in case he hurt her or she got fatally cold without his body warmth. This, Heesha decided, was fun. She tightened her grip in the blond curls and pierced a neat row of six bolts through the edge of his right ear from top to lobe. That made him scream right enough. She put the trid gun back in her pocket.

"Stop it," came Deirdre's protests. "Stop hurting him like that, you fucking bitch!"

"Or what?" Heesha laughed and pointed her Assassin at the woman on the ground. "I was the first one this wanker ever had sex with and he was useless at it. Came and went in two seconds flat. Makes sense now I know he's not one for women. I'm disappointed in Ygoi though. Never had him down for, what do they call them here..?"

Deirdre didn't want to hear whatever it was Heesha was going to say. She reached out with a strength she didn't know she had, snatched the weapon out of Heesha's hand and remembered something she had once heard. Lethe had no idea what she was doing but he pulled his throbbing head free of Heesha's grasp and leaned over Deirdre as best he could while she worked on the Assassin and blocked Heesha's attempts to get at it.

"Six red lights, limb matrix nine," she muttered through clenched teeth and slapped the Assassin on the road. "Fuck it, it hurts. How the hell did he put up with this?" Suddenly six red lights glowed between her fingers and she hurled the Assassin at a stone wall just before Heesha's frustrated hand scrabbled at the ground where it had been. The Catherine wheel of lights sparkled and the useless Assassin fizzed at the roadside.

"What have you done?!" Heesha cried and dashed across to look. "You've disabled it," she exclaimed in disbelief. She spun the useless weapon in her hand. "How did you do that? You're not even from our galaxy."

Deirdre was starting to feel a bit better. "Your father was a good teacher."

"What did you do with him?"

"Nothing. He's gone where nothing can hurt him now."

"He hurt himself, the stupid fool." Heesha spitefully shot another bolt of trid through Lethe's nose.

It was odd, Lethe thought, how when you were in so much pain anyway, another little bit just didn't matter. And when you could see with only one eye, you could hear a lot better. "Car coming," he announced to cheer Deirdre as much as anything.

Heesha looked round. "Can't see anything."

"Listen, it's coming down off the hillside."

The hills were almost pitch black apart from a dim light from the moon but the contours of the land hid the car that was making the sound. They could all hear it now and it sounded quite close but there was no sign of it. It was as though a dark spirit was coming at them from the shadows.

Ygoi drove the valiant Honda down the hillside away from the explosion and even he thought it was getting a bit dark now. The problem with those Assassins was they blew everything up so hot there was no fire afterwards to give any light. He headed back towards the by-road he had noticed and which seemed to be going in approximately the direction of the spaceship. The moon was in and out from the clouds but he didn't notice the dark any more as he concentrated on negotiating the rough terrain. The Honda slid down a particularly steep bit of hillside and it was as he straightened the wheels out again he saw the white van in the moonlight. The odd thing was it looked to be tilted over and it definitely wasn't going anywhere. Realising Heesha would probably have stopped driving when the spaceship blew up, he turned the car in the right direction and set off again, wondering what he would find.

He didn't see the figures in the road until he turned the headlights on full beam and saw his battered and broken wife lying in the arms of a man whose blond head was bowed over hers to protect their eyes from the light. There was no sign of Heesha which he didn't like.

Deirdre clutched Lethe's arm. "Who is it?" she muttered.

"Haven't got a clue." He raised his voice. "Oi! Turn your fucking lights off," he bellowed at the car.

The lights dimmed to sidelights and Lethe raised his face to see the welcome Honda logo between the lights. "It's OK," he told Deirdre. "It's your very own fallen hero come to rescue you."

"Where's Heesha?" Ygoi called from the car. He turned his headset off in case they had to talk about things other people shouldn't hear.

She stood up beside the wall. "Just here," she announced and held up a Tiowing. "Get out of the car and keep your hands where I can see them."

"I'm turning the engine off," he told her calmly. "The car's been hotwired, this could take a moment."

He ducked down as though to fiddle with the wires under the steering column and swiped the Assassin off the dashboard as he did so. One human target, range about four feet, two others and a tank of highly combustible fuel at a frighteningly close proximity. He couldn't hope to send out enough energy to kill her without risking overheating the petrol in the tank.

A white light crackled from the Assassin and Heesha dropped to the ground.

Ygoi got out of the car. "Quick, I've only set it on stun. Let's get you out of here then I'll deal with her when the petrol tank is out of range."

"Got any blankets?" Lethe asked.

Ygoi looked on the back seat of the car and found a beautifully soft and warm wool blanket. "This do?"

"Have to. We need to get this one wrapped up."

Ygoi remembered something. He turned his headset on. "Found them. Deirdre's not good. I'm sending up a flare for you to find." He spun the Assassin once more and a bolt of red shot into the sky.

"You've been eyeballed," Mike Duncan's thankful voice sounded in his ear. "You've been out of contact, thought we'd lost you. Confirm you need an ambulance?"

"Confirmed."

"We'll mobilise the air ambulance. If you're where we think you are the road vehicle will take too long. They'll have lights on so they'll find you."

"OK." Ygoi turned the headset off again. He had to say things he didn't want others to hear. Mike Duncan's chat of criminal charges was still bothering him slightly and so far all he had done was steal a car. "Can you drive?" he asked Lethe.

"So long as I don't have to change gear."

"What the fuck has she done to your face?"

"Done some target practice in it."

The two men got Deirdre carefully covered by the blanket and she thankfully kissed her husband. "He wouldn't leave me," she told him.

"He always was a stubborn bastard. Take the car and just drive it a few yards away so I can finish off Heesha. Why do you keep turning your head sideways?"

"She shot me in the eye. I can't see anything out of it."

Ygoi handed Lethe the Assassin. "In that case, I guess you'd like to do the honours, as they say here. I'll back the car up."

Lethe knew his hand was probably broken but to kill Heesha he would shoot her left-handed. He was glad Ygoi understood his need for revenge. "Move the car first. I don't want to lie Deirdre down as she kind of gurgles a bit if I do."

"Perhaps we should go for the three-way commitment after all," Ygoi remarked as he got up from kneeling beside his wife.

"Piss off, Shit-face," said wife and friend together.

Ygoi backed the car a safe distance away from any chance heat coming off the Assassin. He hadn't seen Lethe's damaged hand and knew he had taught Lethe to level five which was more than high enough to finish off one not very big woman. He could hear sirens in the distance and the throb of helicopter rotors so he turned the headlights on again and went back to his wife.

Deirdre sighed and settled herself as best she could in her husband's arms as the two men so gently changed care of her. "It doesn't hurt as much any more," she tried to reassure him. "I'm going to be just fine."

"Course you are," he responded automatically and kept reminding himself of the medical miracles that could be performed on this planet. "And David will have Lethe's head in a bucket of Coca Cola by tomorrow so he'll be fine too."

Lethe walked up to Heesha with the Assassin primed and he just looked at her as she lay half propped up on the wall. He would never have believed he could feel such hatred towards a human being. All she had wanted to do was hurt him any way she could. From that cutting remark about his first sexual performance to shooting the sight out of his right eye. He lifted his aching head and spun the Assassin left-handed.

Heesha stirred a bit and saw what was going to happen. She raised the Tiowing and pointed it at the man standing near enough to kill her with one bolt from the weapon she could just see in his left hand. She didn't understand how he could possibly have got an Assassin. It had never occurred to her that he was left-handed and she wished she had stamped on both of his hands now.

"Armed police!" a voice shouted so close they both jumped. "Put the gun down, Miss, and you won't get hurt."

Heesha struggled to her feet. "Back off!" she shouted. "This one's mine." She raised the Tiowing and the policeman got the nod from his senior officer and shouted a second warning but he was ignored. The policeman knew now he had no choice. It was the bullet from a gun from another galaxy that ended the career of the bounty hunter from Sunara. The Tiowing dropped from her hand and burst into a tiny ball of white flame then dissolved into nothing.

Lethe pocketed the Assassin now he had got rid of the Tiowing and looked at the woman on the ground. Another policeman came to stand next to him, gun still held ready in case she showed any signs of coming back to life. A third man checked the body on the ground.

"It's all right," he consoled. "She's gone."

FIFTEEN

Lethe had never been in a hospital before and it was all the more scary as he could only see out of one eye but nobody knew this and they kept coming up on his blind side. They had put him in the air ambulance with Deirdre and told Ygoi to follow behind in his car and the sorry cavalcade had arrived at a huge hospital somewhere back in Newcastle and there had been the press waiting for them.

One of the first people Lethe saw in the crowd was Caitlin as she was on his sighted side and she pushed her way through to him.

"How are you?" she asked as though she hadn't been dumping him every night. She reached up as though she would kiss his cheek but a paramedic got in the way.

"Not now, Miss," he told her rather rudely. "Let's get these through to A and E."

Lethe had heard about the Casualty departments of hospitals and this one was certainly frightening enough. They wheeled Deirdre off into a side room but she hadn't said anything since the man in the air ambulance had injected a load of stuff into her arm.

A lady doctor with dark skin and hair took Lethe gently by the elbow and steered him into a curtained cubicle with a bed in it. She parked him on the side of the bed.

"Right then, let's get you cleaned up," she said. "I don't think I've ever had such a famous face to work on before. Why do you keep turning your head?"

"I can't see anything out of my right eye." Lethe held out a tooth in his hand. "Lost this as well. And please don't try to take the rods out."

The doctor shone a light in his eye and that really hurt. "Sorry, looks like massive retina damage. What happened."

"She shone a light in it," he snapped and put his hand over his eye. "Go away. Can I go and see Deirdre?"

"No. They'll be checking her over now and getting her stable then she'll go into theatre as soon as we've called the surgeon in."

Lethe vaguely remembered watching a hospital drama on the TV once and they had talked about theatres then.

The curtain flapped and Ygoi came in. "How are you? They won't let me near Deirdre so I've come to check on you instead."

"Wait outside," the doctor told him curtly.

"Don't you tell him to bugger off. This is the guy who drove all round the hillsides in a stolen car to find us. We'd still be out there if it wasn't for him."

"Lethe," the doctor explained kindly. "You have some very serious facial injuries here and we need to get you treated. Now, your friend here is perfectly welcome to wait for you in the reception area but we really do need to get these metal spikes out of your face first. Then we can get the eye specialist in to look at you."

Lethe got off the bed and got her in his line of vision. "No. You don't know how to get the rods out. They've been burned in. I'm walking out of here and you can't stop me."

The doctor started to protest but Ygoi interrupted her. "You won't be able to reason with him, he's way too stubborn for that. Let me borrow him for a few minutes, I'll go and get him a cup of tea or something and talk some sense into him then you can have him back." He got on Lethe's sighted side and took his arm. "Come on, I may even treat you to a doughnut."

"Not with those teeth you don't," the doctor commanded. "I'll give you ten minutes and don't take him out of the hospital."

"I won't."

They met Caitlin in the corridor. "Half a million each for the exclusive rights to your kidnap stories. And I do mean exclusive."

"Not for sale," Ygoi replied. "Do you know where we can get a drink round here?"

"Vending machine at the end of the corridor or café near the way in. Should he be walking around like that?"

"I'm trying to talk some sense into him."

"Can I help?"

"No. Thank you."

"Want me to sell the story of your nights of gay passion instead? Or how about our threesomes? You know I'll be believed after that poster you two did. Go on, exclusive rights or you two get branded a couple."

"And nobody will care," Ygoi told her. "Get out of our lives, Caitlin."

She watched them go then took her mobile out and keyed in the number for one of the less reputable red-tops.

Ygoi bought some cans of Coke from the vending machine, stole a bowl from a passing trolley then he and Lethe went out into the car park where a very muddy and unlocked Honda was parked. The trid rods were still newly punched through and they only needed to be dissolved a little before Ygoi could pull them out.

"You OK to go back for some more conventional treatment now?"

"Sure. Thanks." Lethe mopped his bloody nose and ears on his filthy T shirt. "You'd better get back to Deirdre."

"She's going into theatre. I'm not allowed near her until all that's over." Ygoi saw a prowler in the car park. "That fucking Caitlin is following us."

"She wants a story to sell. Poor cow. Why she can't get a proper job I don't know. Great fuck though. Come here, I owe her half a one for all the good times she's given me." He leaned over the bowl between them and gave the unprepared Ygoi a long-enough kiss on the lips.

Caitlin took her photo and smiled to herself. That should keep her living comfortably for a few months.

Ygoi scrambled out of the car. "Back to Casualty. Now. I'll stick with you until they find me to tell me how Deirdre's getting on."

So Lethe Miarren went back to A and E and was treated. They strapped up his hand and told him three of the little bones in his hand were broken, but it had clearly been stamped on and the bones would mend. They examined his eye and said they had never seen damage like it and there was nothing they could do but it might get better on its own or it might not. A dentist said he'd never seen damage like it but he mended and patched up as best he could and put back the tooth that had fallen out then wired the others and said the wounds were still fresh enough to hope the teeth would settle of their own accord. His ears and nose were a mess as the trid holes had only been there for a few hours so they bled as they started to repair and the doctors kindly prescribed antibiotics and doses of painkiller for him. Then, when the police had interviewed him, they finally let him go and find his harpist.

Deirdre Hunsecker was in intensive care with her pelvis smashed, her shattered legs pinned and stapled back together and her internal organs cut up by the shards of pelvic bone. She had spent most of the night in surgery and when Lethe finally got to see her she was in bed with a frame over her from her waist to her toes and she was sedated to sleep. Her husband was sitting beside her bed and only Lethe dared intrude on his grief.

"What's the prognosis?" he asked as he sat next to Ygoi.

"Fifty-fifty as they say here. They've salvaged her liver and most of her intestine. Her reproductive organs are in a mess and they say she may never have kids. The bones will mend eventually. The good news is they've patched her legs up so they don't need to amputate. How about you?"

"Lost an eye and they can't promise my teeth will stay in but I'll be OK. Poor Deirdre. Are you staying with her?"

"Just for a bit. I rang Jenni last night and she's coming up from Devon. And we were right."

"We were?"

"She's expecting twins."

"Good old Nurtasia wives."

Ygoi didn't even smile but looked back at the woman lying so still in the bed. "You going on with the tour?"

Lethe sighed. "Don't want to, but I've got no reason not to. I'm playing in York tonight and I'm sure Dan's keyboard can cover your harp for the rest of the tour."

"I'll see you in York."

Lethe hadn't been expecting that. "You will?"

"I can do nothing for her. They're keeping her sedated so I can come down to York for your gig then back here again. I've talked to the doctors and they've agreed she can be transferred by ambulance to Exeter when her body can cope with it. Won't be for a while though. But I'll do tonight for you. Then I can't make you any promises. Sorry."

Lethe gave his friend a shoulder hug and rested his head on the short hair of his harpist. "I'm not asking for promises. Stay with her."

Ygoi sniffed a bit. "No, she's beyond my help at the moment."

Jenni met up with her client in his dressing room in the York theatre. She thought he looked exhausted, his ears and nose were a mess but he gave her a one-armed hug in greeting.

"Twins, huh?" was the first thing he said. "Bet James is pleased."

"James doesn't know what to think. There hasn't been a set of twins in his family in all their history. How's Deirdre?"

"She's OK. Well, no, she's not. But she will be. She must be the bravest woman I have ever met. She was lying in that road with her legs all smashed up and she managed to disable an Assassin. I just hope Ygoi knows how lucky he is."

"Oh, I think he does. And talking of Ygoi, there are some very spicy rumours going round about the two of you."

"I know," he admitted and didn't sound as light-hearted as he would have once. "We started them."

There was an imperious knock on the door and Dan came into the dressing room. "Ten minutes to blast off. You're sure you're good to go on? We've got a harpist on standby. She's about the best in the country and has offered her services for free if you want her, or do you want me to busk it on keyboards?"

"If Ygoi isn't here to play the harp then I don't want anyone," Lethe said stubbornly then remembered his manners. "But it was kind of her to offer and I do appreciate it. Maybe another time, huh? But right now I'm going to go outside for a fag and some air."

"I'll come with you," Jenni offered.

The theatre in York was smaller than many they had played on the tour and the stage door opened onto the street. Lethe was half way through his cigarette when a filthy Honda car stopped on the double yellow lines and the driver got out. He was already dressed in his black stage clothes and had his headset sticking out of his shirt pocket.

"Said I'd be here, didn't I," was his quiet greeting.

Jenni gave him a hug. "How is she?"

"Doped up to the eyeballs but at least she's conscious now and she told me I needed to play this tonight to show us, and her, that Heesha hasn't won. Dan rang me earlier and said there's another harpist on standby but I said I think you and I need to do this one. After that you've only got another three to go so if you want to use her, I really don't mind. I have no idea when I'll get away from Newcastle again now." He handed Jenni a car key. "Would you mind finding a car park for me, please? But I need to get on that stage and get some very loud music through my brain to make the nightmares go away."

Jenni looked at the keys. "Where did you get these from?"

"The guy who owned it. He sold it to me. Said it was in such a mess now he's going to buy a new one."

"You can teach me to drive it one day," Lethe said almost sadly. "When we're all home again." He trod out his cigarette and gave his harpist a hug. "Come on, Shit-face, let's go and blast out some music and look forward to better times."

The two went into the theatre and less than half an hour later walked out under the glare of stage lights together with all the other musicians. The audience stood to applaud as Ygoi Roemtek went across to his familiar harp and Lethe Miarren walked up to the microphone in front of the lead guitarist.

"No guitar tonight," he apologised and held up his bandaged hand. "So tonight the guitar part is going to be played by Pete from the band." Everyone gave Pete a big shout of approval. "Tonight, ladies and gentlemen, you're all aware I've had, as you say in England, a bit of an accident, but I want to dedicate this concert to the bravest lady I have ever met. I didn't have the luck to marry her, that guy over there with the harp did. I owe her my life and I am going to tell that husband of hers every day of his life that he is the luckiest guy on this or any other planet in the universe. Deirdre, this one's for you."

He crossed the stage to sit on the floor at the harpist's feet as the lights dimmed to the effect of moonlight and the gentle harp began the lament of *Fallen Heroes*.

Printed in Great Britain
by Amazon